DEATH BEFORE SLAVERY

On the fateful last night Little Wolf, the war leader for the breakout, announced to Dull Knife the final words he went now to speak to Indian agent John D. Miles.

"I do not wish the ground about this agency to be made bloody, but now listen to what I have to say to you. I am going to leave here. I am going back north to my own Wyoming country. If you are going to send your soldiers after me, I wish that you would first let me get a little distance away. Then if you want a fight, I will fight you and we can make the ground bloody at that other place."

Little Wolf hesitated, putting his hands upon Dull Knife's bowed shoulders.

"Do you understand me now, my chief? What it is that I will do when I have said yes to Agent Miles, and he has said no to me? What it is that will then follow us away from his Oklahoma country?"

It was *death* of which the war chief spoke; death rather than further dishonor; death in preference to continued imprisonment; death in freedom as against life in slavery.

WILL HENRY

THE LAST WARPATH

LEISURE BOOKS NEW YORK CITY

A LEISURE BOOK®

October 1997

Published by special arrangement with Golden West Literary Agency.

Dorchester Publishing Co., Inc.
276 Fifth Avenue
New York, NY 10001

ISBN 0-8439-4314-9

The name "Leisure Books" and the stylized "L" with design are trademarks of Dorchester Publishing Co., Inc.

Printed in the United States of America.

FOR MARC JAFFE
who made it possible.

Acknowledgment

The Last Warpath is a re-created history of the Cheyenne people. The events depicted are essentially true, with enough fictional cement supplied to bind the historical elements together. Source materials include the novels *No Survivors* by Will Henry (Random House) and *Yellow Hair* and *The Brass Command* by Clay Fisher (Houghton Mifflin). A special debt is owed George Bird Grinnell and *The Fighting Cheyenne,* without which no such story could possibly be told.

FOREWORD

The Cheyenne was in many ways the most admirable of Indians; indeed, of men. Kind to the old and the afflicted, gentle with the lost of mind, loyal to friend, devoted to all children, honoring the given word, punishing the broken vow, he was a man who did not understand the forked tongue of the white brother until far too late.

When at last he saw how he had been cheated, and realized that he must fight or languish in the bondage of the reservation system, the Cheyenne chose his way with the dignity and courage which were his prairie birthrights.

If it was a harsh way that he chose, it was noble too, and it was necessary. For there remained but little time to him— scarce time, indeed, to run in the ponies, oil the old guns, make the medicine signs and mutter the sacred prayers to the Allfather.

The white man was demanding war or peace, and peace at the price of slavery. The Cheyenne would not pay that price; he would never live unfree. He would follow the uncaught wind. He would range with the eagle and the wolf. He would live as Maheo had intended him to live, a free thing, out there, under the wide blue sky. And he would fight for that freedom. He would fight until his people were no more, until the last buffalo had disappeared, until the last warrior had grown old and gone forever upon the last warpath. Then, perhaps, the grass would grow where he had been, but not before.

W.H.
1965

THE LAST WARPATH

The Pale Eyes

When Goodfeather was a young girl the Shahi-yena lived in the north country on the headwaters of the Mississippi, and they had never seen a white man. They first met the Pale Eyes when the French came into Canada to build Fort La Salle, about 1680.

Shortly after the arrival of the white men a severe winter fell over the land. Ice locked the rivers. Snow blocked the forest trails. The game disappeared. The stomachs of the Shahi-yena grew small. The faces of the children became gaunt. The old people lost their strength. Famine was upon them, and great fear.

Consulting the smoke of the sacred pine, the medicine man of the band declared that the Pale Eyes were to blame. The Shahi-yena must move away from them, he said, and stay away. The people could not know if it was true that the white man had brought the hunger into their hunting lands, yet as the winter wore into spring and still the warmth did not return, a time of decision was upon them. A council was called and it was determined that the tribe must migrate southward in search of the sun and of something to put into its shrunken bellies.

When starting time came many of the old people were too weak to travel. The kindest thing was to leave them behind in the warm earthen huts of the village. So it was

that Goodfeather came to say farewell to her old grandmother.

"Child, I want to tell you a story." The old lady smiled.
"In the beginning we Shahi-yena lived in a land of many
islands far across the Sunset Sea. Over there in that other
land we had stone lodges with fierce lions and bears to
guard them. When our people left that land they crossed
the Sunset Sea on the ice of winter. But suddenly the ice
split open before them. It was then that a flock of giant
eagles appeared to help them. The eagles flew down from
the sky and took up a number of the people upon their
backs, promising to return soon for the others. Then the
great birds flew away, carrying the people five days, flying over the open water where the ice had split. Upon
this side of the Sunset Sea the eagles put the people once
more upon the land. But when they flew back to bring
over the rest of the people, a great storm made the air
black and the eagles and the other people were never
seen again."

The old woman paused. She held the child close a
moment, then released her.

"Granddaughter," she said, "it is important that you
remember to tell this story to your own grandchildren. If
you forget it, then the Shahi-yena will forget where they
came from. Those others who were left on the far side of
the Sunset Sea will have to wait over there forever. Give
me a warm hug now."

The child did so, promising that she would never forget
the story or the grandmother who told it. Then her mother
entered the lodge and said some low, quick words to the
grandmother. The two women kissed one another and
gripped hands. Goodfeather went out of the lodge with
her mother. That was all that she remembered of the time
when her people lived where the Mississippi had its
sources.

The Shahi-yena argued too much and delayed. The
start southward was made much too late in the summer.
The chill of autumn caught them still upon the trail, still
wandering, still suffering. They halted to pray to Maheo,
their Great Spirit.

The Shahi-yena had no horses, no guns, very little of
any metalwork. They had only a few hatchets sold them

by the French at Fort La Salle and a few crude trade
knives of the same origin. Their arrows and rabbit lances
were tipped with flint. Animal skins were their principal
clothing. They had no cloth for blankets. Fire was made
with the twirling stick and dried leaves. The only traps
were the snare, the staked pit, the deadfall. They tanned
their pelts with human urine like the Eskimos. It was a
cruel existence, not far above the cave and the club. But
they found the courage to go on.

All days were bitterly cold now. The land was devoid
of game. It waited still and empty for the white grass of
winter. At darkfall the wind came prowling with the bite
of ice in its bared teeth. By dawn the hoarfrost silvered
the lowlands. It was an urgent, warning time and the
starving people responded to it, fighting to the southward.
Yet with the forty-fourth sun since the prayer halt and
the decision to continue, they came to a great bluff above
a mighty river and could see no way beyond.

Jagged chunks of ice filled the swollen stream. No human being might hope to cross its raging channel. There
was talk of lying down to die quietly. But the mother of
Goodfeather reminded them of their faith in Maheo, and
the tribe commenced to pray again, chanting the words
of the ancient ones which no living Shahi-yena understood, calling upon the Allfather to send them a sign that
he heard his children crying to him. And as they prayed,
the tops of the river bluffs turned yellow with warm light.
The sun, these many days hidden and dark, had returned.
It was Maheo's sign.

Responding to it, the Shahi-yena went on down the
great stream southward. A little way farther, around the
first bend, they came in sight of the Mandan villages at
the juncture of the Knife River with the Missouri and
were saved.

The Shahi-yena lived with the Mandans a lifetime and
more, well beyond a hundred years. In this time they
came to be called the Cheyenne, and the old name was
forgotten. Also in this time the Cheyenne grew away
from the river tribes. The sons and daughters of Sweet
Medicine and Maheo were born to be free. Freedom
was their passion. They could not forever abide the round
Mandan houses and tilled fields. They called the Mandan,

the Hidatsa and Arikara brothers. But in truth the Cheyenne were more the brothers of the wind, the sky, the prairie, the eagle and the hawk. They deserted the Missouri, moving inland to the west, out upon the great plains, the land of the fierce and warlike horseback Indians. But the Cheyenne did not yet have horses nor did they yet have guns. Still, in the moving away from the river, they met the thunderous herds of the buffalo, and their life was altered from that time.

The meat of these shaggy creatures, hunted afoot and taken with wooden lance and flint-tipped arrow, furnished a diet and way of life demanding the utmost of the hunter yet giving him great returns of strength and skill. Along with the many products made from hide, bones, sinews, hoofs, horns, intestines—and even calloused hocks—the buffalo beef, backfat and organ meats, when combined with the arduous life of the chase, commenced to bring forth a taller, stronger, fiercer, more haughty and independent people. They learned to make lodges of dried spruce poles and cow-buffalo skins, which were light enough to be transported on the backs of women and packdogs. Thus were born the conical cowskin structures, future symbol of the nomad fighting tribe which would not be bound by fields and fences. And all of this was done with wolfdogs, wooden lances, stone-tipped arrows, cheap iron trade knives and travois litters dragged by uncomplaining squaws or yelping mongrels over the trackless grasses of the new-found buffalo pastures.

When Goodfeather had become a mother and a grandmother, the main band was living in the beautiful Dakota roughlands of the Black Hills. The Cheyenne still had no guns and no horses. But now new enemies appeared who had both. These were the Assiniboin.

The horses of the Assiniboin were taken from the Shoshone, Crow, Blackfoot and Piegan of the far western mountain bands. Their guns were secured through barter with the French and British traders of Canada. From these traders, too, they received the encouragement to go out and make war on their brother redmen who might have good supplies of buffalo robes and fox and ermine furs, the things the white men wanted. Thus, when the Assiniboin believed the time was right for raiding the

Black Hills Cheyenne, they did so with no fear of the latter. Their first victims chanced to be the little band of Goodfeather.

As the elder squaw of the lodge of her son Lame Bear, she was preparing the evening meal. Tiny Lighting Swan, the old squaw's infant granddaughter, laughed and clapped her chubby hands in anticipation of a bit of gristle or piece of rib bone upon which to gnaw. At the rear of the lodge lay North Star, Goodfeather's old camp dog. The companion of many trails, he could now no longer hunt. But if the aging limbs were stiff, the ears and nose were still keen. Suddenly the dog lifted his gray muzzle and whined. The sound made the old squaw grow cold. It was the dog's "enemy whimper," the warning he gave when he smelled death approaching.

Instantly Goodfeather strapped Lighting Swan upon her back and went scuttling out of the lodge. Outside she followed North Star. The old dog headed directly for the stream beyond the camp. Goodfeather floundered through the icy current behind him. Upon the opposite bank a hiding place was found deep in a thicket of willow. "Be still!" whispered the old squaw to the child; and the infant, trained from birth never to cry when the enemy was near, lay silently like a wooden doll.

The Assiniboin slew all in the camp—every man, woman, child, dog. When they were gone Goodfeather left her hiding place and set out through the night for the main camp. The Cheyenne went back with her and buried the dead of her band. They then held counsel to see what course the people must now take. The question, since they had no horses and no guns, became that of staying to be slaughtered by the warrior Assiniboin or of leaving the beloved Black Hills.

It seemed a poor choice and Goodfeather would have none of it. "There's another way," she pointed out. "We don't have to wait for them to kill us, and we don't have to leave this beautiful land. We can go and get some guns and horses of our own!"

"And from whom shall we get them?" The council members scowled.

"From the people who have them, of course," answered the old lady. "From the Assiniboin."

The people forgave Goodfeather. After all, she had lost

a son and a daughter-in-law. But the fact remained that the Cheyenne had no guns and no horses and could not fight the Assiniboin. They would have to give up the Black Hills hunting grounds. Goodfeather could not accept this surrender. Neither could she agree to it. Leaving her tiny grandchild with a grieving squaw who had lost her own nursing child, the old woman called North Star to her and set out upon the trail of the Assiniboin. For three days and two nights she followed them. The enemy warriors were not hurrying. They hunted and dawdled along the way, never dreaming of Cheyenne pursuit.

On the third night Maheo sent Goodfeather the sign she had been praying for—a heavy ground fog which blanketed the hills and fell over the traveling Assiniboin. The latter, not knowing the country as well as the old woman did, made the mistake of pitching camp at the very top of an eighty-foot cliff. The Cheyenne had driven buffalo over it to kill them without shooting. Goodfeather could see no reason why the cliff would not serve as well for killing Assiniboin. "Faithful one," she said to the old dog, "let us get on with the matter."

The Assiniboin ponies, because of the dense fog, were picketed instead of grazing free. Had they been loose, one of them would surely have winded Goodfeather and whinnied in warning. As it was, she was able to creep around the horses and get to a place where she was nearly able to reach out and touch the warriors, who were squatted about a fire boiling meat in a kettle with heated stones. Suddenly the old squaw bounded to her feet. With a wild Cheyenne war cry she leaped into the midst of the startled Assiniboin men. Kicking over the boiling kettle, she turned and fled back into the fog. The scalding contents of the kettle struck the warriors, sending their tempers out of control. With cries of rage they ran after the old lady. The result was precisely as Goodfeather had foreseen it. At the cliff's edge she hid in a clump of weeds and the Assiniboin, racing past her, plunged over the precipice and were killed on the rocks of the streambed below.

Goodfeather scrambled down the steep trail. Collecting the precious guns of the warriors, she put them in a nearby cave for safekeeping, then turned for home. Her tribes-

men, following her directions, raced back to the cliff.
There they recovered the guns and the fine Assiniboin
war ponies, none the worse for the waiting. A victory fire
was built and the name of Goodfeather chanted in praise
far into the night.

The people now had rifles and horses. The dreaded Assiniboin had been beaten back and would never again
know a strength to threaten the Cheyenne. Were there
indeed any people anywhere who might imperil Goodfeather's folk? The happy old squaw did not think so.
None of the people thought so. The council of chiefs was
certain there were not. But there were.

With the advent of the one hundred twenty-fourth winter since the arrival of the old Shahi-yena people along
the Upper Missouri, all the major bands of Cheyenne
had departed the villages of the Mandan for the buffalo
pastures of the west.

A few, however, by virtue of mixed Mandan and Cheyenne blood remained with the river tribes. These remnants of the old Shahi-yena days attracted frequent visitors from the outer prairie bands. One of these visitors in
the fall of 1804 was Lighting Swan, the granddaughter
of the old squaw Goodfeather.

Lighting Swan was then no longer a young woman herself. She was perhaps forty and was the mother of a four-
teen-year-old son named Whistling Elk. The father of
this youth was Far Hills Elk, a leader of the prairie bands.
The couple had come to the villages of the Mandan to
spend the deep part of the winter with Big Man who, although an orphan of pure Cheyenne blood, was third
chief of all the villages of Knife River.

Far Hills Elk had not wished to come. Even though
Big Man was his uncle and the godfather of young
Whistling Elk, the settled way of life in the river towns
made Far Hills Elk nervous. He felt trapped among all
the log-walled mound houses and tilled fields. But his
woman, Lighting Swan, had persuaded him to forego his
doubts and conquer his dislikes. She wanted her young
son to see how the Mandan and mixed-blood Cheyenne
lived along the river. She believed it was time to show
the boy, to let him see with his own eyes, the difference
between living free in the land of the buffalo and being

trapped in the mud-log huts and cornpatches of the Mandan.

"How better to teach him to stay free," she asked Far Hills Elk, "than to show him those who have permitted themselves to be captured by the Pale Eyes?" Thus did she refer to the dependence of the river tribes upon the trade with Canadian factors of the British fur companies.

In this matter Far Hills Elk, as free in his heart and mind as any man alive, could readily appreciate his woman's view. Indeed he agreed with it vehemently. Yet he was uneasy. Something was wrong.

At sundown of the twenty-sixth day of October, in the time known to the Cheyenne as Tonoese, an old news crier came shouting into the village of Big Man from down the river. Beyond him, there was already a great number of the Mandan running toward the bend of the stream below the village. Bewildered, Far Hills Elk and Lighting Swan stumbled out of Big Man's lodge. The boy, Whistling Elk, was ahead of them, following the people. The couple looked at one another.

"Did you hear what that old man said?" asked the warrior.

"I heard," answered Lighting Swan, her anxious gaze fastened on the river's bend. "Many white men coming in a great winged house upon the water. They are *hestōhetanes*, unknown ones."

There were three sailboats on the Missouri, two smaller pirogues and a fifty-five-foot keelboat of twenty-two oars. When the craft skimmed around the lower bend and stood with the fair upriver wind for the third Mandan village of Big Man, the Indians following along both banks could not restrain themselves from rushing out into the water. Before this day no white men had ever come in force up the Mother Missouri from the south. The Mandan realized this was no ordinary party of French or British or half-blood traders such as the Loisels, Dorions and Tabeaus of their previous experience. This was a new kind of white man, one for whom the Mandan and Cheyenne had no word in their languages. Indeed, so enthusiastic was the curiosity of the Indian mob ashore that the white commanders could not seem to decide whether its members were peaceable or hostile, and so withdrew to an anchorage under some low bluffs and there stayed the night.

When, on the following day, Lewis and Clark made their landing at the Mandan villages of the Knife, Far Hills Elk, Lighting Swan and Whistling Elk viewed the meeting from afar. The prairie-bred warrior had alerted his wife and son in the dead of night and guided them out of the settlement to the timbered height from which they now watched.

The wary mind of Far Hills Elk was aroused by these alien white men. In his tongue the words for stranger and enemy were frequently interchanged. Yet he had the natural curiosity of the nomad, along with the friendliness of the old Shahi-yena, that tribal good humor to believe and to expect the best of mankind. But the prairie warrior also found himself swayed by another tribal tenet or belief, which warned that constant preparedness was the price of continuing liberty. In years past, when his people had moved into the lovely grass and timberland of the Black Hills country, they had learned a grim lesson. If a people had nothing and lived in a poor land, they would preach of peace and be known to all as friendly; but if those same people then acquired something, became prosperous and strong in a rich land, they would be known as hostile and dangerous, as bad people, certain talkers and makers of war.

So it was that the Cheyenne warrior lingered on the wooded height, looking back to make sure what the strangers, or enemies, were about, before finally departing from their presence. Peering intently below, he saw the sturdy pale-eyed men of the newly arrived company confronting the friendly and smiling Mandans. He saw their shining rifles. He saw the brass cannon fore and aft of the big white-winged boat. He saw the soldierly discipline of all the crew. He saw particularly the riflemen, upon the order of their leader, fire their weapons at small and distant targets to impress the Mandans, and he saw that the targets were struck with regularity and with no missing.

Far Hills Elk was not relieved. "These men are not traders," he said to his wife.

"I can see that," replied the woman. "They bring gifts but will not take anything for themselves. What kind of people will give an Indian something for nothing, do you think?"

"A bad kind," said Far Hills Elk.

"A bad kind, Father?" asked the boy, Whistling Elk.

The tall warrior nodded, reached down, took the boy by the arm. Pointing to the white company on the beach below, he said somberly, "Remember those men, their pale eyes, pale skin. Stay far away from them always."

The lean youngster seemed to understand the warning and to be stirred by it. But his mother shook her head sadly.

"You won't remember it," she said. "You're too young."

She paused, looking below. "Husband," she said, frowning, "down there the Pale Eyes are telling the Mandan they will travel on to the west in the spring, following the river. Won't that take them through a part of our lands? May they not decide to stay with us? To hunt our buffalo? Steal our ponies? Covet our women? Now I am commencing to feel your fear."

"We must go quickly," nodded Far Hills Elk. "The people must be got ready to leave this land; to go and find a new land farther out. We can't fight soldiers who shoot as these do, never missing. Come on, hurry!"

"I don't know," said Lighting Swan. "The Mandan are not afraid. That white chief with the red hair seems friendly. I don't believe I fear him. See him smile and shake hands now."

Far Hills Elk put his hand to her shoulder, voice urgent. "Wife," he said, "do you recall the old Shahi-yena legend about strangers with white skins and bright hair coming among us, who will seem friendly but will destroy the people?"

"Yes," admitted the woman, suddenly nervous. "I do remember that legend. It was told me by my old grandmother Goodfeather. We had better do as you say. The old lady was never wrong."

Far Hills Elk turned to lead the way. "From this time," he said, "we will never forget the old warning; we will stay to ourselves where the white men cannot find us or follow us."

They got upon their ponies, the woman first, helped by the boy Whistling Elk. Quickly they went from that place, not looking back. Henceforward and for many

years—even until Whistling Elk had passed the warning
to his own young son, Spotted Wolf—the white mountain
men who followed the trails of Lewis and Clark called
the Cheyenne by another name and for a singular reason:
the Kite Indians because the white men never saw them
save at great distances and always moving swiftly away.

Thus, for the first half of the new century, the Cheyenne remained a nation of wary, seldom viewed or visited
people. But the times were changing. The ways of
the white man were everywhere. And it was to the worst
of these ways that the proud Cheyenne fell heir. Yet
even in their fall the prairie warriors retained their keen
sense of humor, of human weakness, of man's inherent
superiority in seeing himself for the ignoble clay he was.

"It was not the white man's whiskey which betrayed
us," said Spotted Wolf many years later. "It was his sugar."
He said this with an Indian twinkle in his fine old eyes,
proceeding to explain the matter in curiously Cheyenne
logic.

He recalled that in 1832 a trader named Gantt had appeared upon the Arkansas. He had constructed a scabrous
log hut for the shelter of his wares at the mouth of Foun-
tain Creek. His sole stock in trade proved to be red-eye.
His primary customers were the Cheyenne drawn to the
area by William Bent's greater trading post farther along
the Arkansas.

· Gantt's problem, since his merchandise would alienate
the gorge of any living creature, was to doctor his prod-
uct so that it might be accepted by human throat and
stomach. White sugar proved the answer. Understanding
the red man's insatiable hunger for sweets, Gantt merely
spiked his rotgut with sugar.

The old Cheyenne, grinning again but wincing at the
same time, said that he could still taste that sugar. Moreover, he could still remember the headaches that it gave
him. No matter, though. So altered, Trader Gantt's
liquor had been an instant success. Within five summers,
the old man said, the Cheyenne had become a nation
of drunkards.

It is doubtful that the verminous Gantt deserved full
credit. He was but the first of many in a vicious trade.
Nevertheless the proud horsemen of the plains had no

social experience with alcohol, hence no resistance whatever to its degrading effects. Whiskey, the toxic, foul
trade liquor of the day, proved as deadly to the Cheyenne
as smallpox and cholera, those other gifts of the white
brother to the red.

And now a third enemy, beyond whiskey and epidemic
disease, entered the lists against the Cheyenne: the emigrant. The flow of white-settler wagon traffic out of the
Oregon Trail lay squarely across the domain of the horseback tribes. A mere trickle at first, it was soon a flood.
Indians who in 1835 hunted buffalo at the forks of the
Platte had to go as far as the sunset edge of the Laramie
Plain a decade later, and even to the foot of the Rocky
Mountains in Shoshone country, to find the herds which
supported their tribal way of life. Along with this driving
away of the buffalo and shooting-out of the antelope,
deer and elk herds of the region, the emigrants completely denuded the banks of the Platte of useful fuel
timber and feed grasses, creating a virtual desert from a
former rich game and pasture land.

Compounding this physical injury to the Indian's her-
itage, the white settlers actually petitioned Congress to
furnish them with military protection during the enact-
ment of the spoilage. By 1849, in response to the spurious
outcry against the bewildered Indians, the army had
built two strong redoubts along the Oregon road: Fort
Kearny in Nebraska, 191 miles from the Missouri River
settlements; Fort Laramie in Wyoming, at the mouth of
Laramie River, 573 miles from the settlements.

In these same years a second route of emigrant traffic
was being established along the Arkansas River between
the Missouri settlements and Colorado Territory. With the
Arkansas road in the south, as with the Oregon road in
the north, came renewed sources of drink and disease
brought westward to the Cheyenne by the work crews
and garrison troops sent to protect the honest home-
steader from the murderous savage who now and again
scalped a whiskey seller or burned a settler barn to show
his pique at being dispossessed of his ancestral realm.

As the garrisons grew along the two great rivers, the
horseback tribes clashed more and more with the military.
The Cheyenne, however, stayed away from this warfare.

They kept their weapons bright but rode wide of the "pony soldiers."

Among the noted warriors of this era was Spotted Wolf, the son of Whistling Elk and the great-great-grandson of the ancient Shahi-yena squaw Goodfeather. It was Whistling Elk who as a child had seen Lewis and Clark arrive in the Mandan villages in the autumn of 1804. And Spotted Wolf, now in his middle years, still recalled the warning passed along to him by his father, who had been given it in turn by his father: *Remember those men, their pale eyes, pale skin. Stay far away from them always.*

But the times, once more, were changing. The Cheyenne had not been called the Kite Indians for many years now. Although still reserved and small in number owing to their nomad way, they no longer fled at the mere news that white men had been seen. Yet they did continue to avoid the whites. So persistent was this ban that of all the warlike horseback Indians of the plains only the Cheyenne had not been engaged in a substantial fight with United States troops before 1856.

In the summer of that year, however, they were attacked in peaceful camp almost within sight of Fort Kearny. Their village was but a few hundred paces off the Platte River wagon road. Its lodges had been pitched there by direction of the band's war chief, who had believed the open location near the fort and the emigrant trail would guarantee safety from both troops and passing settlers.

But the commander of the pony soldiers understood only one certain thing about red men. Judging from the Congressional reaction to emigrant petitioning for protection from the savages, the swiftest route to military promotions was to kill a few Indians. And of course the easiest Indians to kill were those in peaceful camp. Reported Captain G. H. Stewart of his charge through the unwarned and friendly Cheyenne village near Fort Kearny:

... Ten Indians were left dead on the field, eight or ten were badly wounded. Twenty-two horses and mules were captured, and a number of saddles,

shields, lances and buffalo robes, etc., were found. I
lost no men, and not a wound was received . . .

But with that charge Captain Stewart had wounded the
white man's cause in a way which would never heal.
From that hour Spotted Wolf, who was the war chief of
the Fort Kearny band, would not aagin forget the ancient
Shahi-yena warnings against the Pale Eyes.

"Let this be the end of it between the Cheyenne and
the white man!" cried the heartbroken chief when the
soldiers were gone, the Indian dead buried, the wounded
bound up and made ready for travel. "We shall become
once more, and stay forever after, as the Kite Indians of
old!"

But the son of Whistling Elk and the grandson of Far
Hills Elk failed to understand that there was now a
deadly flaw in the shield of the old Shahi-yena warnings.
If the present descendants of wise Goodfeather and the
shy Kite Indians were to stay apart from the white man,
who was to guarantee that the white man would stay
apart from them?

For a few brief years it appeared as though the Cheyenne truly would learn to survive the onslaughts of whiskey, disease and settler greed. The livestock thefts, the
barn burnings, the unavoidable deaths of whites in the
continual abrasion between the races in a contest for
land, all commenced to wane.

After a convulsive flaring of Indian resistance in the
bloody "Cheyenne Summer" of 1864, it was all but over.
The red man had finally come to understand, or at least
begun to grasp, the insurmountable nature of the white
man's power. He could see by this time that he *must*
learn to live with the settler, the sodbuster, the gold hunter, the cattle grazer, even the soldier. And he was ready,
or so the peace chiefs among his people insisted, to make
the ultimate effort.

The white man for his part could see no good in the
Indian as a fellow citizen. He had no serious intention of
trying to learn to live with the red brother, or even to
tolerate his continued presence as a free-roving individual.
Peace, if it meant that the horseback tribes were to remain at liberty, was not wanted.

Something had to be done. Drink, disease and sod

dugouts having failed to dislodge the stubborn red man, a new force was needed. It was speedily furnished in the form of the cavalry career officer, the commander of frontier mounted troops hungry for Eastern newspaper space with all its attendant political reward for the man fortunate enough to happen upon, or create, the opportunity for a genuinely big "Indian killing" out west.

The officer had already been selected by the lottery of black chance. He waited now, gathering his troops, arranging his excuses, searching carefully for just the right spot to make his terrible mark upon the map of Indian memory. The place he chose was in Colorado Territory. The Cheyenne had a poetic name for that place; it was Ponoeohe, Little Dried River, one of the great traditional wintering grounds of the nomad bands. The white men called the place by its more prosaic name, Sand Creek.

Little Dried River

In Denver that late November afternoon the weather was lowering and mean. Old snow lay in the mud gutters glazed with soot and scum ice. The wind, always prowling at that altitude, was on the rise. The four men rounding the corner from the direction of the Governor's mansion were leaning against the building gale. They drew in at the doorway of the Overland Express station, huddling there. They seemed ill at ease, not with the weather or with their surroundings, but with one another.

The older two were white men, one in Cheyenne buckskins, the other in city clothes. Their two companions wore Indian wolf coats and winter moccasins of buffalo hockhide. They were in their late teens, either pure or half-bloods, and were not familiar with Denver or with any settlement of its size.

"By damn," complained the roughclad white man, hunching to the cold. "This here wind would cramp a snowshoe rabbit's foot. We won't get far tonight, lads. Be lucky to make the bend timber up along Cherry Creek." The darkskinned youths bobbed their heads but did not speak. The older man turned to his companion in city clothes. "I'm beholden to you, Major," he said. "Letting me bring the lads to meet the Governor and to hear his words on the Indian trouble firsthand was mighty fine.

Eddication is the onliest way we can whup this thing."

The city man agreed. "Yes," he said. "I hope these two young men prove serious about learning to be interpreters."

"Oh, they're serious, Major. They'll ketch on quick as greased weasels. Besides, being half-Injun like they are, they'd ought, both of them, to make the primest kind of interpreters. That's how me and the other lad's father figgered."

The city man nodded thoughtfully. For a moment he studied the two young half-breeds. Both youths had Cheyenne mothers, he knew. The father of the second boy was Ezekial Blunt, an educated man trading along the Smoky Hill and Solomon Rivers. Young Blunt thus showed a faint stamp of something beside buckskin and blanket teachings. But Jack Smith had no whit of formal learning. The boy could neither read nor write and spoke English with the typical fragmented wording of the "ignorant breed," which in frontier fact he was.

Major S. G. Colley, Indian Agent for the Cheyenne and Arapaho in Colorado Territory, was not impressed. A kindly and cautious man, however, he would not embarrass Uncle John.

"Well, boys," he said, "pay heed to your fathers and you will be all right." He paused, waiting to catch their restless eyes. "On the other hand, I must warn you not to listen to the Indians. Work for peace, boys; it is all that can save the Cheyenne."

Jack Smith did not reply, but the Blunt boy made the handsign of respect, touching his fingers to his forehead. "Speaking of peace, Major," he said quietly, "my father believes Black Kettle ought to get his people away from where they are down there by Fort Lyon."

Colley's gentle frown deepened. "Black Kettle's folks have accepted Governor Evans' plea to come in and camp near the army posts, where they can be protected," he said. "Fortunately, Black Kettle understands the situation."

Young Blunt shook his head, stubborn chin outthrust. "Begging your pardon, Major," he denied. "My father says that ain't so. He says the old chief don't understand nothing that's going on. If he did, he for certain wouldn't have camped where Major Anthony wanted him to. Not just thirty miles up a good trail from the fort. My father says—"

"Boy," ordered Uncle John Smith, "be still."

Smith was Colley's man. As chief government interpreter for the area, he had translated for the Cheyenne in their September council with Governor Evans at Denver. This was the council which Black Kettle and the other peace chiefs in attendance had been led to believe was an amnesty agreement for that coming winter of 1864–65. When the venerable squawman spoke now to the Blunt boy, the youth properly subsided.

His own son, however, did not. "Heap cold," said the young half-breed. "We go now."

"The lad's right," smiled the agent, relieved. "Remember, Uncle John, don't go nosing about that camp of Chivington's. You leave him to me. I'll find out what has brought him back down here from the Platte."

"You do that, Major. Meanwhile I'll quieten the Cheyenne. They're apt to fly apart like a busted covey of bob-whites when they learn he's camped over in the Bijou. *Katam!*"

"Yes, I know. Well, do your best; here's my stage. I want your word now, Uncle John—ride wide around that Bijou country. Understood?"

"You betcha, Major. Don't worry. I know the colonel."

"I know you do," said Colley pointedly. "That is precisely the reason I want you to stay away from him."

"Still heap cold," announced Jack Smith expressionlessly.

"Yes," agreed the Blunt youngster, "and getting late."

"*Waghl*" said Jack. "We no leave quick, we no reach Ponoeohe in time. Me get horses."

"Hold on," said Agent Colley, frowning again. "I don't know what you mean by that, boy—about reaching Sand Creek in time. But I must caution you once more that if you are to be of any help to your Indian people, you must be extremely careful what you say and do. I would expressly advise against such talk. It sounds ominous, threatening. I don't like it."

"Pshaw!" assured Uncle John. "He don't mean nothing by it, Major. Jack, he's took extra strong to his maw's side, that's all. He's mainly Injun I reckon. Only wants to get home to his folks down on Sand Creek. Ain't that so, boy?"

His half-breed son eyed him unblinkingly. He did not reply to the question. There was no sullenness, only silence. The Pueblo stage pulled up, easing the pause. Uncle John saw Colley aboard but first dispatched the boys to bring their own mounts around from the livery corral. Alone with the agent, the interpreter spoke urgently.

"Major," he said, "there was something didn't get brung out today. I caught it, so did the boys. The Governor is onto something we ain't. I suspect it's to do with Chivington and them Colorado volunteers over to Bijou Basin. I suspect it ain't the Confederate threat he's down here to chase—Chivington, I mean—I think he's after them hostiles up on the Smoky Hill. What you think, Major?"

"I don't know; there was something held back," admitted Colley. "I'll see what I can learn in Pueblo. Be careful."

"Sure enough I will. So long, Major." The stage rattled away over the frozen mud. Uncle John watched it bounce out of sight, brow furrowed anxiously.

A supremely simple man, he took his greatest reward not in serving the Army or the Indian agents but in leading the free-roving life of his wife's people. And now he knew that something was very wrong with regard to the safety of those people and to their future in that land. Something had changed since the Governor's September council with the peace chiefs. Was it the return of Colonel Chivington?

Uncle John Smith did not think it was. Chivington was the commander of the military district of Colorado. He was an important man in the territory. He held great responsibilities. Certainly he was a hard fighter and had killed a good many Indians. But a good many whites had been killed too.

Uncle John shook his graying head. It was one too many for him. He was no Indian agent, no Army commander. He would have to leave such thinking to Major Colley and Colonel Chivington. For himself, he had done what he could to secure a safe winter camp for his wife's people and he believed that he had done so. Being under the protection of Major Anthony and the troops at Fort

Lyon was the best arrangement old Black Kettle could have hoped for after the bloody "Cheyenne Summer" just past.

When the white dead from those summer-long Indian raids upon the Arkansas settlements had been counted that autumn, it had been a certainty that the troops would strike some winter blow against the hostiles. Black Kettle knew that and so did "Blackfoot" Smith. So, too, did old White Antelope, Bull Bear, Neva and the Arapaho Left Hand, all present at Denver. With these chiefs, their friend and brother-by-blanket, Blackfoot Smith, had worked hard to get from Governor Evans promised immunity which had resulted in obedience by Black Kettle to Major Anthony's direction that he encamp his main band of Southern Cheyenne on Sand Creek.

But there was still something wrong; Uncle John knew that too. Yet what was it? Or whom? And from where would it come, and when? The old squawman shook his head again. "*Kataml*" he growled, in the Cheyenne variant of the white man's favorite curse, and was glad when Jack and young Blunt came up just then with the horses.

Mounting, the three riders looped out of Denver by the Cherry Creek Bridge road. The town was quickly shrouded from view, the gray scud of a sleety rain closing behind them. Indianlike, there was little talk.

Jack Smith crouched to the fire. His father and his tall cousin, young Blunt, were long since rolled in their blankets, backs to the glow of the banked embers. The half-breed youth continued to stare into the popping coals. There was no sleep for him in that day's work. Unlike his white sire, the boy could not dismiss his fears of the giant Colorado cavalryman. Colonel J. M. Chivington was not just another pony-soldier chief. He was an Indian-killer. He believed and professed to believe that the only way to contain the hostile threat in Colorado was by killing Indians—only Chivington did not specify hostile Indians.

"Kill Indians" was his stated creed. "Kill them all, little and big. Nits make lice." It was more than a creed; it was a standing order with the Third Colorado Cavalry. "Take no prisoners" was the precise wording in military terminology, but the Cheyenne knew what that meant, and Jack Smith was one-half Cheyenne.

The boy's dark and narrow face seemed to twist in torment. It was as though he had seen a ghost in the heartflame of the fire. He rose silently, reaching for his rifle where it lay across the roll of his blanket. He had made his decision and he would go, now. No ghosts in the fire would stop him, no nightwinds slow his way.

He had listened to Governor Evans. He had heard him say that Chivington had not returned to the Arkansas to hunt for Indians but to defend Union lands against the Confederate soldiers of the South. These were said by the Governor to be advancing up the Arkansas to take Colorado away from the pony soldiers of the United States. They were said to be sending agents among the Cheyenne and the other Indians, inciting the red man to revolt, promising him the return of those Arkansas lands which had been his since time began its travel across the stars.

Lies, all lies. White man's tortured lies. No such agents had come among the Indians. No Confederate soldiers were advancing into Colorado along the Arkansas. Jack Smith knew that. All the Indians knew it. Chivington must know it too, and Governor Evans—even good Agent Colley perhaps.

Yet Chivington was over there in the Bijou Basin and he had come down from the Platte to hunt *something*. What? Half-breed Jack Smith believed that he knew. He went on feet as light as those of the coyote or the kit fox to the side of his tall comrade, young Blunt. He touched the other breed boy on the shoulder no harder than the fall of a snowflake.

His comrade came awake. True to teaching, he did not at first move a muscle save those of the eyes. Then, seeing it was Jack, he came to the fire noiselessly, picking up his own rifle on the way. They talked with their hands and an occasional whisper, the Blunt boy nodding quick agreement to what Jack Smith said. Jack led the way to the ponies.

"*Ho-shuh, ho-shuh*," they murmured to the nervous mounts, "be still, be confident, it is only your friends."

Taking up the picket pins, they coiled the staking ropes, slipped on the saddles and the split-ear Cheyenne bridles. When the cinches were pulled tight, they led the little

mustangs up the stream, watching that their flinty hoofs
did not strike a stone or scrape upon loose gravel, awaken-
ing the snoring Uncle John. They went half a mile before
Jack was satisfied. "All right," he said finally, "let's go."
They swung up on the ponies, reined them hard left,
away from the Cherry Creek trail. Going east they struck
out across the trackless tawny sea of buffalo grass. Over
there somewhere was the place Uncle John had promised
good Agent Colley not to go. Over there somewhere,
hopefully short of daylight, was the cavalry camp of
Colonel J. M. Chivington and his Indian-killing Third Colorado volunteers.

About 5:00 A.M. the ponies pricked their ears and
began nickering in their throats. They had winded the
soldier horse herd. The boys immediately got down and
wrapped the noses of their mounts, so they would not
whinny to the other horses. Jack left them with the Blunt
boy and himself went up the incline of the rise in the
prairie before them.

Bellied down in the waving grass of the crest the half-
breed youth drew in his breath sharply. Down there in the
vast swale of the Bijou Basin was the camp. But there
was more in it than just Colonel J. M. Chivington and
the Third Colorado. There were hundreds and hundreds of
soldiers down there. The tent rows ran in scores, white
and gray and dirty brown in the streaky darkness of the
coming dawn. Jack could see, beyond the tents, the wagon
park with its dozens of ammunition carriers, ambulances,
field kitchens and ferriers' carts. He could not be certain
in the bad light, but he believed he made out some high-
wheeled mountain artillery—one battery at least of light
howitzers.

Jack Smith knew a great deal about the soldiers. He was
the youngest of the Black Kettle scouts, but he had studied
hardest of them all. The gray was thinning now and he
made out two regimental guidons that he was certain of,
in addition to that of the Third. These were of the First
Colorado Cavalry and the New Mexico Infantry. There
might have been more; the breed boy never learned.
Even as he lay watching and straining to see, the brass
cry of the buglers commenced shrilling reveille through
the camp and everywhere lamps and lanterns and field

candles began to spark and glow. That was not only a very big camp but also a very busy one. Something more sinister than settling in for the winter was going on down there. That camp was not settling for the winter, it was settling to spring upon the Indians. But, again, what Indians?

The Comanche and Kiowa were under the protection of Fort Larned far over in Kansas. And Fort Larned was under the protection of Major Wynkoop, a good man and a friend of the Indian. Wynkoop had been relieved of the Fort Lyon command on the directive of Chivington who was commander of the entire military district of Colorado, the charge being that Wynkoop gave the Indians food and promised them peace. Now Wynkoop was in charge at Fort Larned and the Indians there could close their eyes at night and know they would open them again in the morning. No, it would not be the Comanche or the Kiowa that the Bijou Basin camp was gathering to kill.

So what Indians were left? Only the Cheyenne of course. Well, then, which of the Cheyenne? Would it be the tough and unrelenting hostiles of young Blunt's band, up on the Smoky Hill? Those hard, wild, free Indians who called Evans a liar and Chivington a mad dog loose on the prairies? *Wagh!* Never, not those Indians. Chivington would not dare attack them. But how about Black Kettle's people? How about those sad, foolish Indians camped down there on Sand Creek where the trail from Fort Lyon to the headwaters of the Smoky Hill went across the famous small stream which the Cheyenne called Ponoeohe, the Little Dried River?

Those Indians—his own mother's people—had lost the will to fight. Black Kettle did not even like to let the young men ride out to scout the soldiers any more. The old chief was afraid someone might fire a gun, or forget to run when the soldiers jeered or insulted or shot at the Indians. He wanted peace so much that he would not speak the word war, nor hear it spoken in his presence. "Believe," he told the Cheyenne, "and what you believe will come to pass. Believe and wait," he said.

Jack Smith shivered. What he believed was something more real to him, and frightening, than anything the peace chiefs preached. Jack believed that he knew what those

Indians were waiting for on Sand Creek, and what was waiting for *them*.

Swiftly he pushed back from the crest, ran down the slope. "Go up there and look for yourself," he told the Blunt boy, and took the horses from him, very hurriedly, apprehensively.

The other youth scuttled up the rise, glanced over its top and returned, running faster than had Jack.

"*Katam*, cousin!" he swore excitedly. "I never saw that many soldiers in one place before. Six hundred of them anyway. And they are, all of them, getting ready to go somewhere. *Hail*"

"I agree," nodded young Jack. "It is a true thing you say. It is likewise true that we had better be getting ready to go somewhere. Very fast too, cousin. We will swing to the south, I think, getting into that timber down there where the creek passes through the rocks. What do you say? *Hai*, let's go."

"Yes, all right, *hai*! But wait, listen to me, Jack. I have just thought of something. I can't go with you. I must ride to warn my own people. Don't you agree?"

The other boy seemed strangely, swiftly sorrowful. "Yes, I agree, you're right. Ride carefully. No, wait—" Jack Smith hesitated, dropping his dark eyes. When it came to things like this, things of the Indian side, it was never easy between half-blood brothers.

"My old friend," he said at last to his companion, "it is in my heart to say good-bye to you. I was thinking we would meet again, hoping my pride would leave Sand Creek and come up to join your people on Smoky Hill River. But I had forgotten something. Last night in the fire's glow, while you and my father lay sleeping, I saw a vision."

The Blunt youngster looked at his companion searchingly. He took the hand which Jack Smith held out to him. They gripped hard as they had seen the white man do.

"I don't understand visions," said young Blunt softly. "Yet you know that I honor your own powers to see. Tell me what you saw in the fire."

Jack Smith met his glance, then looked away.

"I saw a Cheyenne lying still in the sands of Little Dried River," he said. "Some soldiers with smoking rifles stood over him. That Cheyenne was dead. The soldiers went away, talking, joking."

Young Blunt felt a chill not of the morning's cold. "You knew the face of that Cheyenne?" he asked.

"Yes, I knew it," answered the other. "It was my own face."

Jack Smith went south around the basin of the Bijou and came to the beginning of the timber along Bijou Creek. Timber, any timber at all in that sea of buffalo grass with no covert larger than would shield a prairie grouse, was retreat to be treasured. Only where bottomland or seepages gave life to the animal or wind-borne seedpods of cottonwood and willow did the trees grow. Elsewhere the prairie creeks wandered off naked of bank, level and wide and lifeless of valley. A mouse might find it difficult to disappear in such an empty space, let alone a man and a mustang.

It was scarcely 6:00 A.M. when Jack reached the timber. The daylight was still gray and murky. He should have been thinking of scouting the shadowy trees before riding into them, but he was not. The young half-breed could not drive from his Cheyenne imagination the fearful image he had seen in the coals of the Cherry Creek campfire. He had been so certain of his recognition of the familiar sandy channel of Ponoeohe. He had known so positively the uniforms of the pony soldiers who had shot down the young brave who lay in the dry streambed of the Sand Creek channel. What Indian would not know the Third Colorado? And he had been so frighteningly sure of the dark and knife-cut features of that pock-marked dead Indian's face staring up at him and at the joking soldiers.

It was a bad thing, looming darker and darker to young Jack Smith. He determined quickly that he would rest but a single hour before traveling on; and that one hour only because his mount had gone the whole night and must be given a grace of water and grass. "Ho-shuh, small friend," he said aloud as the first of the willows closed behind them. "We are safe now for a little while. You can rest."

His words were startlingly replied to by another Cheyenne voice, but a deep and alien one.

"Make no least motion of your body, voxpas," the voice

ordered, and with the order came a clinking of rifle hammer being put upon the cock. Jack froze like a fawn to the doe's snort.

Voxpas was a corrupted Cheyenne term for half-breed, meaning "white belly" and implying that that part of the breed which was "weak," or "white," was his belly, his courage. Jack knew the term very well and knew, as well, when to resist its insult.

"Who speaks?" he asked carefully. "You are Northern, from your tongue."

"We are Northern," admitted the voice. "What are you?"

"Southern. Black Kettle's band. My mother was a Northern. My father is Blackfoot Smith, old Moxtavata. You may have heard his name."

"We have heard it; turn around."

Jack Smith came about slowly, twisting in the saddle to see his captors. They were three in number, and surprising: A chief of indeterminate age but not young—indeed a man who had ridden far, many war trails, seen much and suffered even so; a squaw, the same number of hard-using years, not quite old yet but far, far from youth; and a child, a little slim and elfish girl, perhaps of thirteen summers.

"Do not be embarrassed." The silver-haired chief grinned. "This is my woman and my child. We are alone in this country but not altogether inexperienced. You are young; you will learn." He looked at the young half-breed with a good-humored but keen glance. "So you are the son of that old rascal, eh? I know your father, all right. He lived up north too, you know. A real blanket chief!"

"He's an old fool," said the wrinkled squaw. "Now and then he never had any sense."

"Do not be so harsh," advised her husband. "What are you called, boy?"

"Jack."

"That's all? No Indian name?"

"Just Jack."

"Well, all right; these are Wind Woman, my wife, and Blue Sky, the child. My wife is the sister of Black Kettle. You are lucky, you see? Suppose we had not been related? Ah, you think I don't mean it, young whelp of the white man?"

Jack Smith had allowed himself what, for him, was the rarest of luxuries—a brief, fleeting smile at the chief's evident salty and friendly nature. But, if he had truly read the other's character, he had missed entirely the *nature* of the man before him. The latter, however, was also a gracious man.

"Be easy," he told the young breed. "How could you know whether to smile or not to smile, when I haven't told you who I am?"

"Be prepared," interrupted the squaw, "for a recounting of all the glories of the history of the Shahi-yena, boy. When this old man begins to blow, no wind on the prairie can equal him. You may as well get down off your horse and make yourself into a comfortable position. Sometimes this takes the better part of an entire morning."

The little girl laughed at her mother's caustic accounting of the chief's penchant for oratory, but the latter's delights were scarcely stirred.

"If you giggle again," he said to the child, "I will leave you behind for the wolves. As for you, magpie," he said to the hard-faced squaw, "whoever named you, did a half-job. Wind Woman, indeed. They didn't quite finish that name for you, blustery one. It ought to have been Windy Woman, eh?"

The aging warrior showed yellowed teeth in appreciation of his own small joke, then wheeled on the waiting half-breed youth, serious in the instant.

"These are bad times for us all," he said. "We have had our grins and tauntings here; let us say what must be said."

He paused, giving Jack Smith a moment more to study him. The idea kept haunting the boy that he should know this barrel-chested, iron-faced elder of his people. The haughty bearing, the lines of sorrow and fiery pride in the leathered countenance, the old-fashioned Cheyenne roaching of the middle lock of hair, the long twin braids bound in otter-fur circlets after the ancient custom of the old tribes, everything about this Northern chief of the kindly eye which could turn to fire so fast told young Jack Smith that he was looking at a prince of his people. And he was right.

"Listen to me well, young man." The fierce eyes burned into those of the half-breed boy. "I am *Hone-ehe-hemo*, the Spotted Wolf . . ."

Spotted Wolf's story proved worthy of a careful hearing. Even had he not been one of the three premier war chiefs of the Cheyenne People—the others being Roman Nose and Little Wolf—his words would have struck fear into any red heart.

He and his family had just been down to Bent's Ranch visiting the old father of Wind Woman, who worked as a handyman for Colonel Bent and as a spy for his beleaguered people. At the ranch they had met Charley Bent, one of old William's several half-Cheyenne sons, and the wildest, according to Jack Smith's certain personal knowledge. Charley, only a boy in years, like Jack himself, had ridden into the ranch greatly excited shortly after Spotted Wolf and his wife and daughter had arrived. The halfblood youth had been up around Pueblo and learned from Indians there that advance patrols of the Third Colorado were at large on the countryside. The purpose of these advance horsemen was singular indeed—it was to shut off all traffic on the Arkansas stage road from Pueblo eastward to Fort Larned. Those patrols had already closed down all stages and even the U.S. mail riders from the Pueblo end. They were now moving swiftly out of Pueblo —right behind young Charley Bent—toward Bent's Ranch and Fort Lyon.

The purpose of their advent upon these posts could scarcely be more innocent than their descent upon Pueblo. They would seal off Bent's Ranch and Fort Lyon and thus quarantine the whole of the upper Arkansas in the face of the movement of Chivington down from Bijou Basin. This was an assumption, of course, on the part of Charley Bent and the Indians who had told him of the patrols. But if Chivington were now moving on Pueblo and his patrols were going on from that place toward Bent's Ranch and Fort Lyon, what else could they be doing but clearing the way for their commander to come on past Pueblo?

Spotted Wolf, old in war and old in the ways of the

pony soldiers, did not argue young Charley's evaluation of the patrol movements. For himself, he had not even known Chivington was back on the Arkansas, but he was prepared to accept that part of the report, as he was the Bent youth's Pueblo scouting.

He had, in fact, agreed to leave the ranch with young Charley guiding for him. Their destination was the Smoky Hill hostile's camp. But young Bent had told him that to reach the Smoky Hill they had better go back to the Black Kettle camp on Sand Creek and pick up the Smoky Hill trail at that point where it crossed the Little Dried River. Agreeable to this, since Wind Woman was anxious to see her brothers Black Kettle and Gentle Horse, Spotted Wolf had set out from Bent's place with young Charley leading the way.

Only a few miles out, however, a party of young men from the Smoky Hill band had come along and persuaded Charley he might find more excitement riding with them. Seeing the sense of that, Charley had carefully explained the route of the Sand Creek trail to Spotted Wolf. But when the old warrior tried to continue on his way the weather had changed. A heavy rain began to fall and the wind commenced to change compass with every gust. Wind Woman had promptly lost her bearings and could not find a single one of the girlhood landmarks she had sworn to in her memories of the Arkansas country. They had wandered for three days. At the end of that dreary time they had found themselves where Jack Smith had found them, in the thin timber of Bijou Creek.

They were about to depart when they saw him coming from the upper basin. It then entered their minds that they would put a gun on this ragged and evil-looking half-blood boy and see if they might not persuade him to guide them rightly to old Black Kettle's village upon Sand Creek; or if he proved obdurate or ignorant, either one, they would shoot him through the head and bury his body under a snowbank for springtime to melt out—to the effect that no prowling pony-soldier patrol might find it beforetime and suspect the presence of Spotted Wolf and his woman and his child.

"Now then, boy," growled the famed warrior, concluding his résumé of pathways lost and winter camps misplaced, "it comes to this: I will still shoot you if you don't want

to take us to Ponoeohe, or if you say that you can't do it
—whichever. I will give you the count of five of my
fingers."

He commenced at once to toll the digits of his left
hand, while his young daughter grinned and tittered in the
background; but by this time Jack Smith had learned
that the girl's giggling did not guarantee anything truly
funny was taking place and so, very hastily, he held up his
hand in the halting sign of his people.

"Wait, that's enough fingers, my father!" he said re-
spectfully. "Why would you think I would not guide you
to the winter village of my mother's people? I am glad to
do it. More than glad, very proud, to guide Spotted Wolf."

"Yes, yes," put in the woman quickly, and before her
husband might volunteer more Indian detail. "Now, come
on, we will get our ponies and let us all go away from
here very quickly. I don't like this place. My bones ache
here, and not with the weather. This is a bad place. There
are ghosts here!"

"All right," agreed Spotted Wolf grumpily. "If that's the
way it is, let's go. Are you ready, young Smith?"

The half-breed boy shook his head. Surprised, Spotted
Wolf scowled angrily. He had a temper like a trapped
bear. But this time he was given no chance to explode it.

"I would be perfectly ready, even though I am very
weary," the boy said, "except that my horse must have an
hour's rest."

Wind Woman went to the pony and ran her roughened
hand over its flank. She put her fingers under the root of
the little animal's tail, testing the moisture there. Scraping
off a bit of the lather from between the rubbing rear insides of the quarters, she sniffed it.

"True." She nodded to her scowling mate. "This horse
has been used hard."

"All right, we will rest one hour. Go and get your things
ready, woman. When I say an hour, that is all it will be."

Now Jack Smith held up his hand again in the halting
sign. "One more thing," he said. "It is clear to me that
Charley Bent does not know what he is talking about. I
know him well. He is a good friend of mine. But he gets
excited."

"What do you mean?" Spotted Wolf was scowling again
and motioning with his Winchester to be brief.

And briefly Jack Smith told him. It was a fact that Chivington's troops were not moving down on Pueblo because Jack Smith knew for a fact that they were still in Bijou Basin. Actually, they were only over that outcropping of rocks through which the creek came out of that same basin, the outcrop seen from the spot whence he himself had just ridden into the timber. If Spotted Wolf were the warrior that legend had him, he would have scouted those rocks before holing up in that timber. Then he himself would have seen the pony soldiers in that big cavalry camp and would now know that Jack Smith spoke the truth. As it was, he could still ride up there, if he hurried, and see them. Oh yes, they were indeed breaking camp to go somewhere, but it was certainly not to go down to Pueblo. How was that so certain? Well, look over there and see for yourself.

That, said young Jack, pointing to a plainly visible wagon road which ran along the far side of the wide and flat-bottomed creek channel opposite where they stood hidden in the timber, that was the trail to Pueblo from the Bijou country. Any movement of troops would be going down that road, if they meant to go to Pueblo.

At this juncture the old chief nodded. He held up a hand for silence and seemed to be cocking his gray head and listening very carefully to the voices in the wind now stirring from the north. Finally he seemed satisfied.

"Well," he said, "how do you suppose Charley Bent became so confused?´ He claimed Indians who could be trusted told him Chivington was coming down the road to Pueblo, although I will admit no mention was made of this Bijou Basin up there."

He inclined his head to the north, and Jack Smith nodded back and said quickly that he was convinced that Chivington and his troops were going to Sand Creek, that he had had a vision showing a dead Cheyenne and pony soldiers of the Third Colorado at Ponoeohe.

Spotted Wolf was impressed. He was of the old faith among the Cheyenne. If not devout as were some of the tribe's other great fighters—such as the mighty Roman Nose—he was at least cautious not to anger or insult the spirits.

"A vision," he muttered, "weighed against the word of

a son of old Bent? One half-blood puppy against another, eh?"

Jack Smith did not reply, but only sat waiting on his horse. At that moment a wind flurry blew up spinningly along the creek's channel. Lifting the light cover of surface dust from the hardened dirt of the channel, it filled the air about the timber and within it with whirling motes. For fifteen minutes the visibility was cut off across the channel. When the wind died and the suspended matter stopped spinning and sifted back to earth, the eyes of Spotted Wolf lit up in triumph.

"*Ah-hai!*" His voice hissed warningly. "Look there, coming on that wagon road from the north. Woman, go and keep our horses from whinnying. You too, child. *Nonotovestoz!*"

As the woman scuttled away, Jack Smith's hand reached for the hairy muzzle of his own nervous pony, and his eyes shot to the wagon road winding along the stream's far channel bank. Over there, in a line which did not break from the cross-creek road all the way back up to the rocks buttressing Bijou Basin, came a line of cavalry troopers, two by two and moving in the quick, shuffling trot of a column under orders to force the march.

Beyond the troopers came supply and ammunition and hospital ambulances, rumbling and creaking and popping in the snowy cold. In the short time of the wind flurries the troops had got out of the rocks and moved nearly a mile toward the timber, and were now in fact nearly opposite.

"Is that the road to Pueblo?" asked Spotted Wolf softly.

"It is," answered Jack Smith just as softly.

"And those are the troops of Maxhetan, The Very Big Man?"

"They are his troops, yes."

"Then they are not going to the camp of Black Kettle upon Sand Creek, but to Pueblo as Charley Bent told it?"

"They are going to Pueblo, yes."

"But *we* are going to the village of Black Kettle at Ponoeohe, are we not, young Smith?"

Spotted Wolf asked the question without evident anger and Jack Smith turned to find that the famed war leader was looking at him with the warm twinkle of eye and the crusty good humor which history was to make his trademarks in adversity and want, as it was to make his name feared wherever the war whoop was raised, or the carbine volley thundered in reply.

In return, the half-breed boy flashed his own dark smile. "Father, you see all things with the clarity of the light of the Dog Star." He bowed, touching his brow in respect. "As soon as the last soldier is out of sight along the Pueblo wagon road, we will go the other way—straight across to the sands of Ponoeohe."

"You're a good boy," said the weathered chief. "Smart."

"*Haho*, thank you," said Jack Smith. "Maheo guide you."

"Never mind Maheo," replied the other, nodding. "Just see that young Smith does not lose the way."

Jack Smith did not lose the trail nor did he linger upon it. The Northern Cheyenne were well mounted, and the woman and the sprite of a daughter rode like warriors. The journey to Sand Creek was made by sundown of the second day from the Bijou timber. Their arrival, with its attendant grim story of Chivington's return, caused only enough alarm in the camp of the peacefuls for a general council to be called later that night. Young Jack could not believe this casual reaction to a scouting alarm which ought to have brought down every lodge in the village within the hour. Spotted Wolf joined him in the outraged feeling. Indeed, the battle-scarred old fighter became so angry with Black Kettle that he spat on the ground in front of the gentle-spoken chieftain of all the Southern Cheyenne.

"In my lifetime," raged Spotted Wolf, "I have seen many fools among my people. Of course they are all dead now. A fool does not live forever, and I say to you people that your chiefs are fools. I am saying that Black Kettle and White Antelope have sold your lives to the liars in Denver. What makes you believe these two old cowards who will not fight and will not even talk about fighting? Why do you think they tell you the truth, when one of your own blood, a half-breed boy from your own band, returns to tell you that the mad dog, Maxhetan, is coming down the Arkansas road to hunt Indians?

"Why do you listen to such lies from these old women who call themselves your chiefs? This half-breed boy has witnesses to what he says. I support him, and so do my wife and little child. Don't you know that Wind Woman is the own sister of Black Kettle? Do you think she would lie to her brother, or to you?

"Let me say again that with my own eyes I saw all of those soldiers coming out of the Bijou Basin. They came only minutes after this boy had told me they were there. Now if they are marching to Pueblo, why is that so? Why, except to take that end of the Arkansas road and hold everybody away from it while the troops march on to Fort Lyon?

"Well, maybe you will listen to that Charley Bent boy when he returns. He went back to scout with some young Smoky Hill men who were not cowards. He and those young men will be coming back here soon to tell you what we are telling you—perhaps a great deal more—and that will turn your knees to water and your hearts to stone. No, it is not possible. I say you are already nothing but water and rocks in your insides.

"Look at you, all of you. You are standing there and shaking your heads and turning away, telling yourselves you won't listen to such war talk, that you all know that old Spotted Wolf is a war chief and knows nothing else. Well, turn away, you fools, you old women. Wait and see what young Charley Bent brings you of news.

"But I will tell you something; you are going to have to wait without me, for I will not stay here with this band of gutless sheep and peace talkers waiting to be slaughtered by that murderer of little children and women, that monster who calls himself a cavalry soldier. He marches, even as I cry out to you in this anger, down the Arkansas road toward this camp of cowards and *berdashes* who look like men but think like old women and who ought to wear dresses instead of war shirts and leggings. Pah! I spit again on the ground in front of all of you! Maheo help you; nothing else will do so."

He strode away knocking the people out of his way with his elbows, daring any of them even to look at him in a questioning way. But none of them would, and most of them slunk away like whipped camp curs. For those few who lingered to commiserate with the shamed leader of their peaceful cause—when Spotted Wolf was safely out of earshot—the empty jokes about the famed Northern war chief had a hollow sound and so did their fulsome praise for Black Kettle's magnificent tolerance in accepting the abuse of the Northern war talker.

Jack Smith, staring hard at Black Kettle before he turned away to follow Spotted Wolf, saw that these poor jests and praises did not deceive the weary and harried mind of the peace chief. Indeed, the latter did not even listen to these speeches, but turned and went into his lodge, walking like a beaten man but one too proud and stubborn to admit that his faith was shaken or his heart's trust disturbed.

When he caught up with Spotted Wolf, Jack found the chief borrowing fresh horses from relatives of Wind Woman. The indignant Northern warrior would not stay, even to eat, in the camp of his craven brother-in-law. He begged young Jack also to find a fresh mount and to join him and his little family. They were going on that very night to the Smoky Hill. Those people up there were still Cheyenne. They were still ready and willing to fight for their lives and their freedom. He, Spotted Wolf, would not pause another moment in this camp of shame upon Sand Creek.

He was as good as his word, too. Within the hour of their arrival from the Bijou timber, he had made his last plea to Jack Smith and was sitting his new pony—wife and child also remounted and ready—waiting for the half-breed youth's final answer.

"Father," said the boy, "I am grateful to you. In my mind I want to go with you, but in my heart I must stay with my own band, with my mother's people."

"That is your final word, boy?"

"Almost, Father. George Bent, older brother to Charley Bent who also lives with this band, has heard you speak tonight. He believes you. He wants me to go on a scout with him down to Bent's Ranch right away, this same night. He does not believe in waiting like women."

The Northern war chief smiled sadly. "Isn't it a strange thing," he said, "that in this big camp of our people, only two half-bloods may be found with the courage even to go and see what is happening? Well, the times change, and the Shahi-yena with them. It's not an easy thing to be of the old blood these days."

As quickly, he returned to his former sternness. "Ride swiftly on your journey," he told the half-breed youth.

"You are not a boy any longer but a warrior. You make me proud. I salute you even though you have but eighteen winters."

"Thank you, Father." Jack Smith stood for a moment watching the famed fighter quietly. Then he touched his brow and murmured shyly, "You make me proud, too, Father."

When George Bent and Jack Smith reached Bent's Ranch, they found that Charley Bent had been there and departed up the river that morning to scout for Chivington along the Pueblo end of the road. George became nervous at this information.

The fact that the stage from Fort Lyon had just come into the ranch for noon halt did little to ease the alert half-breed's concern. For another thing, Colonel Bent was not at home. He was away down the river talking to the Arapaho of Little Raven. In charge during his absence was his eldest son Robert Bent, called Jack by his intimates. Like young Charley, Robert Bent refused the white man's way. He still spoke breed English, still cleaved to all things Indian. This intransigence only added to his steadier brother's awareness of impending trouble.

Family council was held. It was decided in an air of considerable tenseness that George should ride back to Sand Creek to continue the effort of arousing Black Kettle. Jack Smith would wait at the ranch for Charley's return. If Charley were not back by sundown, Jack also was to return to Sand Creek, assuming Charley to have run into trouble or to have changed his mind and gone home to Sand Creek by another route.

With George gone, however, and the stage passengers contentedly finishing their noon meal, things quieted down.

"Maybe," Robert Bent said to Jack, "him Maxhetan go chase Injun like Hancock. No catch, no want catch. Just march around, get promotion. You think?"

"Maybe," nodded Jack, then shook his head. "But me no think that."

The noon dinner concluded, the Pueblo passengers reassembled in the yard. An elderly Cheyenne began helping the stage driver harness the fresh teams. Jack Smith and Robert Bent drifted from the ranchhouse to stand near the hitching.

Suddenly the ranch dogs commenced to bark and run out toward the Arkansas crossing. All eyes—all Indian and half-Indian eyes in the group—shifted to pick up the three ominous horsemen splashing through the shallows of the ford. The old Cheyenne helper straightened, shading his rheumy vision with a gnarled dark hand.

"*Zetapetaz hetan!*" Jack Smith heard him whisper to Robert Bent. "Him Big Man. Squaw-killer."

Glancing up from his harness-buckling, the grizzled stage driver cursed uneasily. "Goddamnit," he said. "It *is* Chivington."

Chivington, flanked by his two troopers, rode up to the group by the Pueblo stage. As the passengers fell silent, he informed them that not a living soul was to leave Bent's Ranch until his further order. The Arkansas road, from Pueblo to Fort Lyon, was under quarantine. No one would be harmed who did not resist the injunction. Violators of the ban would be shot wherever they might be apprehended.

The stage driver, no respecter of the military, moved forward to say that he had a coachload of paying customers to deliver to Pueblo and was not of a mind to be delayed by any bunch of ragged-tailed draft dodgers out chasing bow-and-arrow Indians when they ought to be back east fighting for the Union.

Chivington, a literal giant of a man, was down off his horse in one step. "You know me, driver," he said. "If you get in my way, I will run over you."

He did not speak loudly, but the stage driver, as certainly as half-breed Jack Smith now standing fearfully in the shadows of the coach, understood that the impression of real and present danger was no mirage. The driver bobbed his head. "It's your army," he said.

Chivington next instructed Robert Bent to convey the quarantine order to every person on the ranch not already accounted for. Bent scrambled up a ladder to the rooftop of the ranchhouse and called out the order in English, Spanish and Cheyenne, and as loudly as he was able.

"Tell them," Chivington called up to him, "to get

around here in the front yard with the others. This entire area is surrounded by my pickets. Anyone, grown man, woman, child or cur dog, that tries to slip away will be shot on sight."

As he spoke, an unbroken line of cavalry came into view across the Arkansas. The troops were moving fast, Jack Smith saw, and the half-breed shrank back farther still into the shadows of the coach.

"Why," said one of the astonished passengers, a boot salesman from St. Louis, "there must be 300 of them."

"Closer to 400," corrected a traveling companion, a Leavenworth whiskey drummer.

"Guess again, the both of you," said the stage driver, swinging down from the top of his vehicle. "Past the bend where you cain't see from here, there's another 200 of First Cavalry coming along. That's nigh onto 600 troops, all hoss-mounted and moving fast for Fort Lyon."

He paused, looking off concernedly.

"I hope to Gawd," he added fervently, "they ain't after them pore damned peacefuls up on Big Sandy."

Big Sandy was the colloquial name for Sand Creek. Not aware of this, the two salesmen nodded knowingly. "I actually don't think Chivington means to cause any harm," one of them offered. "I never did believe all the bloody stories about him myself. He's a preacher, you know. Yep, regular ordained minister of one of the big churches."

"Yes, that's so, I hear." The second salesman was also an expert on Arkansas lore. "One thing certain: Preacher Chivington's been given credit for a lot of Indian scrapes he was never near. I've been on this run long enough to know that, my friend."

The driver studied the last speaker and shifted his cud of shag-leaf chewing tobacco. He spat toward the drummer's shoes, splattering them nicely.

"You been on this run long enough to know you're a damned mealy-mouthed liar," he said disgustedly. "Shut your mouth."

"Now see here!" cried the drummer. "I don't have to take that from you!"

"True," said the driver, grinning. "Hand it back."

The drummer, caught, took another tack. "Listen," he said, "you don't need to take my word for it. Nor I don't have to take yours. We can ask that young breed yonder. He'd ought to know all about the Colonel's so-called Injun atrocities."

A look, very nearly of pure pleasure, invaded the driver's granite features.

"Go ahead," he said, "ask him. That is," he added with a significant pause, "providing you can find him."

The drummer wheeled about, staring in the direction where Jack Smith had last been standing.

"Why," he said, "he's gone!"

The driver spat again. "Seems to be," he said.

Recovering, the flustered salesman shouted for Chivington to beware, that the half-breed had made a break. The big officer pounced like a cat upon the warning, but he was too late. Somehow, whether with the collaboration of the irate stager or by his own desperation, unaided, Jack Smith had made his escape in broad daylight from the Bent's Ranch stockade.

An afternoon of fine-comb-searching for his hiding place, or avenue of exit, revealed nothing. There was no hint even of the way in which he had evaporated.

Chivington, after an initial outburst, grew calm. The youth could not have gone far, of that he was definitely convinced. He had his pickets ringing the ranch so tightly spaced that they were at actual voice-touch with one another, as well as within uninterrupted sight. Nothing could have passed between them unchallenged. Chivington believed, rather, that the Cheyenne son of old Uncle John Smith had managed to hole up somewhere inside the military perimeter around Bent's Ranch. Sooner or later he would have to come out from whatever badger den or coyote nest he had found. When he did that, the soldiers remaining behind at the ranch would have him trapped. And they had their orders.

Meanwhile Colonel J. M. Chivington had a date with destiny down the Arkansas road. Resting his troops that afternoon, he threw them back upon the march as soon as full darkness was down. Tempo was double-time, destination unannounced. Within the hour of sundown, the last of the roughclad column had clanked back across the Arkansas and were gone.

Jack Smith ran afoot northeasterly through the night.

Behind him lay Bent's Ranch and the river. Ahead waited Sand Creek and he knew not what. But behind waited only the baffled soldiers of the Third Colorado, and death for Jack Smith. The thought of the Pale Spirit caused the half-breed's heart to drop. He slowed his pace to the steady dogtrot which would melt the miles yet not exhaust the runner. He remembered now what waited ahead of him. Death, it seemed, stood in the dark for Jack Smith, whether at the ranch of old Bent or the camp of old Black Kettle.

He turned his dark face upward to the stars showing beyond the scudding rifts of snowcloud. "Help me, Maheo," he said, and ran on. He would trust the Cheyenne Allfather. It was his duty meanwhile to warn the people at Ponoeohe. If he ran well and did not encounter soldiers or other harm, he should be in the camp the following night. He might have made it sooner, except that he had had to wait a long time where he was hidden, until the pickets of Colonel Chivington grew cold and careless with the lateness of the night and he could creep from the hiding place—which must not even be imagined in the mind, lest someone not of Cheyenne blood discover it—and get far enough away from the ranch to cross the river and be free to start for home, hungry, heartsick and horseless.

Where was his friend, young Charley Bent? Had George Bent made it safely back to Sand Creek? What would happen to Robert Bent, who had been impressed into service as a scout and guide by Chivington, as he marched away from the ranch? Had his other dearer friend, young Blunt, reached the Smoky Hill people safely? Would those strong and brave Indians come down to help the Black Kettle people? Would they prepare to fight where they were? Would they flee north to the Republican or the Arikaree River, saving themselves and forsaking their Southern sisters and brothers?

And what of his own people when he reached them? Could Black Kettle and White Antelope listen to him now, when they had covered their ears before? What did he have to show them for proof of what he would report? Why should they accept his word this time, when they had refused it the other time? They would think his mind was going, that his great fear of Colonel Chivington had

disturbed his reason, or that the Bents had poisoned him
against the white man and the military. But it did not
matter. He would do his best. He would get his father to
appeal to the chiefs. They would listen to him.

Heartened, the breed boy trotted on through the darkness. When dawn came, not daring to travel afoot in daylight, he found an abandoned den of the buffalo wolf
and burrowed into it and slept until darkness fell once
more. He chewed some roots which he knew to give
strength, drank a little cold water from a nearby seepage
and set out again.

Midnight came and passed. He trotted steadily. His
moccasins began to break apart. His feet commenced to
bleed. After a while he made out through the eerie starlight the slope which led down to the timber marking
Rush Creek. He nodded at the sight and said some soft
Cheyenne words of thanks. There remained another ten
miles, perhaps a little more, and he would be home.

Starting on, he had little immediate concern over
Chivington and the Third Colorado. Of course the troops
would need to be rested when they reached Fort Lyon.
To have got to Bent's Ranch from the Bijou Basin in
those few days since passed, the soldiers and their mounts
would have to be weary. They would camp at least two
days at Fort Lyon before going on to wherever their commander was taking them. The day after tomorrow would
be the soonest that all those hundreds of soldiers could
be got moving again. There would be many daylight
hours in which to scout them and, if need be, to move the
village out from in front of their advance. *Wagh*, it was
good. Maheo was up there watching out for his half-
Cheyenne child, as Jack Smith had always known that he
was.

Coming a little later to the Rush Creek crossing, Jack
felt compelled to stop. Instead of going on over the small
stream, he lay up in some grasses on an elevated point
just above where the old Indian trail made its fording.

Now the morning was perhaps but two hours away.
The heavens were black as smoke-hole soot, the stars
glittering white as ice. But away to the east a faint be-
traying tinge of gray gave warning of the new day. Jack
was puzzled. His examination of the trail at the crossing

had shown him no fresh pony droppings. With two or three cupped matches he had seen no marks of iron horseshoes to show him pony-soldier mounts had passed this way. The unshod hoofmarks and all of the droppings gave evidence only of Indian travel, and no travel at all in the past hours of the night.

Why then this compulsion to linger on Rush Creek? The half-breed boy rolled his dark eyes. This was the black hour of the morning when the Indian dead, who came above the earth with twilight, returned to their spirit homes. It was their favored time for capturing some living Indian to take back to the lower world with them. Jack Smith wanted to run, and to run fast, but a stronger spell made him wait, made him lie another minute longer in the dry grasses.

It was then that he heard it, the thud in soft trail dust of shod horses' hoofs, the musical tinkling and clinging of the iron shoes striking some pebble or streak of exposed bedrock. Closer now it came; the ringing of bit and spur chains, the clinking of stirrup irons, of buckles against cinches, of bridle snaps and linkings. Then the creak of saddle leather, the squeak of fenders and skirts, the rubbing of riders' boots. Now he could hear the breathing of the horses and their snuffling.

Suddenly he saw the men: four horsemen—two pony soldier officers, two civilian scouts. The leading horseman loomed against the darkness of the trail like a giant shade from the lower places. It was Chivington.

The horsemen halted at the ford directly beneath Jack Smith's hiding place. In the stillness, the snaffling and blowing of the lathered mounts, the rank odor of the horse sweat and wet leather carried plainly to the half-breed. The voices of the riders carried as well. Chivington spoke.

"Well, Scott, how do you like nightriding so far?"

"Not overly, Colonel. But I must say we've made amazing time. We can't have more than eight or ten miles left. We should be in position by daylight."

The crouching half-breed knew this voice, too. It was that of Major Scott Anthony, the commander at Fort Lyon and the man handpicked by Chivington to replace the kindly Wynkoop; the man who had, only that same week, given Black Kettle and a delegation of his worried chiefs tobacco and coffee and assurances of their continued safety on Sand Creek; and the man who, many Indians said, had put the old chief and his people on Ponoeohe only so that he would know exactly where to go and get them when he had enough soldiers to do so. Now he had that many soldiers, with Chivington to lead them. In his thin nest of wintergrasses atop the creekbank, the half-breed boy knew near-panic.

Chivington turned in his saddle. "Beckwourth!" he barked at one of the scouts. "Get up here."

Both scouts kneed their mounts forward. The starlight fell upon them and the half-breed recognized them. They were Robert "Jack" Bent and the legendary Jim Beckwourth, the mulatto mountain man of the days of Uncle Dick Wooton, Bill Williams, Joe Meeks and Brokenhand Fitzpatrick.

Beckwourth was old now, partly blind and bent with rheumatism. His was still a name with which to conjure, or by which to follow the tracks of an Indian band. Yet his many winters and the darkness of the night, together with the bone-aching cold, had conspired to confuse old Jim.

"Well," demanded Chivington, "don't sit there like a yellow lump of mud. What do you say?"

Beckwourth hunched in his saddle. What teeth remained to him were clenched against the freezing wind which cut along the creekbank and rattled the dry brush of its winter bed. The aging mulatto shook his head helplessly.

"I cain't do no more for you, Colonel, suh. I'm that blue with the bone-cold I cain't even get out'n the saddle. Eyes gone to watering so fierce I cain't make out nothing. I'm done, all done—"

Chivington ignored him on the instant. "Well, Bent?"

The son of William Bent raised a hand, signaling for the talk to suspend. He stood in his stirrups, right ear cocked in the direction of the cross-stream darkness and Sand Creek. After a lengthy pause, during which Uncle John Smith's son listened as painfully hard as the white officers, Bent spoke softly.

"Wolf he howl," he announced. "Injun dog he hear wolf, he howl too. Injun he hear dog and listen; hear something else, and him run off."

Chivington made nothing of the breed's broken report. He was plainly angered with Bent's "Indian talk," which he considered spurious in style as well as content.

Robert Bent saw the starlight glint along the barrel of the long cavalry revolver. He stiffened as Chivington put the weapon's chill muzzle against his temple.

"Jack," said the giant officer, "I haven't had an Indian to eat for a long time. If you fool with me and don't lead us to that camp, I'll have you for breakfast."

Bent merely nodded his understanding. "Two hour more," he said, "light come."

"All right," decided Chivington. "Let's go."

Jack Smith came to the Cheyenne pony herds on the south bank of the Sand with daybreak only minutes away. He was able to thread his way among the hundreds of grazing animals because his smell was the smell of an Indian, and of one of their own Indians. At the creek the youth crouched a moment, preparing himself for the last dash over the open streambed, into the silent camp.

All about him, as he had come up to the herds, had been the movements of the Fort Lyon and Bijou Basin soldiers. He knew, with certainty, that there were troops above the village, below the village, and behind him on the far side of the pony herds. It had been no problem in the dark for one slim half-breed boy to slip through the converging ranks of Chivington's and Anthony's men. But now the light was growing and the flat sanded bottoms of the creek were wide and as bare of cover as a hairless dog. And Jack Smith had run out of time.

The breed boy leaped to his feet and ran low through the banks of ground mist which still swirled through the bottomland. His flight drew no fire. The next moment he was in the village and racing for the lodge of his father, pitched in the center of camp near those of the main chiefs Black Kettle and White Antelope. As he ran he saw no sign of awakened or alarmed life among the Cheyenne, save for a few old women who were out with first streak of day to gather the breakfast firewood.

Trying to warn these ancient squaws of the approaching troops, he found they only laughed at him and thought he was playing a poor joke upon them. Desperately Jack raced through the sleeping village toward his father's lodge. The elder Smith had reached home and was bedded with his Cheyenne woman at the rear of the tipi. Entering the smoky darkness, Jack shook the squawman awake and gave him the alarm.

Aroused, Uncle John still refused to believe his son. Nevertheless, he got grumblingly into his leggings, agreeing to go outside and examine the timber beyond the creek for possible sight of cavalry. Jack's mother, as calloused as the older squaws to her son's protestations of "hundreds of soldiers only across the stream," ordered him to lower his voice; he would alarm the younger children. Jack, frantic now, ran back out of the lodge and was met with an incredible sight.

Down by the creek, plainly visible to his keen young eyes and looming by growing hundreds now above the ground mist, were the uniformed figures of the gathering enemy horsemen. That *was* pony-soldier cavalry over there. No sane Cheyenne could doubt it or linger to discuss it. Ye the old women had stopped gathering firewood to throw stones happily and wave their blankets at the fog-shrouded horsemen, calling out as they did so the Indian words which meant "Shoo! Go away and graze another place!"

Jack Smith stood, unable to believe his senses. Those crazy old ladies thought the cavalry to be a herd of buffalo! Wheeling, the young breed leaped down the village street toward the lodge of Black Kettle, crying the alarm to all. But he was too late. Behind him, as he ran, the firing was begun by Captain Wilson's battalion of the First Cavalry, detailed to cut off the Cheyenne pony herds; and, at first rifle crack, the wild Indian mounts commenced to run.

As the stampede set in, the soldiers above and below the camp closed in. The streets of the village were almost instantly enfiladed by a whistling, popping cross fire. Indians, now running out of tipis half-clad or not clad at all, began to scream and to drop writhing or silent upon the ground.

Jack Smith was in the very center of it. He saw Major Anthony's battalion of mounted troops come into the village from the southeast. He saw his father, old Uncle John Smith, run out of his lodge still tugging on his leggings. He heard him beg and plead with the incoming

troops to stop firing, that they had the wrong camp, that
these Cheyenne were the peacefuls of Black Kettle, that
the blind and senseless cross-firing was murdering innocent women and children, that they, all of the officers
there, and many of the men, knew him well. They knew
he was Agent Colley's interpreter. Uncle John Smith!
Uncle John Smith! Uncle John Smith! He screamed the
name at them again and again. One of the officers so appealed to, and clearly annoyed, said to his sergeant,
"Shoot the old fool and shut him up." Uncle John, hearing him, ran sobbingly back into his lodge.

Son Jack now raced through the ricocheting bullets,
actually dodging cavalry horses, saber slashes and the
aimed blasts of cavalry Colts and carbines, to reach the
tipi of his parents. It was in his mind to do what he
might to help his father get his mother and the several
smaller Smith children out of the lodge and somewhere
to safety. But when he lunged into the darkness of his
home, only his father was there, sobbing still and calling
for his wife and little ones.

The rearskins of the lodge were slashed by a knife.
Through this gaping hole, no doubt, the Cheyenne mother
had hurried her brood. Now Maheo alone knew where
they might be in that camp of hell, and whether dead or
alive, hale or in some horror of wound or outrage amid
the welter of dying Indians who already lay in the streets
in windrows. The half-breed youth knew, too, that all he
could do now was to save himself; even as he hesitated,
staring at the knife-slashed exit hole, he heard his father
run out of the lodge behind him and off down the street
crying aloud for mercy and for sanctuary.

But now there was a difference in the plea. Uncle John
was no longer asking after the safety of his Indian wife
and half-blood Cheyenne children. He was begging to
be saved himself. And that was all. Young Jack felt the
last of his world disappear with the form of his weeping
father into the packed, reeking mass of pony-soldier
horsemen.

Stumbling out of the lodge, he made for the streambed
of the Sand, following the earlier exodus of the main
body of fleeing Cheyenne. He was in time to catch up
with the last of that fugitive group and to see—only in
time to stay back and save himself—that they were being

driven squarely from the rear by the mounted troops of
Anthony into the massed dismounted rifles of Chivington's Third Colorado, thrown into a solid dam of gun barrels across the channel of the creek. It was a planned
ambush.

Seeing this, the approaching Indians called out to the
waiting Colorado volunteers that most of their number
were women and children. This the troops could see for
themselves, they implored. Why not let the women and
children go back, turn away? Then the soldiers could
shoot them, the men. Chivington's reply to this was to
flick his gauntlet and instruct his men in drillground calm
to "fire at will."

Jack tried then to turn back into the village. He got
far enough to see Black Kettle standing in front of his
lodge pointing to the American flag which fluttered upon
its white pole to mark the tipi of the chief. He heard the
old man pleading with the soldiers to see that, beneath
the Stars and Stripes, a while cloth of surrender had also
been run up. This was a friendly camp, already surrendered, already given up to the cavalry at Fort Lyon,
long ago. Some say the soldiers laughed, some recall
that they did not. Jack Smith heard no laughter. But he,
and all who saw, agreed upon one thing—the soldiers
never quit firing.

The young half-breed saw White Antelope, seventy-
five years old and most honored of the old-time Cheyenne among the Southern people. The white-haired warrior refused to run when his friend Black Kettle at last
came limping past with his squaw and urged his old
comrade to come with them, to try to make it to the
streambed and join the fleeing people there.

White Antelope folded his arms across his chest. He
shook his head and stood erect before the entrance of his
lodge, and Jack heard the croaking of his feeble voice
intoning the ancient Shahi-yena prayer of those about to
die:

> *Nothing lives long, nothing stays here,*
> *Except the earth and the mountains. . . .*

The half-breed boy saw the hail of soldier bullets cut
through the fringes of the old chief's beaded doeskin

shirt; saw the proud old man buckle and slide down into a sitting position, dead and starey-eyed in the open doorway of his lodge.

Mercifully that was the last of the nightmare memories in that camp for Jack Smith. A blast of soldier fire, the same volley which cut down White Antelope, turned him for the final time back to the streambed. Minutes later he had got beyond the blockade of Chivington's riflemen and was striking up the narrowing bed of the creek for the Cheyenne rifle pits which he knew to exist above the encampment.

But there was, in truth, one other last thing which he witnessed in leaving the village. However, it was not a nightmare memory. Indeed, it should have made Jack Smith happy, but for some uneasy reason it did not. It seemed wrong to him; a thing an Indian would not do; a thing only a white man, even a white man with an Indian wife and red children, would do. It worried Jack Smith but he never dishonored himself by telling it.

What he saw as he turned away was his father. Uncle John was alone. Jack's mother was not with him. None of their young children were with him. But Uncle John was looking for someone, and it was not them. He ran a few steps this way, then that way. Some new troops, just driving into the village, bore down upon him. At their head was Chivington. The giant had left his bloody fortress in the riverbed. Uncle John did not see him, but Chivington saw the old squawman. He flung up his gauntlet with a friendly roar. "Ho, Uncle John! Run here!"

The squawman saw and recognized the Colonel of the Third Colorado. He scuttled to the side of the latter's horse, jumping and stumbling over the dead bodies of his wife's and his children's people in doing so. Seizing the officer's stirrup, he clung to it and ran along in that craven manner with Chivington and his murderers.

When the haze and gunsmoke of the heavy soldier firing hid the two from Jack Smith's view, the half-breed's father was still clutching at Chivington's boot, still cringing by the side of the squaw-killer's horse to save his own life.

The breed boy tried to remember his father in a better way than this. His mother's people, the Cheyenne, owed much to Uncle John Smith. The old white interpreter had perhaps prevented many such slaughters as this terrible one. He had worked his entire life for the red man. But Jack Smith was not able to make his mind obey and believe that better thing. He could only remember his father clawing at Chivington's boot, saving himself, white man turning to white man in the final bitter end of things. That was the last haunting memory which the son of Uncle John Smith bore away with him from the main camp at Ponoeohe.

After that came the rifle pits. These natural entrenchments were located where the banks of Sand Creek, above the village, narrowed and grew high and honeycombed with the time gougings of wind and water. The Indians called the stronghold Voxse, the Place Where the Pits Are. When Jack Smith reached the site, there were some 400 troops ringed about it, and the cornered Cheyenne fugitives crouching within its shallow depressions were already in desperate plight. Yet the fact that plunged the half-breed's heart to blackest depth was not the number but the identity of those troops. They were *all* of the Third Colorado Volunteers. Colonel J. M. Chivington had found the main blood trail of the Sand Creek survivors before any of the other commanders might do so. The people, barring a miracle of Maheo, were doomed.

In the pits themselves it was like an animal-killing pen. The sand and soft stone of the bank were slippery with blood and the shot-away parts of intestine, lung, bone and brain which lay everywhere. Living Indians rested in the same slime with the dead. After the first hour which saw Jack Smith reach the Cheyenne redoubt, the stench of human urine and bowel matter emitted by the wounded made of the battle offal in the pits a thing of separate terror in itself. The half-breed youth became ill. He wretched repeatedly until there was nothing, not even the yellow-green bile, to empty from his tortured gut. All that kept him sane, kept him in the pits, was the presence of the Bent brothers there with him. Of the two, Charley, who had returned only in time to join the retreat up the Sand, was the one he would longest remember.

The soldiers, as the hours wore on, would not charge the pits frontally and so bring a merciful end to the fight. From time to time, as their officers determined through field glasses that the men in a certain pit were all dead, an assault would be made upon that pit. The other Cheyenne could not stop these individual attacks because they had only a few guns, a few rounds of ammunition, and must wait for the last wave. They had to huddle and watch as the soldiers cleaned out the fighterless pits, took rifles and clubbed each woman, child, old person, even nursing infant left thus to their civilized charity.

Jack Smith did not care to remember time or detail, but he would never forget the final atrocity at the rifle pits of his mother's people. As with the chanting of old White Antelope and the surrendering of his squawman father, the last action at the pits was such a thing as stupefied the Indian mind.

The Cheyenne women in the central pits despaired of life toward the end. Seeing their sisters and little children of their sisters shot and clubbed in the other pits, reason abandoned these poor mothers. They told their men that the soldiers were doing those other killings because in the excitement of rushing the various cut-off pits, the troopers did not have time to distinguish between man and woman, between adult and child, between old and young. They cried out to their men, "If the soldiers knew that we were women, they would not shoot us or knock out our brains like that. Have they not always said, the white men, that they do not kill women and children? *Ai! Ai!* We must run out there and show them that we truly are women."

The men in the pits were aghast at such wildness. "Shame, shame!" they cried out in return. "Have your minds left you? Don't say such crazy things. Those soldiers know you are women. Be still. Die here with us like Cheyenne."

But the women had seen too much of blood and death. "Care for the children!" they said, weeping in farewell, and before their men might stop them, leaped from the pits and ran toward the white lines calling out, "We are women, we are women!"

As they ran, they lifted up their skirts to prove to the soldiers that they did not lie. The riflemen of the Third Colorado shot them down as they came on. The few which survived to reach the ranks of the executioners were clubbed to the last squaw.

It was after that that the soldiers lost their belly for the fight and went away downstream to loot and bicker among their own number for the spoils of the burning village. The Cheyenne, after waiting to be certain they were gone, left the pits and began the slow, terrible retreat up Sand Creek and away from the horrors that had been Ponoeohe. But Jack Smith did not join that retreat.

The Cheyenne people had no horses with them at all. Everyone understood that some ponies must be procured to transport the many injured, aged and infants among them. Six brave young men, all of the young men who were with the survivors—save for George Bent, who was crippled with a bullet in or through his hips—wanted to go back and try and get those few ponies. Black Kettle, however, ruled that four of the young men must stay to help the weak and wounded. Only two would return to the village. They would be the best and wiliest of the six, experienced in such things. They would be young Charley Bent and Jack Smith.

There was no argument. The two youthful half-bloods went at once downstream. The Cheyenne, with Black Kettle at their head, began laboring up the windy and freezing channel of the Sand. For Black Kettle, as for his remaining tribesmen, the parting with the quiet son of Blackfoot Smith was not to be "until the next time."

The long hours wore on. The whistling cold increased. The people longed to be far away from the deathholes at Voxse, but their progress was a continuing agony of slowness due to the many wounded and the high number of small children among the survivors—children who had to be given particular attention and love because their mothers had left them to run toward the pony soldiers crying, "We are women!"

But the wounded walked, or crawled, or were dragged along by the unwounded. And the children, somehow, found arms still strong enough to carry them. Then at last, as the icy twilight was shutting down, the first joyous sight was seen through the winter gloom—men, Cheyenne young men, with a few ponies, were coming in from the darkling prairie to join the fugitives. These warriors had caught up the horses early in the fight; they had seen nothing of Charley Bent or young Jack Smith.

The precious mounts were given to the most sorely wounded and the retreat went on another ten numbing miles from the rifle pits at Voxse. Then, in utter arctic cold, the halt had to be called. The human spirit would bear no more.

Still the weather deepened. By midnight the temperature stood between freezing and zero Fahrenheit. The men and women and older children, all who could still walk, went out into the black void and dug in the old snow for grass to bundle and burn for warming fires. The grasses were also matted beneath and heaped over the wounded, the old and sick, and the young babies, to keep them from dying in the plunging cold. None of the people had their winter clothing. Many were half dressed. All had been driven from their beds by the attack, except for the old squaws out gathering breakfast wood; and the old squaws were all sleeping back along the trail that night, sleeping forever.

All through the night hours the Cheyenne called plaintively into the surrounding darkness so that any wandering survivor might know they were there, might come in and be with them, not die alone on the prairie with no Indian hand to comfort him or calm his terror. But no one came in out of the darkness.

By 3:00 A.M. the warriors knew that the people could not live there in that icy ravine. All were ordered up. The ponies were again loaded with sick and injured. The strongest men carried the little children. There were very few women left to do this. Of all the drifts and moundings of silent red bodies left behind in the Sand Creek bottoms, two out of three were women and children, and more women than children.

In the noisome pits at Voxse itself, apart from the camp, seventy dead were counted when the soldiers left and the Indians tottered away. No Cheyenne knew how many other dead were left that day of Preacher Chivington's last Indian service. The Cheyenne knew only that somewhere across that freezing blackness lay the Smoky Hill River and the camp of their relatives who had not trusted Governor Evans and Major Anthony. So it was that their warriors aroused them out of the ravine and led them on through the blind night, praying to see daylight and the sight of their friends on the Smoky Hill.

And this time Maheo was listening. When the day broke across the frost-rimed buffalo grass, they saw their friends and relatives coming through the sunrise toward them. Some other young men with ponies had reached the Smoky Hill people with the news of Sand Creek. Now the kinsmen and friends were rejoined. Cooked meat, warm blankets, riding horses and medicines for the wounded were given the fugitives, and all were carried swiftly back to the Smoky Hill encampment. There the farewell prayers and the keening of the women for their dead made a sound in the prairie morning that each Cheyenne would remember until the Allfather gathered him to the Land of the Shadows.

Scouts from Smoky Hill went out immediately to watch the trail from Sand Creek and from Fort Lyon, and to find what they might find on the deserted slaughter grounds of Ponoeohe. But they found nothing and they returned with no word. The pony soldiers were gone. No living thing, Indian or white man, stirred along the sands on the Little Dried River.

On the morning of the third day, a gaunt young ghost of Black Kettle's people drifted in through the dawn mists of the prairie. He was riding a bony Cheyenne scrub, leading behind him a riderless buckskin. Black Kettle knew that buckskin pony. So did a tall Cheyenne squaw of the Smoky Hill people standing with the Sand Creek welcomers.

Charley Bent rode up to them. He said no word to Black Kettle, but spoke to the tall Smoky Hill woman.

"You are the mother of young Blunt?" he said.

"Yes," said the woman.

"And you know this buckskin horse that I lead?"

"Yes, that is the horse of my son's friend, Jack Smith."

Charley Bent nodded. He got down stiffly and handed the lead rope of Jack Smith's pony to the woman.

"Jack would have wanted your son to have this horse," he said.

The woman took the pony, nodding in return.

"The pony soldiers caught Jack Smith and me," said Charley Bent. "They were of the Third Colorado, all of them. They had both of us captive for a full day, then took us out into the river bottom and stood us against a bank. Because our fathers were white, some of the men were afraid. They said Chivington better be told. Men went to him and came back and laughed and said the colonel only repeated his orders, 'no prisoners,' when told of our capture. The soldiers shot Jack then. They were still laughing, some of them. As they turned to shoot me, some friends of my father in the New Mexico Infantry came up and made them stop. Those New Mexican boys took me away from Chivington's men and saved my life."

Bent's son paused, looking back toward Sand Creek. "The last thing I saw of Jack Smith," he said, "the soldiers were prodding at his body with their boots and joking about something. I remember that the muzzles of their rifles were still smoking. I could see Jack's face underneath that smoke. He was dead with his eyes wide open."

The Cheyenne woman who was the mother of young Blunt touched her brow in respect toward Charley Bent. "Thank you for this fine horse," she said. "I will tell my son how his friend died at Little Dried River. Ride with Maheo."

Charley Bent said nothing. He shrugged and turned his pony and disappeared back into the dawn mists toward Sand Creek. After him rode the legend.

Half-Blood Brother

Young Blunt turned restlessly upon his straw pallet. It was hard to find sleep. The confinement of the Fort Dodge stableyard, where he had spread his blankets, made him uneasy. Moreover, the thumping of the dance drums from the Cheyenne camp just beyond the stockade was of a tempo and insistency to pry at the nerves of any half-blood such as himself.

It had been a difficult day for the youthful interpreter. Sired by a white father, reared by a Cheyenne mother, he was suspected by both sides, accepted by neither. This dual standard by which he was compelled to work and by which he could certainly be held responsible was inhumanly critical, he thought. As the son of Ezekial Blunt, the Smoky Hill trader, the white troop commanders would expect him to remain constant to them. As the son of his Indian mother, the Cheyenne would count upon him to "speak with a red tongue."

Blunt sat up and looked around the stableyard for what seemed to him the hundredth time since raking up his straw bed at prairie nightfall. Lord, it was quiet on that post. And Lord, it would be easy to go over that stockade without anyone being the wiser. What he wouldn't give, too, to do it and so be free of sitting between the two sides as translator in tomorrow's continuing session of the

Fort Dodge peace talks between Custer and the Southern
Cheyenne. The strain, the temptation, was intolerable.

"Be still!" he snapped at his saddled pony. "I can't sleep
with you stomping around." The pony pricked its ears
and whickered.

Young Blunt nodded wearily. "Sure, sure," he said. "I
know it ain't your fault."

He rolled a smoke, using the cigarette tobacco given
him by Custer's executive officer, Captain Benteen. After
a few puffs he nodded to himself. Of course it was not
his pony's stompings which were keeping him awake. It
was that Indian girl. Young Blunt smiled and lay back
against his saddle. Ah! how he would like to see that girl
again.

Then, as quickly, he thought of her fierce parentage and
lost the dreamy smile. Spotted Wolf, her father, was one
of the Stone Calf band of war chiefs—Indians who wanted
to fight the white man—as against the peace chiefs, headed
by Black Kettle, who understood that any such militant
course was suicide for the Cheyenne.

Wind Woman, the girl's mother, also had great in-
fluence with the hostile elements of her tribe. She would
scarcely be partial to "educated" half-bloods like young
Blunt who were paid to interpret yet talked for peace.

The dark-faced youth sighed heavily. Few in years or
not—he had turned twenty-three that past summer—young
Blunt was still the son of Ezekial Blunt. He was the best
friend of the Cheyenne among the white men; the best
friend of the white men among the Cheyenne. Not even
his trusted father could claim such common-blood distinc-
tion. Young Blunt was all that stood between the
Southern Cheyenne of Stone Calf and Black Kettle, and
an Indian War that could sweep the prairies of the Arkansas and the Smoky Hill free of settlers and pony
soldiers alike that autumn of 1868.

The half-breed punched at his saddle. He squirmed on
the prickly ticking of the straw pallet. He thought of what
another year of war along the Solomon, the Smoky Hill
and the Arkansas might mean in terms of disaster to his
mother's people. For the past two summers the Cheyenne
had raided and murdered along these rivers, and a dozen
other rivers north and south of them. In 1866, after Sand
Creek, they had gone to the high country of Wyoming to

help the Sioux wipe out Colonel Carrington and Captain Fetterman and Fort Phil Kearney. It had been the great Cheyenne hero Little Wolf who had actually put the starting torch to the burning of that ill-fated post. In the other raids—the bloodiest of all—against Julesburg, Platte River Bridge, Cimarron Crossing, scores of white lives had been lost. In that last summer of '68 alone, 117 settlers had been killed and seven women carried away into Indian slavery—a fate not always as kind as death.

To let the mind dwell upon such statistics against the Cheyenne half of his blood was to court desperation. Another year of war by the Indians was unthinkable. Young Blunt loved his mother's people. He was himself a Cheyenne in his soul. And not alone in his soul. He looked like a Cheyenne and much of the time behaved with the peculiar dignity and restraint of the horseback Indian of the high plains. But his thinking and reasoning was partly white. So it was that he understood the present situation which kept him within the stockade. So it was, too, that he realized the danger of that situation to his red relatives more than they themselves possibly could.

If the coming summer did not bring peace it would bring savage destruction to the Cheyenne. The cavalry was ready, even eager to carry out the death sentence against them. If they made so much as one premature mistake—scalped one settler, shot one soldier, sent one war party north of the Arkansas River line of the Medicine Lodge Treaty, stole a settler horse, cut up a settler cow, took away one white woman or one white child or even burned one settler barn—the pony soldiers of Custer would be sent out to hunt to earth the Cheyenne people of the South. This much young Blunt knew from the kindly Benteen, as good an unsung friend as the redman ever had and, in young Blunt's opinion, a better soldier than Yellow Hair Custer on the best day the latter ever had against the Indians.

But how was a half-breed interpreter to impress this mortal danger upon his mother's people? He could not do it in open council, for there he was merely repeating for the chiefs the words of the pony soldier chiefs. And the Cheyenne had never worried a great deal about such words, or such chief. What must be done, if anything were to be done, was to go to the Cheyenne and tell them what

the good Benteen had told him, young Blunt: that Custer
had been told to start killing Indians at his own discretion
along the Arkansas, awaiting only such excuse as would
serve to placate the Eastern papers and the sobbing hearts
in the Bureau of Indian Affairs. Now, judging from the
temper of the proud warriors in that day's exchange with
Custer and his juniors, the Cheyenne were in gravest
jeopardy of supplying the army with its excuse.

The youthful interpreter sat up and made another cigarette. He cursed again the stillness of the stockade, the
continuing throb of the drums, the heat of the night, the
switch and slap of his pony's restive tail. Then he looked
up into the blackness of the prairie sky. He saw up there
the blazing trail of the Hanging Road—Ekutsihimmiyo, as
the Cheyenne called it—that great bridge between heaven
and earth up which the Indian dead departed and which
the white man named the Milky Way. The star trail reminded him of his mother and of his Indian blood. He
grinned quickly and with good nature said aloud, "Shucks,
I ain't worrying about Custer and Stone Calf; it's still
that Cheyenne girl!"

If he did not get to see her before the people of Stone
Calf departed the council for their winter camp, he might
never see her, the tide of events between Indian and
white being what it was that autumn. She would never
know that her glance had smitten him. True, she had
seemed to catch his eye upon her where she stood with
the squaws beyond the ring of chiefs and warriors. And,
he believed, she had returned his look with some degree
of interest. Perhaps even of real meaning. But the affairs
of the palaver had swept onward at too rapid a pace,
leaving no time for further acquainting glances or possible handsigns to signal a future meeting place and time.
It was only by the rarest of luck that he had noted a
former Cheyenne comrade of boyhood standing among
the watching Cheyenne and managed to speak with the
youthful brave. From him he learned the girl's name and
lodge of residence, together with her blood kinship within
the tribe.

But what of that now? He had not even thought swiftly
enough to ask his old-time friend to speak to the girl for
him until he might do so for himself. And then Captain
Benteen had come up quickly to suggest he stay aloof

from the visitors, lest Custer and the others grow suspicious and discharge him as interpreter. Naturally his subsequent request for permission to visit the Indian encampment that night had been refused.

"*Katam!*" he said, uttering the Cheyenne curse acidly. "No man should be born half-white and half-red. It's a bad color." Then suddenly his scowl had melted and his quick smile had replaced it. "However," he added, getting lightly to his feet and giving his inquisitive pony a warning neckpat, "it does blend well with a dark night. *Hoshuh*, little horse; I am going over the fence . . ."

Fort Dodge was built in a half-moon, the two horns of the moon based on the Arkansas River. Once past the barracks, there was no stockade to scale. Blunt had only to slide by the sentries at the riverbank to be moving free upon the open prairie. For a man used to prowling where a mouse's sneeze of sound could cost his hair, it was too simple. The only obstacle he encountered was a band of night-grazing cavalry mounts being held outside the fort under heavy guard. He passed so near these horses he was able to identify them, when one of the guard troopers struck a light to his pipe, as the mounts of Captain William Thompson's troop of the Seventh.

Ahead of him now, in the position chosen by the red nomads between themselves and the enemy, lay the Cheyenne pony herd. But he had no trouble. His buckskins were deeply cured with the woodsmoke of many years of lodge fires. His odor was the odor of their own red masters to the scent-curious ponies. They only whickered low welcomes and fell to grazing again.

The camp itself was another matter. It was a very large camp. It spread half a mile over the plain. Few lodges were erected, the majority of the visiting redmen preferring to eat and sleep in the open. In the center of the nomad gathering were some six or eight tipis of important treaty chiefs or famous warriors. Young Blunt recognized the distinctive lodge of Black Kettle, and believed the lodge of such a noted fighter as Spotted Wolf would be pitched near that of the principal chief. But how was an uninvited half-blood brother to reach those lodges without being discovered?

As far as the Cheyenne were concerned, such discovery

was not critical. They all knew young Blunt. All he had to do was simply to stand up where he was and cry out his name and he would be welcomed. But if he did that, Custer would hear of his visit. Then whatever Blunt hoped to do for his mother's people in the continuing treaty talks would be endangered, perhaps destroyed. Custer was quick to suspicion. He had ordered no fraternizing with the Indians. Any violation of that stricture would arouse the mercurial officer, possibly to hasty, and disastrous, punishments. On the other hand, Blunt could turn around right where he was and beat a shadowy retreat to the stockade, forgetting the slim girl and his duty to his mother's people, all in the same moment of nervous indecision.

But that was not the way of young Blunt. Setting his jaw, he commenced his approach to the lodges. He was careful to keep the shadows of the cowskin shelters between himself and the light of the fires about which most of the tribe was dancing, or gathered to watch the dancing. Checking off the tipis he was sure of—Yellow Bear's, Red Moon's, Little Robe's, Eagle Head's, Gray Eyes', Curly Hair's—he made for the only one he was not certain of, praying it would prove to be that of Spotted Wolf and Wind Woman. Circling this final lodge, he dropped to one knee at its rearskins. From this position he was less than fifty feet from the barking cries and pulse-thumping din of the dancers and the drums. Gritting his teeth, he lifted the rearskins and slid under them into the tipi. He was more fortunate than any half-white man deserved to be who would go sneaking in among 500 hostile Cheyenne. His only greeting was the soft glow of a lit pipe and the rasping croak of a notably hoarse voice.

"Who is there?" queried the voice.

By the glow of the pipe, Blunt could see some other things beside the homely face behind the stem and bowl. One of them was the muzzle of a rifle staring at him, held virtually to his nose by a Cheyenne squaw who appeared to know precisely how to squeeze the trigger should she have any need to do so. Blunt gulped, grinned, gambled all the way.

"It is I, your friend," he answered cheerfully.

The woman nodded, sucking on the pipe, still aiming the gun.

"What friend?" she asked.

"Why, it is I, Nahahan, Blunt's son."

Again the woman regarded him without lowering the rifle.

Nahahan was young Blunt's Cheyenne name. It meant "Our Son" and was a term of endearment bestowed by his mother's people. But the Cheyenne woman was not looking at him endearingly.

"We don't call you by that name any more," she said. "When you talk for the white man, we give you back your white man's name. We call you young Blunt now. *Nohetto.*"

Nohetto was the Cheyenne term for "that's all." The people used it to signify the end of anything, or of everything. The interpreter was badly surprised to hear it used for him, and to learn the Cheyenne had dropped his Indian name. These things boded ill for him in that camp. But he was there and he had one more card to play—the squaw's name—if she *were* the squaw.

"Mother," he pleaded, "listen to me. I know you. You are Wind Woman, the wife of Spotted Wolf, the mother of the girl Moheya, Blue Sky. My own mother was of your blood and band, you know that. Do you then still say you won't use my name? That you won't welcome me as a son?"

In the Cheyenne way a married woman of middle age, or older, was always "mother" to her nieces and nephews, as well as to the much more distantly removed kin of her own offspring. By similar tribal usage these various and distant relatives would call themselves her daughters or sons. Thus, when young Blunt addressed Wind Woman as "mother," he was properly respectful of the ancient ways and rules; this also put upon the hoarse-voiced squaw an obligation of response.

"How do you know that I am Wind Woman?" she demanded after a lengthy pause of pipe-puffing.

Blunt touched the fingertips of his left hand to his brow and waved them toward her in the sign of respect for greater age and wisdom. "Mother," he said, "who else could you be, so pretty and well-formed in your own charms?" This produced the needed reprieve. The suspicious one put down the rifle.

"A liar!" she snorted. "A half-blood and a liar. But young and tall. And yes, handsome, too, as a spotted stud colt. Go on, liar. What is it you want of Wind Woman?"

"I need your help," Blunt told her quickly. "And I come to offer the Cheyenne my help in return. The matter is urgent."

"A liar," repeated the woman, "*and* a fool. Don't you know you could have gotten yourself shot sneaking around this camp? I might have shot you myself!" She broke off, snickering evilly. "Except that I was waiting in hope that it would prove to be a man who scratched at the rearskins of my lodge. It has been a few summers since that happened!"

"You will have to forgive me," said Blunt, ignoring her giggled remembrance. "I could not help the way I had to sneak into this camp. Yellow Hair has forbidden anyone to leave the fort. His good chief, Benteen, especially forbade me to come over here tonight. I must not be seen here. I gave my word."

"And your word is not better than that, young Blunt?"

"My word is good enough, I swear. It's my heart that's bad."

"Aha, the girl! I knew it! That she-coyote has been flirting her tail at you!"

"Mother! She's your own daughter!"

"Pah! Exactly why I know her so well. What do you want of her? She is already given, you know. To a good man, too."

"No, I didn't know that, Mother. What man?"

"I said a good man."

"Well, how good then?"

Blunt was abrupt if good-natured, fearing few men, red or white. But he was not prepared for the answer he got.

"I will give you his name," said the squaw. "Then you tell me how good. Try the sound of Naevhan'hotoavesz."

Blunt grew pale.

"Death Horn?" he asked, small-voiced and hoping he had misheard.

The woman grinned, knowing the nature of his dread.

"That's what the white men call him," she chortled. "You know our old Cheyenne name for him, though: 'Death Horn Bull.'" She bobbed her head again, not grinning now. "By either calling, how does he sound to you, young Blunt?"

The youthful interpreter swallowed with some difficulty. He glanced toward the tipi entrance flaps and the flickering light of the dance fires. Death Horn Bull was unquestionably one of the great Cheyenne fighting men of tribal time. Except for Little Wolf and the recently dead Roman Nose—killed by Forsythe's men at Beecher Island—Death Horn was the most feared warrior on the south plains; and he was, too, the most implacable hater of all with white blood in their veins.

Moreover, as second to Tall Bull in command of the Ho tami tan iu, he was the dedicated enemy of peace with the pony soldiers. In the present talks it was he who headed the forces which were undercutting Black Kettle's advices to trust Custer and to have faith in the peace promises he was offering the Cheyenne. Since, in the frontier translation, the Indian term Ho tami tan iu came out "Cheyenne Dog Soldiers," Blunt now took a renewed chill at the woman's mention of Death Horn.

If the second chief of the dreaded dog soldiers was the promised one of the girl Moheya, then the half-blood son of Ezekial Blunt had come awooing in a very bad time and place. But Blunt's son was a stubborn man, and a smitten one.

"I still want to see the girl!" he demanded of Wind Woman. "Bring her to me. At least let us talk, Mother."

The squaw shook her head quickly. "There is no chance of that," she answered, "and no sense in it. If you want to die, I do not. Now I warn you, go from this lodge, and very swiftly. Go the way you came, by the rearskins. There's nothing here for you, young Blunt."

"Wait!" ordered Blunt, touching her arm, when it appeared she was rising to go out of the tipi. "When you speak of warnings, we are returned to my other reason for breaking my word to the pony soldier chief and coming here at night."

Wind Woman hesitated, peering hard at him. Then she nodded carefully and, reaching out, touched his arm in return.

"Go ahead, young Blunt," she said. "Talk."

Quickly the interpreter did so. Wind Woman, he insisted, must call a council that same midnight—the moment Blunt had safely departed the camp—and warn the peace chiefs to watch the war chiefs with all vigilance. Above all were the dog soldiers to be prevented from any rash acts of hostility which might give Custer the excuse he needed to drive the Cheyenne people away, to pursue them, and to kill them where he caught up to them.

"Very well," agreed the squaw when he had concluded. She arose and went to the entrance of the lodge. Pausing there, she looked back at Blunt. "Now you will see," she told him, "what I really think of your peace talking."

She was gone before the interpreter could speak. He waited a short while, not knowing if she had departed to summon her shapely daughter, her fierce old husband, or Death Horn Bull, the daughter's promised man and second chief of the dog soldiers. The uncertainty lengthened. Suddenly a stir outside the lodge's entrance flaps choked off his breath. The bent form of Wind Woman loomed against the starlight beyond the opened flaps. Behind the squaw, Blunt could make out the wide shoulders of her famed mate. Instantly the half-breed youth found his decision—not caring for the arrival of gruff Spotted Wolf—and with the thought he rolled under the rearskins of the lodge. Coming erect outside, he listened intently, relaxing slightly as, within the lodge, he heard Spotted Wolf commence to tell Wind Woman about the dance she had called him away from. Then the squaw was interrupting to say that she had more urgent things than this to talk about.

The chief wanted to know *what* urgent things. He accused the woman of coming to the dance fires saying he must follow her and must not behave as if anything had happened, yet something very much had happened nonetheless. Now he wanted to know what it was. And quick, too, *katam!*

Wind Woman encouraged him to seat himself and light his pipe. She poured him a buffalo-horn cupful of red willow tea, calming him. As she did this, she talked quite loudly, explaining her every action, as to some blind child. Of course she was talking for young Blunt's benefit, in case he was still crouching outside the lodge listening. But the monologue irritated her mate who was scarcely simple-minded.

"What do you think you are doing, woman?" he demanded. "I have eyes. I see what you are doing. Why

must you announce it to the entire camp? Be still and
tell me your urgent news."

Wind Woman then informed him that her urgent news
came from a friend of the tribe inside the pony soldier
camp, a man who had just spoken with her pleading
that the peace chiefs be warned of Custer's orders to kill
Indians at first excuse.

At once the crusty old fighter wanted to know who this
friend of the tribe might be, and why Wind Woman took
such a one into her confidence when she knew Spotted
Wolf was not with the peace chiefs in this matter? The
squaw replied that she could not reveal her visitor's identity but Spotted Wolf would know him well enough. The
chief grumbled some more but Wind Woman was too sly
for him. It was evident to Blunt that the council would be
called, the peace chiefs alerted. His mission done, the
interpreter turned and faded into the darkness.

It was some few minutes past midnight. On his return
journey to Fort Dodge from the Indian camp, Blunt had
just begun to breathe easier and was in the process of
swinging wide to circle upwind of Captain Thompson's horse herd, when the herd commenced to run.
Startled, the interpreter dived into the shelter of a narrow gully. In another instant the herd was thundering
past his hiding place and any doubts as to the cause of
its stampeding were harshly removed: *Cheyennes!*

Blunt saw three warriors that he knew riding in the
whooping van of the raiders. The leader was a lean,
hawk-headed devil with a buffalo-horned headdress dis-
tinguished by a single huge horn on the left side. Flanking this man was a hulking brave, naked but for a
breechclout, and a second warrior wearing a cougar's
gleaming white skull, teeth intact, for a war hat. *Death
Horn. Fat Bear. Yellow Cat. Ai-ee,* brother! Those were
the dog soldiers riding by out there!

Blunt watched until he saw the driven herd hit the
waters of the Arkansas by the main Cheyenne camp. Then
he was up and running for the fort. Curse the red idiots!
If there had been any chance that Black Kettle and the
peace chiefs could cool down Custer and the cavalry, that
chance was now as gone as Captain Thompson's horses.
And more. The dog soldiers had fixed it so that the theft

would seem the guilt of the whole camp, running the herd right past its sleeping people and practically right through the tipi of the old headman himself. Poor Black Kettle!

Even worse—poor Spotted Wolf, poor Wind Woman, poor Blue Sky! The raiders had fixed it so that Blunt would, in all likelihood, never see the girl again. *Katam!* Maheo's damnation upon that murderous Death Horn Bull, and all his crazy dog soldiers with him! Blunt sped on with a final oath. If it were the last Indian young Blunt ever put under, he was going to put *that one* under for certain keeps.

When Blunt entered Custer's office, it was to find the Colonel struggling into his boots, the sleep still heavy in his pale eyes. As he finished his brief report, the long-haired officer was on his feet, face livid, voice wild.

"What the devil are you saying, man?" he demanded.

"I already said it, Colonel." Blunt shrugged. "The dog soldiers just run off G Troop's horses."

"By the Lord, sir, I don't believe it!" Custer's face and voice seemed less strained now. "Who told you?"

"I never take anybody's word for such things. I reckon you know that, Colonel."

"You've been outside the stockade, sir?"

"Somewhat."

"With the Cheyenne?"

"Somewhat." The second shrug was as calm as the first. "You want to hear about my life with the Indians, Colonel, or what happened to Thompson's horses?"

"By thunder, sir, Benteen had your word! I want to know what you were doing outside the stockade. I *demand* to know!"

The third shrug compounded the imperturbability of the prior two.

"I didn't like the way the dog soldiers stayed away from your council today. I figured they were up to something."

"And—?"

"They were. Running off Thompson's horses, for starters."

"You're absolutely certain it was the dog soldiers?"

"Absolutely. I seen them hand-close. Black Kettle and the others wasn't mixed into it at all. Just the dogs."

"Nonsense! You're defending those people again!"

Before Custer could continue the charge, the door crashed open to admit the bug-eyed front-runner of Thompson's horseguard troopers. When the latter had panted out the news that the Cheyenne had just run off the herd, Custer nodded coolly and asked with pointed deliberateness if there had been light enough for the trooper to identify any of the raiders.

"Yes, sir, Colonel, there surely was, sir!" the latter responded. "There was mighty good light and I seen old Black Kettle himself riding square up in front and leading the whole shebang. They was a hundred or better of them!"

"That's a damned lie, soldier!" Blunt was towering over the trooper, dark eyes blazing. "It's black as a bear's gut out there, and you never seen nothing!"

Custer was between them, bristling with anger.

"Stand away, Blunt. I'll not have you bullyragging my men. Was there anything else, trooper?"

"Yes, sir, they was," said the latter. "Corporal Bonners and me was running together to get clear of the stampede and we was able to get a good look at the main camp. Sir, the whole kit and kaboodle of them Injuns is clearing out, tipis acoming down, pony herd being run in. They're shagging it, sir, right on acrost the Arkansas, every last one of them!"

"You hear that, Blunt?" Custer wheeled on the interpreter.

"Yes, sir, clear as a brass bugle."

"Well, what do you say now, sir?"

Blunt knew what he was supposed to say, that Black Kettle was a liar and a thief and talked peace with a split tongue. But he was still Blunt's son and still stubborn.

"I say, figure it this way, Colonel. Supposing you was the old chief, what would you do as soon as your pony herd guards woke you up with the news that the dog soldiers had just run off some of Yellow Hair's horses? Black Kettle knows you, Colonel, remember that. And he knows what damned liars your troopers can be. He figured it just as sure as though he was standing here listening to us right now, that you would put the blame on him for *anything* that happened. So he just told the people

to pack and he got them out of there as fast and as far
away as he could manage it. Now you tell me different."

He did not add the customary "sir," and he knew Custer
was raging inside. But the colonel was a consummate
actor, and an enlisted man was present.

"You may go now, Mr. Blunt. I shall want you back
here ready to take to the trail by 4:00 A.M. When you
come, I suggest you bring some better manners and be
ready for a long ride."

Blunt looked at him and nodded. He turned and left
the room without added assurance that he heard, understood, or had any idea of complying.

"A good man," said Custer to the wide-eyed trooper,
"but half-Cheyenne, you know. A pity."

The Loafer, Blunt's prized Sioux buffalo pony, whickered a soft greeting as the door to Colonel Custer's office
opened and the familiar gaunt figure of his rider came
striding toward him. Blunt repaid the pony with a heel
in the ribs and terse instructions to "light out." Loafer
broke into a lope. He came up to and passed the column
of troopers already moving out of the fort on the trot.
Blunt reined the mustang in alongside the youthful officer heading the troopers.

"Morning, Lieutenant. The colonel tells me you may
need an interpreter where you're bound for."

"True enough, Blunt." The younger Custer grinned.
"We're off after G Troop's horses. Glad to have you
along."

Blunt nodded and rode silently a moment.

Tom was as different from the colonel as cavalry officers came. He was a head taller, six heads handsomer, at
least three heads more human. He was friendly as a
spaniel, if not too much smarter. Of course, he worshiped
Custer. He was so convinced that his older brother was
the greatest cavalryman since J. E. B. Stuart that he tried
to make his own life a looking glass for the colonel's, re-
flecting every claim, idea, order or afterthought the
other might see fit to hold or to hand along. But he was
still all right with young Blunt.

"Thanks, Lieutenant," he now said belatedly. "Glad to
be along. Might even say, if I hadn't told the colonel

there was only thirty head of the dog soldiers made that run-off, neither you nor me would likely be here."

"What's that? You told the colonel a lie to get me the chance?"

"More like to keep *him* from getting it, Lieutenant."

Tom Custer slowed his horse, frowning.

"Blunt, are you saying you went out of your way to prevent Colonel Custer from going out after these Cheyenne?"

"I am."

"I don't believe I like that, Blunt." The young officer was affronted and worried.

Blunt showed him small sympathy. "Like it or let it lay, Lieutenant, but get it straight. There's not thirty of them dog soldiers but more like 200. Now, you know if the colonel had come along I couldn't have held him away from them, or persuaded him to go at them in the right fashion. You I figure I can handle."

The youth grew flushed, started to remonstrate. Blunt cut in on him. "Think of it this way, Lieutenant. I'd rather chase 2,000 ordinary Indians than some 200 of them dog soldiers. Now you remember that when the track gets hot up yonder. You hold up when young Blunt tells you to. You hear me?"

Tom Custer shot an uneasy glance back along his small column of mounted men. The line of troopers looked much thinner than it had closer to Fort Dodge. He turned a sober face to the waiting half-breed.

"Sure I hear you, Blunt. You don't have to worry about me."

Blunt nodded, satisfied. "We'll get along, Lieutenant," he said. His accompanying thumb jerk flicked over his shoulder toward the dusty troopers. "Tell them to pick it up a bit, eh? We don't want to keep the dog soldiers waiting."

Tom Custer tried a grin, let it fade. His "Forward ho!" rang out with a slight crack in the bell of its authority. The column responded, moving from trot to lope. It swung left to ford the Arkansas and veer away from the river due east into the trackless shortgrass of the open prairie.

Ten hours later they had still seen no more sign of Captain Thompson's stolen horse herd than the wide trackline of its passing over the endless plain. Frowning, Blunt pulled up Loafer and told young Custer to wave halt to the following column. Pointing ahead to a rising swell of the prairie hiding a range of salt-earth hills beyond, the interpreter spoke tersely, his eyes never leaving the silent rise before them.

"All right, Lieutenant, let's do it this way: you and me will take ten troopers and top out with them on yonder swell. The rest of the column waits here with Lieutenant Law. That's bad country, them salt hills past the rise. I've an idea we will find something we're looking for when we poke our noses over that ridge up there."

Custer agreed. Law was brought forward and stationed with the main column near the top of the rise. With Blunt, Custer and the ten troopers went up and over the crest. There, indeed, they "found something." It was Captain Thompson's missing horse herd grazing peacefully in a wide prairie swale below. Beyond the herd the salt hills baked silently in the late sun.

"Wait up," said Blunt to the now eager Custer. "That's a trap down there. The dog soldiers are hid up in them hills."

"And—?" queried his companion.

"And when we ride in to round up the herd with our ten soldiers, they rush us—200 of them. Only when they rush, we hightail back here, leading them into Law and your eighty good Spencer carbines back of the ridge. Let's go."

Down the slope they went. Blunt led the way at a brisk lope, a natural speed for men just discovering an unguarded herd they hoped to recover. The hidden Cheyenne waited until they were within seventy-five yards of the horses before they made a prophet with honor out of young Blunt. Then they did it in style, screaming and whooping out of the dried ravines with terrifying effect. But Blunt held the troopers together and the grain-fed cavalry mounts, once the race back up the ridge was lined out, steadily opened up their beginning narrow lead over the pursuing warriors. No fire was exchanged, the troopers under order not to use their guns, the Indians evidently confident of success and wanting to save ammunition. True hostiles and horseback redmen, they never used a bullet where a knife or lance or stone ax would do equal work. Or where a squat osage or ironwood warbow could smash out a man's ribcage at point-blank, buffalo-running range. And do it *quietly*.

Blunt's counterbait worked perfectly. The dog soldiers came yelping over the ridge in typical Indian order, the fastest ponies and best riders first. These vanguards threw their mounts on their haunches the instant they saw Law's waiting line of rifle steel, but the halt only piled their following fellows into them, full tilt. In less than ten seconds the Cheyenne attack was hopelessly snarled.

"Go ahead," said young Blunt to Custer. "Hold low."

The crash of the heavy-caliber Spencers shattered the sunset stillness. The troopers could hear their lead thudding into the packed ponies of the Indians. The little mustangs began to go down. Blunt counted twelve of them thrashing on the grass from the first volley. The count was twenty ponies with the second volley—twenty ponies and perhaps a dozen of their riders. Yet, with their usual marvelous horsemanship, the Cheyenne survivors managed to rally and to scoop up their wounded before fleeing back over the ridge to safety.

One warrior, alone, lingered too long in this business of brave mercy. Recognizing him, Blunt put heels to Loafer's ribby flanks. The warrior saw him coming, tried to turn his Cheyenne scrub away. Loafer slammed into the other pony with the force of a wounded bull, knocking the smaller mount off its feet, unseating its rider. Blunt had the fellow in a bearhug before he might recover from the shock of his heavy fall.

"Don't move, cousin," he said, his knife in the other's ribs. "I don't want to hurt you."

"*Nahahan!*" gasped the Cheyenne, eyes widening. "It's you!"

"It's me," Blunt told him. "But I mean it with the knife."

He did not need to repeat the warning. The captive knew him well. It was Nisimá, Young Brother, the comrade of his youth; the brave who had told him at Fort Dodge of Moheya's kinship with Wind Woman and with Spotted Wolf.

By the time Tom Custer returned from chasing Death Horn and the dog soldiers back over the ridge—and from gathering and driving back the recaptured horse herd—

Blunt and his knife had made quite a coverage of old times with Nisimá.

Adding up the information his former comrade of the Cheyenne days had surrendered, the interpreter frowned uneasily. He was riding outflank of the retiring trooper column, eating the dust of both soldier and horse herd. It was hot and late and dry and Blunt did not feel well at all.

No matter how he turned the thing in his mind, he could not free his conscience from the core of the information he had coaxed from Nisimá: somehow, Death Horn had learned of his, Blunt's presence in the Cheyenne camp; had hastily timed the G Troop horse herd run-off to abort any possible good result of a meeting of the peace chiefs that midnight.

Young Custer's column came to a halt. A courier from Dodge slid his lathered mount to a halt and saluted. He had been sent to find the lieutenant in the field, he reported. Colonel Custer had decided to go on an Indian hunt of his own. He had already started from the fort with the entire Seventh. Lieutenant Custer was to change his own route, swinging due west to intercept the main force on its line of march over the Jornada or Dry Crossing between the Arkansas and the Cimarron. It was at this point that Blunt pushed Loafer forward to object: they could not possibly follow the long dry route specified in the colonel's orders, he told young Custer. Without water for their mounts since leaving the Arkansas, they must now find a drinking place quickly or face serious trouble.

Tom Custer was a simple man but no fool. "All right, Blunt," he said. "We will take your way."

They drove all that night. At daybreak they used the last of the water in the troopers' canteens to wash out the horses' nostrils and to squeeze some of the priceless moisture onto each animal's swollen tongue. A four-hour, horse-and man-wilting march brought them, however, into sight of Lower Cimarron Spring. There was a hoarse cry from the men. Three cheers for old Blunt's half-breed boy. He had done a fine job of guiding them to water in time.

Tom Custer, soldier enough to know when a condescending cheer was not fit pay, called Blunt aside at

the spring and seriously expressed his gratitude. The
young interpreter shrugged the praise aside, but wondered how differently the other brother would have responded to similar circumstances. In his entire experience
with the older Custer the half-blood interpreter could not
recall having been thanked a single time for a job well
done. Plenty of back-pattings and smiled promises of high
reward beforehand always. But let the chancy affair be
brought off, and the colonel invariably managed to end
up with his own thumb stuck squarely in the middle of
the victory pie. Yet Tom was only a boy lieutenant who
drank too much whiskey, and Custer was Custer. It was a
strange world, that white man's world, even if a man only
half belonged to it.

They rested at the spring until sunset. Shortly before
dark the senior Custer's column moved in off the prairie.
Blunt was astounded by its size. There were twelve full
companies of Seventh Cavalry, together with an ammunition and supply train of forty wagons. Among the officers
he recognized Majors Joel Elliott, Gibbs and Tilford;
Captains Benteen, Keogh, Hamilton and Yates; Lieutenants Moylan, Brewster, Longan, Cook. The selection
told Blunt that Custer had handpicked his companies with
dangerous care. Outside of Benteen, Joe Tilford, Miles
Keogh, and perhaps young Cook among the juniors, the
officers of the Fort Dodge column were all cut to the
colonel's own slapdashing pattern. A Cheyenne interpreter
might accompany many a long column of Indian-chasing
pony soldiers without seeing a better combination of bad-
reckless white commanders.

Despite his professional misgivings, however, Blunt was
pleased to hear, via camp rumor, that his primary employer was in high mood. And why not? Had not General
Sheridan's latest directives to "kill Indians" put the colonel
and his gallant Seventh Cavalry back on the military
maps? And back, too, on the front pages of the Eastern
newspapers where those maps were always so prominently
printed when the quarry was dark red of skin and the
huntsman bright yellow of hair?

Kataml as the Cheyenne would curse in their phonic
adoption of the white man's "goddaml" That "kill order"
had done the business. Yet anyone in Blunt's position
needed to find Custer in just this roused and rising spirit in

order that he might wheedle from him the favor he had in mind. The commander of the Seventh liked to keep his interpreters in close where he might accompany their work word-for-word, the better to improve their advice with his own. And Blunt had no intention of being "in close" under the circumstances. He must get away from Custer and the cavalry—get out ahead of them—if he were going to have any last chance, whatever, of finding the Cheyenne in the field.

Regardless of the fact that someone in the Indian camp had sicked the dog soldiers onto the horse herd, and regardless of whether that sicking had anything to do with Blunt's having been in the camp that night, it was the interpreter's determination to attempt once more to warn the remnants of his mother's red people away from the vicinity of the pony soldiers.

If it were not too late to call Custer off, if the running off of G Troop's horses had not unleashed the cavalry beyond recall, then there might still be time to find the Indians and warn them out of the country—frighten them into fleeing for their lives with the news that Yellow Hair was coming—*after them*. Blunt meant to get his permission from Custer to scout ahead of the Fort Dodge column, or to get arrested in the process.

The interpreter was lucky. He found the "boy general" in the headiest of moods and easily won from him the approval of his suggestion that he ride on down to Middle Spring of the Cimarron to determine if one of his half-Indian blood might not "see" a little something of his red relatives that the other scouts had missed. Something which might be hidden from mere pony soldier eyes.

It was the sort of imaginative adventuring which appealed to Custer, who sniffed the winey air of intrigue as eagerly as he did that of the war trail. Blunt did not linger to elaborate upon his good fortune. He caught up his horse and departed the cavalry encampment immediately.

A short way out, however, he stopped and made his bed upon the open prairie. His eyes and ears must be good tomorrow. The very surest way to have them so was to hone them with eight long hours of sleep. Picketing Loafer near his blankets, he lay down and looked upward toward the star trail of the Milky Way. As always, the glittering pathway of the Cheyenne's departed ones led his mind along its mysterious road into the Indian glories of the past, lost him in a reverie of empathy for his warrior brothers and for all the people of his dark-skinned mother. He was not a white man in that drifting moment. He was not even a half-white man. He was a pure Cheyenne. "*Ha-ho, Maheo,*" he murmured in his deep voice, and in a minute's time was fast asleep upon the warm breast of *escheman*, the grandmother earth.

He came awake at 4:00 A.M., saddled up, moved out. He saw nothing in that morning's wary ride. He stopped to graze and water Loafer at ten o'clock, mounted up and moved on, frowning as he rode. Where were the Cheyenne?

It turned blazing hot for a November day, as it freakishly would in that Cimarron country. When at last Blunt saw ahead the dark cottonwoods and willows of Middle Spring, he was panting with dehydration. Scouting the entire perimeter of the grove, he rode in to find the spring, with its large eighty-foot pool, as beautiful as it had ever seemed to his wanderer's weary limbs and sun-reddened eyes.

He did not seem unduly concerned with thoughts of ambush in this nigh-perfect place for such entrapments. After enough years at this sort of thing, a man developed a feel for spots like Middle Spring of the Cimarron. Right now Blunt's "feel" was telling him to lie down and turn his livestock loose. Accordingly he did so. Following a long slow drink from the spring, he carried Loafer's saddle over to a sun-dappled clearing, loaded his stone pipe and stretched out gratefully on the short curl of the buffalo grass.

Ah! Nothing like a charred stone pipebowl of aromatic shag-cut trade tobacco and a ten-minute cat nap to lift a man's troubles. Or perhaps his hair . . . The first hint Blunt had that all was not well along the Cimarron was a chance, sleepy-eyed glance at Loafer flaring curious nostrils toward the cottonwoods behind him. Feigning a yawning stretch, the interpreter stole an eyetail glance toward the trees. It was enough.

Sitting their potbellied ponies over there, soundless as hawk shadows, were some twenty Cheyenne dog soldiers. In their van, looking neither notably pleased nor resent-

ful, Death Horn Bull was silently fitting an arrow to his
bowstring. The rest of the warriors were grinning, slack-
lipped, waiting for the fun to come. Blunt could read their
red minds.

*By Maheo, what a wonderful way to happen upon a
traitorous kinsman. To repay a once-trusted son of a Cheyenne mother who had sold his honor to the white man.
Who talked now for the pony soldiers, trying to trick his
own red brothers. Be careful now, Death Horn, feather
him just so. Wound him only in the thick of the leg, so
he can't run. We will hold our guns. Go ahead. Don't
miss him, but remember you promised to catch him alive
for us, so that we could have some fun with him. . . .*

While the dog soldiers waited for Death Horn, Blunt
did not. By a miracle of Maheo, a chance of life had just
turned his way and was coming toward him in the splay-
footed form of the Sioux mustang Loafer. The Cheyenne
warriors paid scant heed to the grazing mount. Again
Blunt chose otherwise.

Bounding to his feet, he ran for Loafer and his life.
Such was his speed that he reached and mounted the bony
animal and spurred him away before one warrior could
raise his rifle, or Death Horn could release the arrow he
already had upon the string. With a chorus of wolf cries
the Cheyenne were after him, the chase driving toward
the Cimarron.

Once across the river, Blunt did not trouble looking back
to gloat over his great luck in the initial escape. Cheyenne
rifle balls were now whistling close enough to him that he
could feel the wind of their passage. It seemed to him
that the ponies of Death Horn and the dog soldiers were
now running up so fast on his rear that their riders could
spit on Loafer's shaggy rump. He yelled at his big dun
horse in Cheyenne, Sioux and profane white man language. Loafer responded by pinning his loppy ears and
really starting to run. Gradually the twilight distance
opened between pursuers and pursued.

Blunt relaxed, sat up straight on his easing pony. To be
certain, they were both a long way from Custer's camp.
But the homely buckskin gelding had given them a brave
start. Failing any of a dozen chances for trouble along the
trail, or for yet being hit by stray, near-spent Cheyenne
lead, he and the Sioux horse would win the biggest race

of their hard-running lives. His dark face was lit momentarily by the lantern of his bright, good-natured grin. *Waghl* he yelled joyfully upward into the gathering night. Turning in the saddle, he drew breath for a final shout of derision at the fading dog soldiers. As he did, he felt a sudden twist in Loafer's withers, heard the gelding's grunt of pain.

He knew instantly that his mount's reaching forefoot had found and driven through the treacherous crust of a prairie dog hole. He tried desperately to throw himself clear of the falling horse. The bone-cracking shock of the flinty ground came up and into him with shattering force.

When Blunt regained consciousness there was enough of the early-night moonlight filtering through the cottonwoods to let him see he was once again in Middle Spring grove. And to let him see a few other things. Not far from him stood Loafer, apparently none the worse for being thrown by the prairie dog hole. Squatting rifle-guard over Blunt himself was the porcine Fat Bear, twin to Yellow Cat, both being the favored twain of Death Horn's subchiefs. By the spring the remainder of the dog soldiers were saddling their mounts. Their guttural talk told Blunt the band was preparing to force a night ride for the hostile camp at Willow Bar of the Cimarron. Yellow Hair was drawing near. His scouts, some of them—Hard Rope, Micah Carmody, California Joe—had been seen that same day not ten miles from the grove. Praise Maheo, they had had good hunting; it was time to go.

Beyond this information, the interpreter had time only to realize that his entire body ached as if fractured in detail, before the gentle Fat Bear was kicking him to his feet and ordering him to get to his pony and mount up. To this insult was added the injury of lashing his feet together under Loafer's belly to prevent him, in Fat Bear's solicitous words, "from falling off and hurting yourself."

The start from Middle Spring was now made. Fat Bear and Blunt rode at column's head with Death Horn. Behind them came Yellow Cat, Black Dog and the other soldiers of the Ho tami tan iu. In all of the long, bone-jarring ride, the Cheyenne warriors held their stony silence, refusing even to look at the half-blood captive. It was as though young Blunt were already dead.

It was a big camp. The shadowed flood of the moonlight showed Blunt 250 lodges strung along the silvered strand of the Cimarron.

The hair-raising howls of the buffalo wolf, with which the dog soldiers announced their arrival on the rocky ridge overlooking Willow Bar, brought a swarm of Stone Calf's people rushing from the lodges to look upward. Descending the ridge in the lead of his savage troops, Death Horn was soon speaking to the hastily assembled crowd of his war-party followers. The ensuing account of the Middle Spring entrapment of young Blunt gave the half-blood ample evidence that Death Horn was not alone a war leader; he was, as well, a politician of considerable and dangerous talent.

"*Eahato*, listen to this, my friends," began the returned hero. "With our trap we have caught this traitor at the Middle Water of this river. I, Death Horn Bull, planned the whole thing. We could have killed young Blunt easily, but it would have been like stoning a helpless rabbit. Besides, I had more plan to use him. If we keep him captive, letting Yellow Hair know that he lives among us again, Yellow Hair will think young Blunt has turned against the pony soldiers. He will think the traitor stays with us by choice. The life of Blunt's son will then be finished among the white men also. They, too, will call him traitor. Then we will kill young Blunt, and his life will be really finished. Are you agreed?"

The people—what sounded to Blunt like the major part —shouted angrily that they did indeed consent to this plan. But Death Horn had only begun. He now boasted of having deliberately run off the Fort Dodge horse herd to bring the pony soldiers and Yellow Hair out to fight. He explained his intention that Black Kettle and the peaceful main band of the Cheyenne should be blamed by the whites for this. He even pledged that if the troops of the Seventh Cavalry lost their way in the search for the old chief, he and the dog soldiers would point it out to them again. After the big fight, he concluded, the men of the Ho tami tan iu society would rule the tribe. There would be war to the death against the white man south

of the Arkansas River. The peace chiefs had had their way
for a long time. They had brought only the blood and
tears of Sand Creek Massacre to the people. Now let the
war chiefs have their way. To die fighting was preferable
to living as dogs and slaves. Follow the dog soldiers!

There was some evident disturbance among the listeners at this further exhortation. The older chiefs who had
been courting war talk in the council at Dodge now hesitated. Had they fanned too hard at the fire? Were they
encouraging their own ends by furthering those of the
dog soldiers? It was a poor choice, but better late than
not at all. In the morning, first thing, the bands of Spotted Wolf, Stone Calf and Little Robe would all take down
their lodges and return to winter with Black Kettle on
the Ouachita. They had changed their minds; they did
not want war.

Blunt was pleased to hear this, realizing that the departing chiefs would warn Black Kettle of his great danger. So much for that concern. Blunt could have done no
more than the same thing, even with freedom; and the
old chief of the main band would listen more to such
as Stone Calf and Little Robe and the tough fighter Spotted Wolf than to young Blunt, *the traitor.*

There remained but one thing for Blunt to do now; the
thing he had set out to do in the beginning. Yet how?
How to kill Death Horn Bull? And if, by some miracle, he
should manage this, what then? Should he escape, where
would he go? The Cheyenne would not have him. Custer, quite possibly, would hang him if he went in again
to Fort Dodge. His father? Yes, he could live with his
father. But he would not. His Indian pride would never
yield to that.

What then? Blunt did not know; but he was a difficult
man to discourage. As usual, when the tides of ill fortune washed hard against him, he traded the dark frown
for the bright, quick smile. Doing so, he turned to Yellow
Cat and Fat Bear, his constant companions now.

"My friends," he said to them, "it's the Devil's fate
but I accept it."

"A brave thing to say," grunted Fat Bear. "I salute you."

"I, too," nodded Yellow Cat. "It isn't easy to accept
death, especially for a traitor to his people."

"No," said Blunt softly. "I wonder how *he* will take it."

Neither of his listeners was alert of mind. While both still scratched their heads at this odd statement, Blunt noted Death Horn had left the fire and was coming toward them.

He was walking alone, none of the people even talking as he drew up before the doomed interpreter. There was an eerie stillness.

"Young Blunt," he said, "will you speak now?"

Blunt knew the Indian mind. To Death Horn, fear—to show fear of any living thing—was the greatest shame of life. It was taboo with him. There must be no chance that in the legends of the dog soldiers some distant tribal historian might say that Death Horn Bull showed fear to let young Blunt be heard that night at Willow Bar.

The interpreter came to his feet. The stillness of the camp endured as the two men stood facing one another. Death Horn was thin and hawk-headed. He looked like a bird of prey. He was the essence of the wild thing, the creature of the free winds, a thing to be killed perhaps but never caged.

In the same instant the dog soldier chief was seeing across from him a man of alien blood, yet kindred. Blunt had humor and kindliness in his dark face but was scarcely a delicate or an easy fellow to study. Six feet and three inches tall, weighing 215 pounds, born and reared and taught "hard," young Blunt was a man whose pleasant nature invited few familiarities and no mistakes. Wise men watched him carefully, or wished they had.

Death Horn was no simpleton. He watched Blunt, now, as he nodded to him and broke the growing stillness.

"I am waiting for your reply," he said. "Will you speak?"

"I will," answered Blunt.

They returned to the fire amid a growing silence and there, voice unraised, the Fort Dodge interpreter told the Cheyenne people the truth.

Young Blunt was no traitor. Not to his mother's people, not to his father's people. He had seen with his own eyes the paper ordering Yellow Hair to kill the Indians, and he had tried then to keep the Indians from doing a foolish thing which would give the pony soldiers an excuse to start that killing. When Death Horn led the dog soldiers down upon Captain Thompson's horses, perhaps he knew what he did, perhaps he did not know what

he did. But what he did was wrong. And what he had
just asked the people to do was wrong. Yet the old chief,
Black Kettle, was wrong also. His peace-seeking would not
save him. His death sign was written on that piece of
paper at Fort Dodge. The shamans and the holy women
and the warrior societies might smoke and make medicine and dance until their moccasins wore through; it
would do no good, no good at all. War was coming to
the South Plains. The Cheyenne themselves had brought
it there.

Now if the people did not want to hear this, let them
cover their ears. But let them remember young Blunt's
farewell, as they would remember Death Horn's call to
war. Young Blunt was his father's son, but he loved his
mother's people more. His heart had two bloods in it, and
he had tried to make it beat true for both. In this he
had been vain and foolish. No man stays a white man
when his Indian blood calls to him. Neither can any man
be an Indian altogether whose blood is partly white. Let
the Cheyenne remember their half-blood brother as the
man who loved his mother's people too well, who served
his father's people not well enough.

Blunt, finishing his speech, stood a moment, throat
tight, lips dry, an ache in his breast for all the things he
had wanted to say and which he had not said.
"*Nataemhon,*" he said finally, and touching his brow toward them, "good hunting to you all. . . ."

Stationing Yellow Cat and Fat Bear at the entrance,
Death Horn went into his lodge, taking Blunt with him.
A chaste man, like so many of the great Cheyenne fighters, the dog soldier chief kept no women in his lodge.
Thus when the flaps dropped behind them, he and the
interpreter were alone. By the dim light of the tipi fire
the two men studied one another's faces. For the first
time, they were meeting within the reach of a half-broth-
er's hand and without the eyes and ears of others upon
them. It was a disquieting moment for young Blunt and,
somehow, a strangely poignant one.

Something had happened between him and his warrior
host. Looking at Death Horn now, Blunt could feel this.
The dog soldier seemed about to put words to this something as they waited for the strangeness to pass. Blunt

thought he saw the shadow of this something mirrored far back in the war leader's dark eyes, a something which was neither savage nor cruel, bred neither of hatred or hauteur.

"Be at ease," said the chief. "Sit down with me."

They seated themselves cross-legged on opposite sides of the small fire. Death Horn produced his pipe and lit it. He then offered it to Blunt. The latter made a sign to wait a moment. He then made a cigarette, lit it and passed the lit smoke to his companion in exchange for the pipe.

Death Horn was pleased as a child, albeit a most fierce and desperate-looking child. He drew upon the priceless white man's "little smoke;" savoring its rare fragrance, letting its light blue smoke curl out through his nostrils in a long, slow exhaling of curious delight.

"Good," he said to Blunt.

The interpreter merely nodded. It was the chief's place to speak, to guide the talk. The guest would listen.

"You came on my trail to kill me," said Death Horn.

"Yes," answered Blunt.

"You heard my vow to kill you just now."

"Yes."

"Well, young Blunt, what is to be done about this?"

Blunt shook his head, puzzled. "Something has changed," he said. "In the departing of the old chiefs. The silence of the people just now. Some feeling of blood between us two. I don't know. But something has changed."

Now Death Horn shook his head. He was not puzzled but definite, yet seeming regretful too.

"Nothing has changed," he said. "Not for us. Our feet, yours and mine, are set on different trails. All that has happened is that the people suddenly do not know which trail to follow. But we, you and I, we know where we are going—we know the name of that trail."

Blunt shivered despite the close air of the lodge. The dog soldier chief was referring to the Hanging Road, the pathway to the other land. He meant that either he or young Blunt must die. For warriors there was no other way.

They had made their separate vows. The feet of Death Horn were on the war road. The feet of young Blunt stood across that road, blocking its passage to Death Horn and the dog soldiers. Someone's feet must move.

"How will it be?" nodded Blunt. "Still the burning-pole?"

"No." Death Horn shook his head quickly. "In your talk you challenged my way. The people, if I burned you, would say I feared to face you now. So that is how it will be."

"You mean *we* will fight?"

"We must fight."

"If so, how then?"

"As men of our people."

"The knife?"

Death Horn nodded. "The knife," he said. "Tonight."

The Cheyenne trial-by-blade was a legal simplicity. When two litigants of the tribe had reached the impasse where one or both of them was unwilling to settle for less than the life of the other, they were stripped naked, given knives and told to fight as "loud" as they had talked.

Knife duels were by no description strange to Blunt and his frontier world. But the dog soldier society of the Southern Cheyenne had certain refinements of the contest not calculated to calm white blood. For purposes of better dramatic entertainment of the spectators, always a prime consideration with Plains Indians, the duel was staged at night.

A circle of fifteen paces' diameter was drawn on bare earth. About this, boundary fires were built, providing illumination for audience and principals alike. Between boundary fires and around the perimeter of the circle squatted selected lancemen, each armed with his favorite buffalo javelin. If either fighter got outside the circle for any reason—tricked, forced or frightened there—the nearest lancer was leased to "remind" him back into the contest.

Sitting now on the near side of the boundary fires' lights, watching the final arrangements of circle-drawing and lancer settlement, Blunt felt his insides draw up as if they had been salted. He licked his lips, looked nervously at Death Horn waiting on the far side of the fires.

Perhaps an hour had passed since the chief had emerged

from his tipi to announce the trial. It seemed an eternity to the interpreter. Try as he might, he could think of nothing save the sliding feel of cold steel entering his intestines. There were two ways in which the trial could end. First: one of the fighters killed the other. Second: the combatants signaled that they were unwilling to kill one another. In this eventuality, the waiting lancers moved in and satisfied them both. The Cheyenne had no word for "a tie."

As to the survivor, whatever his status prior to the contest, he was entitled to the rights of tribal membership upon victory. In Blunt's case this meant one thing: if he killed Death Horn he went free, riding Death Horn's best horse, wearing his best weapons, taking with him the choice of the dead chief's wives or daughters or other chattels.

If these other chattels of Death Horn's would include the girl Moheya, Blunt did not know. In the loneliness of his waiting he wondered about her, however, and hoped that he might see her again. He wanted to tell her that in some other time, in a kinder, less brutal land, in another life than this harsh one of his half-blood, he could have loved her very deeply. But now the knives were near and the time was gone. Very well, so let it be. Man lived alone, he died alone.

About midnight Spotted Wolf came to Blunt and told him that it was time. "I am to be *nis'en*, friend or second to you," he said growlingly. "Come along."

"I am grateful to you, Father," said the youth. "I touch the brow in your direction."

"There is no debt. Forget that. I knew your mother, boy."

He would talk no further but then, as they reached the outskirts of the crowd, he stopped.

"Here," he said, giving a slim knife to Blunt, "this is a blade said to have belonged to Mangas Coloradas, the great man of the Gila Apache people. Perhaps it did. Who knows these things?"

Blunt took the long thin weapon, aware instantly of its unusual crafting and balance. He had never before held such a knife in his hand. It seemed alive, to move of its own will.

"Thank you, Father," he said. "I accept it gladly."

"Use it then," was all the war chief said, and turned and was gone in the darkness.

Alone Blunt went forward, the cold rising from the ground, creeping through his legs, settling in his belly. A guttural rumble of Cheyenne sound ran around the ring of the waiting people. Every eye swung in the interpreter's direction, as those nearest him parted to let him through. He walked looking neither right nor left, head high in the manner of a warrior, or as nearly as he could simulate that manner while experiencing that crawling fear.

Then the eerie heavy silence which pervaded Indian crowds at ceremonials where death is the invited guest descended again. Blunt could hear the fall of his own moccasins in the dust of the fireground. Before him the circle loomed. He entered it, standing irresolute for several seconds, eyes temporarily affected by the flaring boundary fires.

Death Horn was not yet in the ring. Blunt took the respite to examine the knife Spotted Wolf had given him. It was a Spanish blade, a rare Toledo, its mirror surfaces as polished and gleaming as untold decades of bathing in soft flesh and warm blood could keep them. The haft was of leather washers pounded down over the tang, Apache fashion. Blunt assumed it had been rehafted many times in its long history. The blade itself was scarcely more than one inch in width, some eight inches in length, very thin and straight after the custom of Iberian blades, with a shallow blood channel grooved in either side from guard to point.

Peering at the shoulder of the blade, Blunt made out the flowing Spanish inscription, *M. Villalobos, Toledo, MCDLIV.* Mangas Coloradas indeed! Cortés himself may have sheathed that slender *cuchillo*. The half-breed's fingers tightened on the aged haft. A warmth flowed up his knife-arm, seeming to pulse in waves from the alien blade lying so alive and light in his grasp. Some of the ice of his fear thawed away. He raised his head, proud again, ready.

It was then that he saw her. She was with Wind Woman in the first row of squaws behind the warriors and rules-lancers. They were not near Death Horn's position.

Neither was Spotted Wolf with them. They seemed apart from the rest even while among them and of them. Blunt, impelled by what curiosity he knew not, moved toward the two women. When he drew up, it was the older squaw who greeted him.

"It was the girl who sent you the knife," she said. "She came to me asking for some medicine. 'Something to save that young Blunt,' she pleaded. I gave her the Taos knife. It's supposed to be *mómäta*, very blessed." The homely squaw favored Blunt with the friendly evil of her bad-toothed grin, and a knowing wink on top of it. "I don't know how sacred the damned thing is," she said, "but I do know that it slips right through tough old meat—*zuttt!*—like buffalo butter!"

Blunt bowed to her, touching the haft of the knife to his forehead. Then he and Moheya were looking at one another. Neither could speak. Blunt thought that he saw the firelight glistening against her cheek. Was it a tear? Did she shed it for him?

"Courage!" interrupted Wind Woman. "Give a good fight!"

Behind Blunt, the growl was in the throat of the crowd again. He wheeled, half-crouched, to face it. Death Horn had entered the circle. He was dressed, as was Blunt, naked as the day of his delivery, save for breechcloth and fighting knife. The half-breed interpreter, noting his easy slouch of stance and the muscling of his lean body, was scarcely reassured. At the same time, however, he realized that Death Horn was examining his own appearance in turn and, for some reason, that brought him a fleeting comfort.

What was the dog soldier chief seeing? Did young Blunt look dangerous to him also? Was he knowing, too, a trace of doubt? Blunt could not believe it. Yet he knew his own strength, his own worth as a fighting man. Since boyhood he had done little but practice the protection of his own life, at the usual price of such a profession in Cheyenneland—someone else's.

Death Horn may well have been adding up his total picture of his adversary, Blunt knew. Yet, if he was, his expression gave no indication that he found the sum impressive, much less fearful. He stood relaxed, slowly flexing his knife arm and watching the half-breed with the curious detachment a cat shows when its prey catches sight of its approach in midstalk.

Unknowingly Blunt found himself imitating his gestures, flexing his knife arm aimlessly. But the palms of his hands poured forth perspiration. His breathing suddenly was as though he had just run a hard-pressed mile. He saw Stone Calf, the Master of the Trial, entering the circle. With the time finally run out, there remained no doubt in Blunt's breast of his true feeling toward the dog soldier opposite. He was mortally afraid of him.

Stone Calf strutted his brief moment in the glare of the fires. He was not the regular master, but only serving because Tall Bull, the First Chief of the dog soldiers, was absent on a raid. For all his posturings, the tribal chief seemed to call off the rules' statement with unseemly haste. *Any fighter stepping out of the ring would be lanced. The fight could end only with the death of one or both fighters. The survivor held full rights to all the status of the vanquished, except for his membership in a warrior society or his civil chieftainship within the tribe, but including all of his real and domestic chattels, not excepting his women.*

"*Evetázistoz!*" shouted Stone Calf, stepping back. "Fight!"

Death Horn was moving with the word. He struck across the ring at Blunt with a speed the latter could not follow. The interpreter saw the glittering arc of the chief's broad-bladed knife coursing like a fire streak directly for his lower belly. He leaped and fell over backward, expecting to feel the bite of the steel in his vitals as he went. Instead he felt a searing bolt strike through his right buttock. Instinctively, he rolled over and forward. His rearward fall had taken him out of the ring's boundary and into the ready lance of one of the watchful referees.

Death Horn had meanwhile recovered from his thrust with ease and, even as Blunt rolled back into the ring, launched himself toward him once more. This time Blunt drew up his knees to protect himself, still on the ground. He turned a hunched side and buttock to the chief in the next instant and felt the latter's blade enter his side. But the momentum of his own twisting contortion to roll free

ripped out the steel as quickly as it entered. Death
Horn's momentum carried him past Blunt and tripping
over the fallen interpreter. Both men regained their feet
simultaneously, some ten feet apart.

Blunt knew that if his opponent struck for the third
time, it was over. His eyes were full of dirt and ashes
from his fall out of the ring. The lance wound in his
haunch had momentarily spasmed the muscles there,
rendering his right leg nearly useless, while the blood
released from the ragged knife rip in his side contributed
also to his dazed shock.

But Death Horn did not strike for the third time. Evidently he had not noted the lance wound, could not
know of the other's impaired vision, could see only the
knife rip and knew that was not handicapping the big
half-blood. He waited a fateful moment, then began
moving to his left, coming around on Blunt's right.
Blunt turned with him in the age-old circling tactic of
fighting animals.

The interpreter had a few seconds to realize why he
had been so badly used thus far. He had made the gross
error of applying his own thinking to the mind of the
enemy. He had envisioned the fight starting with the wary
circle they were now making. Death Horn by his un-
orthodox opening lunge had very nearly eviscerated
him. Blind luck and a superior set of reflexes had saved
him. Now, twice wounded, half blinded and blunderingly
humiliated, Blunt's son was beginning to think.

The answer to his original fear, he knew, was in the
weapons. The knife is not the choice of those who bear
white blood. They fear it, hating those who use it. But
with his knife fear Blunt now remembered an old Cheyenne fighting move taught him by his grandfather, Elk
Bounding, in boyhood. It had been a game then but the
old man had known that one day it would not be, and
he had schooled the grandson well.

Blunt felt strength return. Dropping both hands to his
sides he moved forward directly toward Death Horn. His
opponent stopped, puzzled. Then, as Blunt continued to
come at him, the dog soldier struck hard, lunging in with
the blade. Blunt moved to his own right, shifting the
Spanish steel into his left hand and whipping it at the
passing Death Horn in a backstroke as the Indian's body
brushed by his joltingly.

Blunt made the shift of the knife beautifully but was so jarred by the impact of Death Horn's body that the backstroke was deflected. His knife found not the soft kidney fat but the iron fiber of the Indian's back muscle.

Death Horn turned in mid-air as the steel entered the muscle, freeing himself of the blade. But Blunt had felt it go in deep. Spinning on his left heel he was in time to slide under the chief's return stroke and lock his knife arm. At the same time he felt Death Horn's left hand lock his own right-hand knife wrist. Arm-bound, they struggled, the Indian's skill and quickness driving Blunt back. And more.

The pressure of his enemy's hand was paralyzing the interpreter's knife grip. Another moment and the blade must drop. Simultaneously Blunt's left arm was yielding to Death Horn's right, the point of the latter's broad blade coming with quivering, agonizing slowness down toward the shoulder juncture of the half-blood's neck. A second more would bring it thrusting home, but even as its point pricked skin Blunt sensed the sudden weakening of the other's left hand. The injured great back muscle was giving way.

Exerting his whole force Blunt threw his knife arm up and forward. The Toledo's slimness found Death Horn's left side, low down, just above the hip joint, and once more Blunt knew it had gone in deep.

Yet in staggering back from the blow the Indian nearly tore the knife from his grasp. Blunt could not follow him either. Neither of his own hands had survived the pressures of Death Horn's unbelievable strength-of-grip without damage. They had not enough force left in them to grasp the haft properly for the deathstroke. He could not risk losing the knife by striking with it.

Luckily the other hesitated also. Blunt saw why. His left arm dangled uselessly; the slashing kidney wound and its twin just delivered had made control of that arm impossible.

The dog soldier chief began to slide toward him crabwise, wounded left side forward. Blunt gave ground and soon they were circling again, neither able to gain an opening.

At once the dark-faced audience commenced to hoot, whistle and beat their palm heels together. The warriors, women, even the small children joined in the chanting and shouting.

"Fear, fear! Cowards, cowards! Shame, shame—!"

It mattered not, Blunt knew, if he or his adversary were of primary blame. If they did not quickly "make a fight" of it, the Cheyenne would intercede and finish it themselves.

He stopped and spread his feet. His knife arm swung free. He was determined to stand and force the Indian to come to him.

There was no other course. It was Death Horn's fight and the interpreter knew that the Indian would have to make it.

And he was right. Almost instantly, the other moved toward him. Watching him, narrow-eyed, Blunt saw something. A little thing. The kind upon which battles turn. Just before the other commenced to move in, the fingers of his left hand, the supposedly "useless" one, flexed and unflexed three times. Blunt's mind leaped. Either that dangling arm had been a ruse all along or Death Horn had just regained control of it. At any rate he was playing it as a ruse now, and he did not realize that Blunt had caught him at it.

Now was the time. What did the dog soldier intend to do with that arm? How would he use it when Blunt attacked or when he attacked? Seeing him come in, Blunt thought he knew, and acted on the thought instinctively. If he were right the fight might end instantly or it might continue. If he were wrong it would simply end instantly. But time was gone. Blunt moved to meet the Indian.

When they were six feet apart the latter erupted into violence. Blunt saw his jaw muscles twitch and tense before he leaped and released his own entire power toward his one objective, the "useless" arm, *and the shift of the knife to it.* The gamble paid. Death Horn switched the knife from his right hand to the supposedly injured left hand just as Blunt's strong jaws, aimed in desperation at the suspected left hand, closed on the wrist of that hand. The last thing the dog soldier chief might have expected was to be bitten, to be attacked as an animal might attack him, in a knife fight with another warrior.

He grunted in intense pain as the half-blood's teeth buried themselves in his wrist. There was the sound of a bone snapping. He dropped the broad-bladed knife. His senseless fingers could no longer close about its haft. The weapon thudded into the thick dust. The fighters went rolling over and over. The dog soldier snarled and growled as he sought for his opponent's knife.

Blunt felt the Indian's left arm close about his waist. Then his right hand seized Blunt's knife arm below the elbow. With the same move, he twisted atop Blunt, pulling the half-blood toward him with all his strength. As he did, his right hand began to inch its deadly way down Blunt's arm toward his knife hand.

Surging upward, Blunt bridged his body. The maneuver freed his pinioned right arm. Flinging the arm outward he swept the knife safely to one side the moment before Death Horn's creeping fingers reached the weapon. His head was now buried in the Indian's right shoulder, looking over the shoulder and down the dark-skinned back.

Looping his left arm behind the dog soldier's neck, he pulled his head forward. In the same fragment of time he struck downward with the knife. The blade plunged into the meat of the right shoulder, where it was soft near the pit of the arm. And Blunt ripped it down the arm, deep-buried, from shoulder point to elbow. The whitish bone showed sickeningly as Blunt let the nearly severed arm go limp, and rolled free of his stricken enemy.

He regained his feet in time to see Death Horn, incredibly, stumble upward and come for him again. The dog soldier's right arm was a dangling sodden mangle of dirt and flesh. His left groped floppingly at itself and at his tortured body, unable to direct itself by virtue of the shattered wrist where Blunt's crushing teeth had almost met.

Blunt was certain, afterward, that the Indian was in shock these final seconds. He was no longer a human organism but a gray-faced, staring-eyed atavism from the pit of time. Magnificently vital as he was, he had taken three grisly wounds, of which either of the first two would have killed an ordinary fighter. He had been suffering untold pain and weakening loss of blood for six or seven minutes. He wobbled lurchingly as he came for Blunt. He gestured with the futile club of his left arm. His step slowed, the thigh muscles jerking and fluttering in failing spasm. The knees were going. And all the while those fierce dark eyes kept looking from beneath the peregrine brows at Blunt and through him. But now in truth those eyes were not seeing Blunt and were in fact fastened on some more distant view.

The half-blood stepped mercifully inside his blind gropings then, slipping the lean length of the Toledo blade quietly into its full depth. A slight shudder ran through the thin body. It slid hesitatingly to its knees in the dust. The fingers of the right hand felt aimlessly across the chest. They found the half of the buried knife, plucked wonderingly at it, fell away. With the falling hand, the body went forward, twisting down into the trampled earth. Blunt knelt swiftly by its side.

He raised Death Horn and held him there. For only a little time—the time of a sigh perhaps—the fierce eyes focused, the dark lips moved. Blunt bent to catch the word. He was never sure of it but he always thought that he understood it.

It was *"Nis'is."* My brother.

That night Blunt slept in the lodge of the departed warrior. Next morning he refused to take the belongings of the dead chief. He gave them instead to Spotted Wolf and Wind Woman. The couple, when he came to their tipi with the sun, were grateful. They would remember him, they said. They would faithfully carry, also, his warning words to the old chief Black Kettle.

As for the dog soldiers, with the elevation of a new Second Chief, or the return of the First Chief Tall Bull, things would be different perhaps. Why did not young Blunt come along with them to the Ouachita? It was always a fine winter camp. The evenings would be long and cozy in the lodge, and the older people like themselves went early to blanket those cold nights. The young people could tend the fire until daybreak without being watched.

Besides, they had no sons remaining to them now. The lodge needed a hunter. If young Blunt could track and shoot as well as he fought, he would be a blessing to their home.

"What are you going to do?" asked Spotted Wolf. "Live out on the prairie like a coyote?"

Blunt, for a fleeting, nostalgic moment, considered it. But he knew it could not be. His lot lay neither with the Cheyenne nor the cavalry. Death Horn had been right.

When the chief had looked upward in that last moment and said what he had said, it had been so. Blunt *was* the brother of the falcon, the coyote, the wandering wild, free wind.

He shook his head now to Spotted Wolf's invitation.

"I have sat in the middle," he said. "I heard the Cheyenne, I heard the soldiers. Both were wrong."

"Nonsense!" snorted the war chief. "Come along with us. Who cares who is right and who is wrong? Will it bring back the dead of Sand Creek or Arickaree Island?" Arickaree was the Cheyenne name for Beecher Island.

Again Blunt shook his head.

"Father, I know where my trail leads," he said. "It leads alone."

"*Hotoahemas!*" interrupted Wind Woman. "All that is so many buffalo chips. Do as my old warrior says. Take the girl and join our band. We'll make a Cheyenne of you."

Blunt touched the brow to both of them. They understood it was farewell.

"If it must be so," said the squaw, "let it be thus between us at the parting. From this day we call you *Nahahan;* you are 'our son' once more."

"Thank you," said Blunt. "I will carry it in my heart."

He caught up Loafer's trailing reins, swung to saddle.

"Where is the girl, Mother?" he said softly.

"Up on the hill," said the woman. "Crying for you."

"Her tears will dry. Tell her Blunt's son said goodbye."

He paused, the ache in his chest very great.

"Tell her," he said, "that in another time things could have been different for us. Happier. Better for all of us. *Nataemhon,* old friends, good hunting."

He swung the Sioux gelding quickly.

The two Cheyenne watched him ride to the river and across it. They watched him until he was no more than the dot of a buffalo gnat against the tawny mane of the autumn prairie; and watched him still until the tawniness gave away to the faint blue haze of last seeing.

Then Wind Woman turned.

"Too bad," she said. "A good man."

"Yes," said Spotted Wolf, "a pity he was half-white."

Red Runs the Washita

Custer had halted his command in a snow-filled wash. The general's tent, pitched in the lee of the field ambulance, was the lamplit beacon toward which Carmody now guided the gray mare. The windrows of freezing troopers, huddled behind the ammunition wagons or seeking the animal warmth of the picket line, paid no attention to the tall rider coming in out of the storm. Grimacing, Carmody dismounted. At the tent flat he hesitated, peering in. The grim face relaxed. Had there been a carpet inside, his fellow scouts of the Seventh Cavalry—California Joe, Apache Bill, Ben Clark, Jimmy Morrison, the Mexican "Romeo," and the Osage old Hard Rope—would have been standing squarely on it. Custer, flanked by his three field-grade officers, along with Captain Benteen and Lieutenant Tom Custer, was giving hell to his vaunted scout corps. The familiar thin voice was tart as pickling brine.

"Well, gentlemen, I suggest that despite your elevated reputations you have gotten me as thoroughly lost as though I had hired one of Black Kettle's Cheyenne to do the job." He shook his head disdainfully. "Indeed, were it not for my own skill with the compass, we would not even know that we are eight hours due south of the Canadian River. Any arguments?"

"None at all, General." California Joe wagged his black beard. "We're just as lost as Bo-Peep's sheep."

"That's the mortal truth," agreed Apache Bill.

The other scouts nodded wordless sympathy, Hard Rope adding the long postscript. "Once we find village, me do you good job. Get in close like hell."

Outside the tent, Carmody nodded. Hard Rope was right. The Osages were not good long-range scouts but could work better at close range than the whites, since they smelled right to the Indian dogs and horses. But Custer and his staff were unconvinced.

"Well, Colonel, here we are." Benteen's slow voice took up the burden. He did not call Custer "General," but gave him his reduced rank. "We have accomplished everything but what we set out to accomplish—find Black Kettle's camp on the Washita. And the only man who might help us is six hours overdue, evidently as lost as we."

"That's a fact, General," said Ben Clark. "Carmody's hair may be freezing over some Cheyenne smokehole right now. I surely do wish he would show up fair sudden."

"I join you in the wish, Ben." Custer made a rare admission of concern. "But if wishes fed horses we would not have to haul oats along. Fretting over Carmody is not going to whisk him in through those tent flaps."

Carmody could not resist the introduction. Grinning shyly, he stepped into the tent. "Depends on how hard you fret, General," he said, "or how easy I whisk."

Only Custer remained aloof in the ensuing flurry of glad backslaps and handshakes which greeted the missing scout. As soon as he decently could, he cleared the tent, reserving Carmody to himself. Whatever the latter might have to divulge of the location of the rumored big Indian camp along the Washita was going to belong to Lieutenant Colonel George Armstrong Custer and no other officer of the Army. And any history-book credit for leading the lost column of Seventh Cavalry out of the blind gut of that blizzard of November 26, 1868, was not going to be split up with California Joe, Micah Carmody or any other scout of record. It was going to stay with Custer and his West Point compass.

Crouched over the colonel's war chest, Carmody labored

at the final details of a field map of the hostile encampment along the Washita. Impatiently Custer snatched the map from beneath his hand. "Are you certain of all this?" he demanded. "Are you dead sure that Black Kettle's camp is isolated from the other bands? Can be cut off quickly?"

Carmody shrugged. "You pay my salary, General, and I try to earn it," he said.

Custer stared at him, then bent to the map, concentrating intently. In a moment he picked up the drawing and returned it to Carmody. "Keep this for your memoirs," he said grinning. "I won't need it again; I've committed it to memory." He wheeled about and strode toward the tent's flaps. "Come along, if you wish," he said. "I'm going out for a breath of air."

Yes, thought Carmody, not moving to follow his employer, and likely to see if it hasn't stopped snowing so that you can find those poor miserable Indians yet tonight. His resentment was scarcely formed when Custer was back through the tent flaps, face flushed, voice rising high with excitement.

"Carmody, come quick! Look at this! It *has* cleared off. We can see the river ahead. By heaven, sir, we've got them now! Well, come on, man! Don't just stand there gaping. Orderly! Get Captain Benteen up here. Ho!"

Wondering if the column commander had read his mind about the weather lifting, Carmody went to the flaps and peered out. As far as the eye might travel there was nothing but clean black starlight. Not a snowflake whirled nor stirred. It was as though there had been no freakish blizzard, or that it had pulled back at Custer's command. And the moon was due to rise in less than two hours. Nothing could stop the general now.

"Sir," pleaded Carmody hopelessly, "don't you try it. The troops aren't up to it yet. They've got eight hours hard riding behind them already. They've had no hot food. The horses are spent. Even the wagon mules are done in. You couldn't gamble on them to get the ammunition up promptly. General, sir—!"

But Custer was listening only to the tunes of his own trumpets, and they were blowing "Garry Owen."

"Orderly!"

"General, for God's sake, listen to me!"

"Orderly! Get Captain Benteen, Major Elliott, Gibbs, all the rest. On the double, sir, do you hear?"

"Yes, sir! Corporal of the Guard! On the double, ho!"

"General, please, in the name of reason, will you listen!"

"Carmody, be still! Plague it, man, you've done your part. Now get out of the way and let me do mine. Get out, do you hear me, sir? Get out!"

"Yes, sir."

Carmody watched the wild race of Custer's orders break the huddled cavalry encampment from its snow-bound bivouac. Within minutes the column from Camp Supply would be on the move. Within miles Carmody and the coming harsh moonlight would be guiding it toward the long-sought winter camp of the hostiles. And within six frost-clear hours the troopers would be grouped on the crest of the ridge overlooking Black Kettle's lodges. The Seventh Cavalry was committed. The Washita was waiting and Yellow Hair was coming down upon it.

The light within the Cheyenne lodge came only from the chief's pipe bowl. The alternate rise and fall of the reddish glow limned the old man's impassive features, tracing upon them the unmistakable prescience of tragedy. Across from him the slim girl crouched, waiting for her father to speak. Outside, the wind, quiet for the first time in three days, let the cowskins hang slack along the gaunt ribs of the lodgepoles. From downriver came the muffled thumping of the scalp-dance drums in the lower, main camp of the Cheyenne. It was a big dance and a wild one. But there was ominous reason for the silence holding between Black Kettle and his slender daughter in the isolated lodge of the weary old "peace chief" of the Southern Cheyenne.

Two days gone, a dog soldier patrol had returned to report hearing rifle fire along the Canadian. It had sounded like pony soldier fire but the snow had been too heavy for a full view. Last night Red Bird had come back from a lone scout to say he had seen a long line of horsemen marching south of the Canadian. But again the snow had been too heavy. He could not say if they were pony soldiers or just other Indians. This same morning two of White Bear's Kiowa had passed through camp with a tale of crossing a line of iron-shod pony tracks lying south of where Red Bird had seen "the many horsemen." With those iron shoes the horses must belong to the pony soldiers!

Black Kettle sighed and stirred the ashes in his pipe. "Bring up our ponies now, my daughter. Tie them outside the lodge where they will be ready. I am uneasy. My heart is bad."

Bright Hair nodded quickly. "Magpie has been on guard upon the watchtower hill above the ridge since sundown. It is very cold. It is time he was brought down. Who shall I send up in his place, Father?"

"Double Wolf. He can be trusted. Send him."

The lithe figure of the girl moved quickly through the flaps of the lodge, leaving the darkness within to the last thoughts of Moxtaveto, the Black Kettle, deposed patriarch of his people.

The dry cottonwood logs of the downriver dance were piled even higher. This was turning into a real celebration. From the northeast within the hour had arrived two new large parties of dog soldiers, the premier fighters and tribal police of the Cheyenne. Both parties were from Kansas where they had been raiding even while the senile Black Kettle had been whining his peace talk with the soldier chiefs at Fort Cobb. Both of these new parties were big for war. Both were led by real true chiefs—by Crow Neck and by Black Shield! And these new parties had fresh white scalps with them, twenty-three scalps by honest count. Now that was something to dance about!

The drums thundered the news. The cracked voices of the village criers carrying along the lodges of all the tribes summoned a second and third wave of dancers from the far-flung encampment. A true scalp dance, brothers! Come running now! Bring your squaw or sweetheart! This is that rare time that you dance with her! Hour after hour the driving chant of the drums continued. The white flood of moonrise served merely to augment the frenzy of the wild bodies beneath the blankets. Ten o'clock came and was pounded under by the drums. Another hour passed, another began.

On the lone hill overlooking the long ridge west of Black Kettle's lodge, Double Wolf, the trusted sentry, pulled the heavy shroud of his buffalo robe more closely about him.

Curse this bone-cold midnight. But then what of it? The dance below was going splendidly, all was clear to the West, with not a pony soldier in sight and no chance of one appearing. What was the real purpose in huddling here like a homeless dog when, down the hill a few steps, he could be snug in his own lodge? A warm fire waited there, and the sweet arms of his woman, with perhaps even a bit of fine boiled young dog left over from supper. Hah! Black Kettle was an old squaw to expect the soldiers to be traveling on a freezing cold night like this, and after such a blizzard. Enough was enough. It was time to go below and warm up a little. Seconds later Double Wolf was gone down the hill to his snug lodge and only the moonlight guarded the glistening snows of the long ridge and of Black Kettle's watchtower above the Washita.

Carmody held in the gray mare tightly. Beside him Hard Rope sat his paint gelding, slant eyes narrowed as Carmody pointed to the long ridge ahead. Behind them a hundred yards moved Custer with the remainder of the scouts. Behind Custer a hundred yards came the thin column of the Seventh Cavalry, the muted harness jingling of its advance carrying too clearly to Carmody and the Osage. Carmody reined in the gray mare. Custer, seeing him do so, waved the halt to his troops. Dismounted, the entire scout group inched its way up the moonwhite slope of the ridge. At the crest Carmody spoke softly.

"You're in luck, General; they haven't even got a sentry out."

"How can you tell, man? I can see nothing save snow."

"That lone hill yonder, General. You see it?"

"Yes. What of it?"

"That's Black Kettle's lookout. He calls it his watchtower. They had a sentry on it all day yesterday. Now you can see it's bare as a new baby."

"Good Lord, Carmody! You don't suppose they've pulled out?"

"No, they're not gone, General. They're just not as crazy as you are. They would never figure you to come down on them under such a blizzard as this one has been."

Custer shook his head stubbornly. "I can't believe there's a big war camp beyond that hill, Carmody. You've missed your landmarks, sir. We shall move on down the river."

Carmody's lantern jaw grew hard. "You'd best not, General. Come on over to the top of that deserted hill with Hard Rope, Joe and me. After all, even Yellow Hair doesn't walk 850 ironshod cavalry horses up to Black Kettle's front door without knocking. Not in the dark."

Custer's brief peg-toothed grin showed his appreciation of the reminder. He knew his own weakness for snap decisions. "All right," he nodded, "let's go. We can't give the troops time enough to get on the edge though. Move out quickly please."

Carmody led the way on a snow-crunching trot. Atop the distant hill, they bellied down once more and peered hard into the darkness below. They saw nothing but the jumble of small hills and dark river timber of the Washita's Big Bend. They heard nothing. Custer was convinced there *was* nothing. But Hard Rope had Indian ears.

"Me hear dog yelp just now," he muttered.

"I didn't hear a thing," said Custer sharply. "And I don't see a thing. Carmody, you've blundered. I should have listened to California Joe."

"No, General," said the black-bearded scout, "Carmody's right. What you'd ought to listen to is that there Injun dog yonder."

"Listen good," growled Hard Rope. "You no hear dog now?"

Custer heard. There was not only one dog barking now, there were several. And they weren't baying at the moon.

"Me see Cheyenne pony herd," said Hard Rope suddenly. "This side river. Right below hill here. You see-um, General?"

"Where? Where?" Custer's straining glance shifted to follow the Osage's pointing arm. "Why, bless you, man, those aren't horses; they're buffalo! I know buffalo when I see them in a herd like that. By the Lord, Carmody, you *were* wrong!"

"Well, General, you're right about them being a herd, but they're not buffalo." Carmody's voice was raw. "And hold your talk down; we can't afford to be spooking those crazy Cheyenne horses. Happen we work it right, we can gather in that herd on our way through the lodges. But if we work it wrong, they'll stampede on us and rouse every Indian for fifteen miles down the river. Let's go, General—those *are* ponies yonder."

"I'm not satisfied, Carmody. Dogs or no dogs, those are buffalo. I believe your Indians are gone, sir. A few curs always linger behind any big camp. You know that."

"Me know too," complained Hard Rope. "Them Cheyenne ponies!"

"If they're buffalo," put in California Joe, "I would purely like to know who hung the grazing bells on them."

Custer's scowl faded. Up from below now came the musical tinkling of several neck bells. Unabashed, Custer patted Carmody's shoulder.

"As you said, Micah," he smiled excitedly, "let us go."

The smile faded in the instant of its flashing. The pale-eyed stare which replaced it put the gunsteel of reality into the rasping conclusion: "And may God have mercy on Black Kettle's soul; for I shall not . . . !"

Beyond the mile-long shelter of the first ridge, Custer readied his column. The lean ration of coffee and hardtack for a single day per man, brought forward from the base camp on the Canadian, was dumped on the frozen ground. It was followed by saddlebags, nosebags for the horses' oats, even overcoats. Nothing was taken forward save unbooted carbines and 100 rounds of ammunition per trooper. The scouts and officers gathered swiftly to Custer.

There would be four attack columns, they were informed. Two would move straight ahead under Custer. One, under Major Elliott, would swing wide and attack from the east. One, under Colonel Meyers, would go to the right and attack from the south. Of Custer's two units, the left would be under young Captain Thompson. All clear? Good. Quickly now.

Elliott and Meyers moved out. Custer sat his horse studying the crawl of the minute hand around the moonlit face of his gold pocket watch. Carmody looked at the famed cavalryman and cursed under breath. Beyond the watchtower hill waited Black Kettle, the Indian who had done more than any South Plains chief to bring peace and a rule of law to the wild tribes. Now Black Kettle would get his reward and Yellow Hair would get his promotion. Carmody's stomach turned within him. He knew the old chief well. He had spoken with him many times

in many councils. It seemed to Carmody that Black Kettle
was the truest, the gentlest of men. Yet now 850 white
soldiers stole through the night into position all about him
and his trusting followers. And who was it that had
brought these 850 white soldiers down upon the old chief
and his gallant Cheyenne? Was it Custer? Elliott? Thompson? Meyers? Was it California Joe? Apache Bill? Hard
Rope? It was not; it was Micah Carmody.

Custer snapped shut the case of the gold watch. "Captain Thompson," he said, "hold your command to a walk
until we are seen."

The 400 troops of Thompson and Custer split like a
snake's tongue around the base of the watchtower hill.
On the far side they converged toward a solitary tipi
pitched beside the trail to hill's top. Double Wolf's woman, out with the first light of the new day to gather firewood, stared in blank terror at what she saw. Double
Wolf was not yet out of his blankets when his woman
dashed in, seized up their two small children and cried
out the dread words, "Pony soldiers!"

Following the squaw outside, Double Wolf was still
loading his rifle when the first soldiers rounded the hill.
Double Wolf had signed the peace treaty at Fort Cobb.
He had been with Black Kettle on that recent day when
the Southern Cheyenne touched the pen with Yellow Hair
and the other white men. But Double Wolf had also been
with that other peaceful camp at Sand Springs when Major Chivington had come to visit his red brothers in the
early dawn. He had seen his first squaw and four small
first children shot down and ridden over. He saw now the
blood of those innocents once more in his memory and
he forgot Black Kettle's careful plan to raise only the
white flag of surrender if the soldiers should come. Instead
he raised his old muzzleloader and fired it with his war
cry into the advancing troops. His body was nearly severed by the answering hail of soldier lead. His last memory was of the blare of Yellow Hair's bugler sounding
the charge. The instantaneous mercy of his death spared
Double Wolf the shame of hearing the regimental band
begin to play "Garry Owen," the war song of the Seventh
Cavalry; and thus the Battle of the Washita was begun.

Custer's column splashed through the shallow Washita

and up the opposite bank. Beyond stood the fifty lodges camped with Black Kettle. Carmody, riding with the colonel, saw Black Kettle's old squaw hobble from the lodge and toward the two tethered ponies. A moment later the chief himself ran out shouting and waving for the soldiers to wait, that there would be no war, that there had been some bad mistake, that these lodges were at peace with the white man. He had no time to bring out with him his flag of peace which he had so carefully prepared. The surprise had overcome him. The panicky thought of Sand Creek came back to Black Kettle with too much power. The tatter of dirty white feed sacking laced to its proudly painted willow staff was afterward found in his lodge furled atop his buffalo-hide war shield and broken lance —the symbol of his promise to make no more war upon the white man.

Seeing his frantic pleas ignored now, the old man also ran toward the tethered ponies. The latter, wild with fear, were rearing and lunging, defying the squaw's efforts to approach them. Black Kettle seized the mane of the nearest one and swung up to its back. Slashing it free, he lifted the squaw up behind him and, mounted double, spurred for the Washita.

Carmody's yells of protest to Custer and the nearest troopers, apprising them of what Black Kettle had said, were drowned in the burst of carbine fire poured after the escaping chief. Custer himself nearly rode the scout down in his eagerness to join the chase. Wheeling the gray mare free of the mad-dog rush, Carmody saw a third figure dash from the tipi of Black Kettle. He recognized the slim body and long auburn-tinged hair: it was the old chief's niece, the one called Bright Hair. He tried to intercept her, thinking to save at least this one of the old patriarch's family, but the girl was too swift and too wild for him. She reached the second pony, vaulted to its back, cut it free and drove it toward the river-edge cottonwoods. He did not see if she made this shelter or not, as the onward rush of Meyers's troops, closing belatedly, caught him up and carried him with their charge up to the crossing of the Washita. There he was in time to witness the macabre close of a Plains Indian era.

Black Kettle's pony, both riders still mounted, ran the gauntlet of trooper fire trying to reach river's edge. But it was not to be. The pony staggered, bit by a volley of

.54 caliber Spencer bullets. It stopped, sprawled, went
down, struggled unbelievably up once more. Yet now only
the squaw was on its back, as it went toward the stream,
unguided. The animal took perhaps a half-dozen strides.
Then its lone remaining rider screamed, threw hands
high, slid off and lay still on the icy earth not twenty feet
from the body of her dead husband.

Carmody fought the nausea which welled up. He
turned from the river, his sole thought to try and do
whatever small thing he might in the continuing carnage
to redeem his part in bringing it about. But he was helpless. Custer's military planning was too skilled. Thompson's troops held the south bank—the opposite shore—
of the river, as well as the entry into Black Kettle's village from the west. Below the lodges of the old chief, seal-
ing them off from the larger hostile camps downstream,
were the 225 troopers of Colonel Edward Meyers. Yellow
Hair had his Indians where he wanted them, and where he
wanted them dead.

In Black Kettle's group of lodges were 175 warriors
and teen-age boys. There were half that number of squaws
and small children. Eighty of the braves, led by ancient
Magpie, reached the Washita and slid over its bank to
begin fighting their way down the current toward the main
Cheyenne camp and possible safety. The remainder of
Black Kettle's warriors, cut off from their pony herd by
Meyers, and from the Washita by Custer, were trapped.
The colonel now coolly stationed Lieutenant Billy Cook
with forty sharpshooters on the south bank below the village. He himself then swung around above the village
and drove eastward through it. As the braves broke and
fled before him, they ran into the crossfire of Cook's picked
riflemen at the river and of Meyers's men on the inland
side. The few warriors who won through this ambuscade
and turned for the Washita were cut down by Thompson's rifles holding the far north bank of the stream.
Carmody's earlier estimate of five minutes needed for
cutting off Black Kettle's small village from the main hostile encampment had not been exceeded by sixty seconds
when the last of the old chief's men were shot to pieces,
the last of his women and children killed or captured.

Custer, shouting Carmody to his side once more, now
turned his skills to the surviving warriors of Magpie holed
up beneath an overhanging shelfbank of the Washita. Or-

dering Cook's sharpshooters across the stream, he turned
their fire into the huddled Indians. When the braves could
stand no more and began to swim eastward, along the
shore, Carmody counted seventeen dark bodies bobbing in
the reedy shallows or sprawled against the naked clay
of the cutbank.

From downstream now, in the direction taken by the
fleeing Cheyenne, came the booming of a Spencer volley. Custer's light eyes blazed. He whirled on Carmody.

"By heaven, Micah!" he cried. "That's Elliott down
there! He's got the devils on the run. Come on, man, or
we'll be too late!"

He was grinning his wild grin, and Carmody knew he
meant "too late to be in on the fun." But the big scout
had counted the Indians in those lower camps. He knew
how much "fun" waited for Custer at the Big Bend of
the Washita. Yet he only nodded and turned the gray mare
to follow Custer's bay.

Rejoined on the south bank by his main command
and supported by Cook's riflemen, Custer led the 250
troopers down the river at a gallop. Overhead the day
was bell-clear, the sun just breaking over the low Washita hills. Horses and men shed the weariness of the long
march down from the Canadian. A good omen came moments later when Elliott's fire slacked just as Custer rode
into the first of his officer's retreating troops. The retirement was in fine order, commanded by a young lieutenant.
The latter reported calmly that Elliott had killed thirty-
eight Cheyenne in a narrow ravine just ahead. Then the
hills had begun to fill with fresh warriors. Troops commenced falling back and although the lieutenant had received no direct order from Elliott, he had assumed the
retreat had been called. Not disturbed by the slackening
of Elliott's fire, nor the young lieutenant's report, Custer
was on the point of waving his own command forward
when he felt Micah Carmody's hand on his arm.

"Wait along, General," frowned the gaunt scout. "I had
best go first. I smell a rat somewhere. Look yonder."

Custer obeyed. He saw the bobbing rows of war bonnets and the sun flashes of the rifle barrels beginning to
sprout on every elevation both in front and flanking him.
He glanced at Carmody.

"The Arapaho, General." Carmody had not lost his

GET YOUR 4 FREE BOOKS NOW—
A VALUE BETWEEN $16 AND $20

Mail the Free Book Certificate Today!

FREE BOOKS CERTIFICATE!

YES! I want to subscribe to the Leisure Western Book Club. Please send my 4 FREE BOOKS. Then, each month, I'll receive the four newest Leisure Western Selections to preview FREE for 10 days. If I decide to keep them, I will pay the Special Members Only discounted price of just $3.36 each, a total of $13.44. This saves me between $3 and $6 off the bookstore price. There are no shipping, handling or other charges. There is no minimum number of books I must buy and I may cancel the program at any time. In any case, the 4 FREE BOOKS are mine to keep—at a value of between $17 and $20! Offer valid only in the USA.

Name_____

Address_____

City_____ State_____

Zip_____ Phone_____

Biggest Savings Offer!

For those of you who would like to pay us in advance by check or credit card—we've got an even bigger savings in mind. Interested? Check here. ☐

If under 18, parent or guardian must sign.
Terms, prices and conditions subject to change. Subscription subject to acceptance. Leisure Books reserves the right to reject any order or cancel any subscription.

GET FOUR BOOKS TOTALLY FREE—A VALUE BETWEEN $16 AND $20

PLEASE RUSH
MY FOUR FREE
BOOKS TO ME
RIGHT AWAY!

Leisure Western Book Club
P.O. Box 6613
Edison, NJ 08818-6613

AFFIX
STAMP
HERE

frown. "I told you they'd mix into it. This is real trouble now."

"All right, how do we handle it, Micah?"

"You'd best stay here and steady these boys down while I go on up and locate Major Elliott for you. That rat is smelling worse by the minute."

Custer nodded abruptly. It was occurring, even to him, that the morning had passed all too quickly. "Very well, go on, sir," he ordered. "Find Elliott and bring him back here to me. I'll hold, don't fear."

Carmody touched his brow, wheeled the gray mare and dug her hard with the spurs. She ran like a deer along the silent bank. On her back Micah Carmody bent low, gray eyes searching the unnatural stillness ahead. He could smell that rat for sure now. It smelled *dead*.

Five minutes later he rode into the abattoir in "Elliott's ravine." He found the thirty-eight dead Cheyenne along with something else the young lieutenant had neglected to mention—six mutilated troopers. One man was still alive. Carmody was off the mare and down beside him in an instant. He held the man up—he was a boy really— and spoke to him. The lad opened his eyes. "What's your name, soldier?" asked the scout. "What happened here?"

The youngster nodded. His voice was low. "Corporal J. B. Mercer, Company E, with Major Elliott. The rest of this bunch of Cheyenne we walked into got on down the river. Major called for volunteers and went after them, hell-for-leather. Wouldn't you say that was right foolish, mister—?" His gaze strained to focus on the face above him, then the eyes set and locked, staring upward. The hemorrhage welled silently from the hanging mouth. Carmody cursed and put the boy gently down. Stepping back up on the gray mare, he turned her downstream. He had his orders; find Major Elliott and bring him back to Custer. The boy had done his duty. He had told him where Elliott was—somewhere on down the Washita, still chasing Cheyennes and a new commission.

Carmody cursed again. "It's wrong!" he said suddenly aloud. "It's *all* wrong!"

But the bull-throated roar of a Spencer volley just ahead cut off his protest, and he spurred the mare around the last low bluff before the open grassland of the Big Bend. He was too late. Elliott and his volunteers had cornered

the last of Black Kettle's Cheyenne—twelve men and older
boys—and they killed them like herded cattle, even as
Carmody rode shouting over the meadow toward them.
It was not until he slid the mare in among the cheering
troopers that he saw they had taken four captives. These
cowered now under the soldier guns. Startled, Carmody
recognized the bleeding, powder-burned girl as Bright
Hair, the old chief's niece. She stood shielding the three
smallest children of the warrior Magpie. The tall scout's
mind went black with rage. He leaped from the saddle, his
rifle swinging by the barrel. He knocked down three soldiers with the steel-shod butt of the weapon before his
brain cleared and control was his again. He wheeled on
the remainder of the men.

"*You filthy dogs!*" he said, low-voiced. "*I'll kill the first
one that even looks at this girl and these kids.*"

"Good lord, Carmody," one of the troopers managed
to blurt. "We wasn't touching them. We was just holding
them prisoner. We ain't no squaw-killers!"

"Where's Major Elliott?" snarled Carmody, ignoring the
trooper's claim.

"Here." The officer, coming up behind Carmody, spoke
for himself. "What's all this fuss, Carmody? Where's
Custer?"

"That's what he wants to know about you, Major." The
scout eyed him angrily. "General says you're to fall back
right now. You're to follow me. Let's go while we can."

Elliott sensed the urgency in the other's manner and
dead-flat voice. But he was blooded now. He waved aside
the order.

"I mean to go just beyond the creek," he told Carmody.
"Then we'll turn back. I think there's another pocket of
them toward the bend."

"Toward the bend, Major, are 3,000 Indians. If that's a
'pocket,' you're right. What the general sent you was an
order, sir, not a suggestion. He made that clear to me."

Elliott's laugh had the sound of battle wildness in it.
"Let's say you didn't make it clear to me, eh, Carmody?
I'm going over that creek! Sergeant!" A burly noncom
came forward, saluting and grinning. "Take these captives," Elliott told him, "and move them back to Custer." His grin widened. "That girl is the one the general
'admired' at the fort, I believe. There couldn't be two
like her. Custer will want her under his wing."

Carmody faced the gray mare in front of Elliott's horse.
"Major, you're already cut off. I saw hundreds of warriors on the hills *behind* you. But there are thousands *ahead* of you. If we go now and stay tight together, holding the girl and the kids with us more or less as hostages, I believe we can get back to the General. If you go over that creek and if you separate the captives, we're all dead."

Elliott's face paled. He pushed his mount past Carmody's. "I think you stayed with the Cheyenne too long when you were scouting them," he cried. "Get out of my way, sir!"

Carmody heeled the mare aside. Elliott and his remaining eighteen men forded the creek and galloped out into the open grassland of the bend. But they did not gallop far into it, just far enough to clear the Washita River timber and get a look at the mounted Indians swarming the cross-bend hills, north, east and south of them. Too late the rash officer saw the situation. Far too late he realized that the scout, Carmody, had done his Cheyenne homework exceedingly well. Fighting for calm, he ordered his small command back across the creek. But as the troopers started for the marshy banks, that avenue, too, was shut off. From the stream's small canyon through the hills issued a howling torrent of black-feathered warriors—the Cheyenne dog soldiers! Their speed and course were certain to cut off Elliott's recrossing. Carmody, who had trailed the command into the grassland, was determined at least to guard the rear of the Company E survivors. He stood in his stirrups and shouted, "Come on, Major! You've one chance only. Ride back through them before they get set at the ford. Follow me, sir!"

But brave Elliott had lost his blood edge. He hesitated. "Good lord, Major," yelled Carmody, "come on, *give* the order!"

Elliott was as pale as a man in shock. Carmody never knew if this was from fear or hard anger. But the officer did not reply to the scout's pleas. The order he did give was the last order in the Indian fighting world that he should have given: *"Ride for the tall grass, dismount there and turn all the horses loose to fight afoot."*

Watching the troopers obey the suicidal instruction, Carmody himself grew pale. What the big scout could not know was that, as Elliott had dashed off with his volunteers in pursuit of the last of Black Kettle's Cheyenne, he had shouted to his men, "Well, here goes for a brevet or a coffin!" And now Major Joel Elliott was already standing within his creek-grass burial box. His men could see nothing. Their 360-degree field of fire was completely blinded by the waving beards of timothy and gramma hay which grew taller than the heads of many of the troopers yet did not shelter them from the elevated view of the Indians. Nor were the latter in the least slow to realize and to take merciless advantage of the ambitious officer's tragic blunder.

In the open flat of the bend grasslands to the east the hostile Cheyenne of Stone Calf's main village were now forming by the hundreds. The dog soldiers of the famed fighter of Mad Wolf were between them and Custer. Right and left, on the low hills, the Arapaho were completing the circle of death. A patrol of dog soldiers had gone after the sergeant sent back with Bright Hair and Magpie's small children, and Carmody had seen them engulf the lone soldier just as he shouted for Elliott to turn back and charge the forces of Mad Wolf at the crossing. With the sergeant had died the last hope of getting word to Custer in time, unless Carmody could get through—Carmody and the gray mare who ran like a real Kehilan, Drinker of the Wind.

"Major Elliott"—Carmody's flat words were not a request but a statement—"this mare of mine is still sound. She's a runner. Give me a burst of covering fire toward the crossing. I'll try to reach the general." He dropped his voice, edging the mare close to the young officer. "And don't waste your lead on long shots while I'm gone, you understand? Save it for pointblank and fire in volleys only. Hang on, Major, *hard*."

Elliott nodded and gripped Carmody's big hand. The scout wheeled and was gone, spurring the fleet mare in a belly-flat gallop through the limpid creek and up the far shore. His only remembered view of Major Joel Elliott was the one glance he flung back, just as he got over the creek, and during which the young cavalryman waved gallantly to him. It was the last any white man saw or knew of Major Elliott and his men. All that was ever learned of the manner and swiftness with which they died would come years later in the croaking voice of Roman Nose Thunder, one of the Cheyenne survivors, speaking from the distant remove of an Oklahoma reservation.

"The shooting was over then," said the ancient brave. "All the soldiers were dead. The fight did not last longer than it would take a man to smoke a pipe four times . . ."

Across the creek the dog soldiers saw the gray streak of Carmody's mare go over the narrow ford and race for the Washita. The burst of Cheyenne wolf howls this discovery sent up among them was at once cut off by Mad Wolf's barking command. "That white man is mine!" he cried. "I claim the first coup on him. All of you know why."

All of them did indeed. Carmody was generally disliked beyond the rest of Custer's scout corps because of his well-known friendship with the old chief Black Kettle, the despised "peace talker." But Mad Wolf also had a special reason for hating the big white man. It was a slim and dusky reason. The dog soldier chief had been told that Bright Hair had spoken in shy tones of the white scout Carmody. He had thus charged the girl with giving her heart, unasked, to the white man when by tribal understanding all knew she was promised to Mad Wolf. But Mad Wolf's warriors knew, as well, that Black Kettle's niece called their leader a camp cur's whelp, and a murderer whose life was sworn to making war while Black Kettle sought peace with the white man. So now the warriors only nodded and growled their polite agreements with Mad Wolf.

"Go and get him," said one of his cronies, a gross brave called Big Body. "He is yours alone. Who will deny it?"

"Aye," said another crony, Yellow Buffalo. "Who will say no to Axhonehe, the new Second Chief of all the dog soldiers?"

Clearly none of the dog soldiers present were of a mind to steal this honor from their leader. Moreover, yonder in that tall grass there were plenty of other white scalps waiting to be plucked. And more. That other hair would not be as tough as Carmody's. *Eee-yahh!* Go and get the soldiers. Right now!

Mad Wolf, not waiting for this approval, was already racing his spotted stallion after Carmody's mare. Watching him go, his two lieutenants hesitated to join their fellows in the war-crying charge across the creek toward

the dismounted troopers. Yellow Buffalo looked at Big
Body. He made a quick hand sign and Big Body returned
it grinningly. They turned their ponies away from the
creek. After all, where went their leader, there went
they. Were they not his noble friends? Of course.

But swiftly as the two braves turned their mounts to
follow Mad Wolf, a third Cheyenne had departed before
them and on the same errand. Unnoticed in the excitement to be in on the kill of the pony soldiers, Bright
Hair had slipped away from her darkskinned rescuers
and driven her sorrel mare westward along the banks of
the Washita. She had no trouble following the course of the
fleeing white scout, Carmody. She needed only to listen
for the wild wolf cries of his sworn destroyer, Axhonehe,
war chief of all the Cheyenne dog soldiers.

Carmody had exhausted his ammunition. He had between himself and Mad Wolf his courage, his knife and the
gray mare's speed. The odds were not handsome. Mad
Wolf's pony was fresh and gaining. He would bring his
savage rider up to the gray mare in another half-mile.
If by some wild chance Carmody should best Mad Wolf
and continue toward Custer, he could expect the rest of
the dog soldiers to be on him before he might reach the
general. And if he reached the general, he would find him
cut off by hundreds of Big Mouth's Arapaho now moving
up the Washita on the far north bank. To Carmody it
seemed hopeless. For if he did *not* reach Custer, then the
general was sure to move on down the Washita and into
the same trap that had closed on Elliott. It was a damned-
if-he-did, damned-if-he-didn't thing for the big scout. And,
as he saw it, it was the same thing for the ambitious
commander of the Seventh Cavalry. Carmody found himself not caring greatly. The girl, Bright Hair, was with
the dog soldiers and would stay with them. She was
bound to Mad Wolf and would live to mother other bad
Cheyenne like the sire, who, in their later time, would
hate the white man and be hated by him. What was all
the running for? Where was Carmody going that it mattered one thin dime to anyone, red or white?

He threw a glance over his shoulder, and grinned his
frosty grin. Well, one place he was going was *down*. He
was, if he didn't think of one awful fast way to deal
with a dog soldier war chief now one pony-jump short

of closing on him. The grin warmed a little. There was always a ray of cheer in the darkest sky. At very least he could go under in good company. Or rather in bad company. He could take Mad Wolf with him.

The dog soldier, of course, had his Winchester carbine in its saddle boot. The Cheyenne did not count any coup made with bullets. It had to be strictly "by the hand." Carmody well understood this and owed his chance at life to the knowledge.

As the Indian's pony came up to the gray mare, the scout pulled her to one side, hard into the racing stallion, and both horses staggered and went down from the collision. Mad Wolf, a superb rider, struck the ground lightly and was on his feet in an instant. Knife drawn, he came for Carmody. The scout, managing to get his left shoulder beneath the chief's thrust, seized the knife arm by the wrist, twisted and threw the Cheyenne over his back and jarringly to the ground. The force of the fall dislodged the blade from Mad Wolf's grasp and Carmody kicked it out of his reach. As he did, the brush behind the scout opened to reveal the hulking forms of Big Body and the other subchief, Yellow Buffalo. Noiselessly Big Body glided out of the cover and took Carmody in a crushing bearhug from the rear. Sweeping him off his feet, he held the white scout helplessly in midair, unprotected stomach toward the recovering Mad Wolf. In the same moment, Yellow Buffalo retrieved Mad Wolf's knife and returned it to the chief.

"Go ahead," he grunted. "Hurry up and put it in his navel and let us get back to those trapped pony soldiers before all the good hair is taken."

Mad Wolf grasped the knife and moved in to open Carmody's abdomen. As a man will do when he believes his final second of life is ticking away, the white scout looked in desperation at the prairie world about him, hoping wildly and against all reasonable hope to see something—anything—which might hold a promise of extending that last instant of life.

In this rare case, he saw it. It was from the river timber across the Washita, a distance of not more than forty yards. No, less than that. Not more than thirty. Since he was facing the same way as Carmody, Big Body saw the same vision as the white scout, but Carmody saw it the longer. As Big Body's eyes widened and his mouth

opened to cry out the warning to his brothers, the rifle
spoke from across the Washita and the .44 Henry bullet
smashed through Big Body's fine white teeth, into the
roof of his opened mouth, and out the back of his burly
head, carrying his small brains with it and dashing them
onto a meadow boulder behind him. Carmody, in the instant of the bullet's blow, writhed from the dying brave's
grasp and kicked the stunned Yellow Buffalo in the groin
with all his skill and power. The second warrior doubled
over in intense pain and, free of the cross-river brush
and kneeling for better aim now, the Cheyenne girl
Bright Hair shot him calmly the long way of his bent
body, buttocks to throat. He went down twisting like a
run-over snake. Carmody, scooping up the Winchester as
it fell from Yellow Buffalo's hands, was barely in time to
raise the weapon overhead and take the knife blow of
Mad Wolf, who had been momentarily impeded by Yellow Buffalo's thrashings.

Now Carmody literally beat the dog soldier chief to
the ground with the curved-steel buttplate and walnut
stock of the carbine. He was blind with rage for the time
that it took him to do it, and for Bright Hair to swing
up on her sorrel mare and splash across the river to
his side.

"Do not kill him, Carmody!" the Cheyenne girl cried.
"His life is not yours!"

Carmody did not try to understand the Indian logic.
But his rage had cleared and he stood back from the
still-breathing dog soldier. "Catch up my horse," he told
the girl. "We've got to get shut of here." Bright Hair
spurred away, returning in moments only, with the gray
mare. Carmody took the animal, legged up and turned her
away upstream. "This way," he said, "and stay low on
your horse. If we can get to Yellow Hair, we may be safe."

The slim girl nodded and Carmody thought she meant
to obey. But she had a Cheyenne debt to pay. At the
first of the shots, the white scout turned back to see her
calmly levering in a fresh shell. She fired it and the four
remaining rounds in the Henry straight down into the
motionless body of Mad Wolf. Then she heeled the sorrel around and sent her toward Carmody.

"My God," said the scout, "what was that for?"

"That was for my uncle," said the girl soberly. "And

for my old aunt. And for all the others up there in our village."

"But what of me?" asked Carmody incredulously. "Why do you save *me?* Why do you shoot *him?* It was *I* who brought the soldiers down upon your uncle and your aunt and the others."

The slender niece of Black Kettle shook her head quickly. "You are wrong, Carmody," she said. "It was Mad Wolf who brought the pony soldiers to kill us. My uncle said this was the way it was. Our own people killed our own people. There is no more to it; we better go."

Carmody still did not comprehend the girl's Indian thinking. He understood the last part of it, however. They sure as sin had better go. And *now!*

Crossing the Washita, they put their horses westward along the southern bank with its friendly cover of cottonwood and willow. Ahead of them, from Custer's position, came only the infrequent boom of an Indian trade musket with some scattered replies of Spencer fire. Behind them, toward Elliott's creek, all sound of firing had ceased. Keeping to the timber, they reached Black Kettle's deserted village without discovery either by Indian or cavalry patrol. Carmody at once led the way past the empty lodges to Custer's position, where he reported the extreme urgency of Major Elliott's situation.

For some reason forever a mystery to the weary scout, the ebullient "little general" treated the report with callous indifference. He reminded Carmody that Major Elliott was a competent professional soldier, well able to fend for himself, and that he would doubtless rejoin the main column in due order.

"You're not a military man, Carmody," he said. "These Indians are whipped, sir."

Carmody nodded, glancing up at the surrounding hills.

"I don't know what Indians you got in mind, General," he replied. "But the girl Bright Hair tells me there are some 800 more lodges spread three miles on down the river. The braves you see up yonder on the ridges are only the first of what's coming. And they look like plenty to me. I saw what they did to Elliott and it's my guess they've got the same thing in mind for the rest of us." He moved the gray mare closer to Custer's mount. "General," he said, "believe me, it's time to go home."

"Blast you, sir, be still!" commanded Custer. "You will upset the troops!"

"If I don't upset them, General, the Indians soon will, and for permanent."

Now Custer was feeling some of the urgency in his tall scout's acrid words. Belatedly he glanced up at the hills which circled his position along the river. The hostile horsemen were swarming by the hundreds now, their mass movement lower and lower by the minute, down the slopes toward the stream. A concerted Indian attack seemed certain to be mounted within minutes, and it was already plainly too late to "go home," except at the price of what appeared to be inescapably heavy casualties. It was precisely at this moment that Carmody learned the little general was correct, that good scouts did make very inferior military thinkers.

Custer, flaxen curls aglint, sat studying his tactical situation on the banks of the Washita as unhurriedly as though he had still been safe at Camp Supply. Even as he sat there, the sergeant left in charge of the abandoned march rations beyond the first ridge stumbled around the watchtower hill to report hordes of Indians coming in from the west. They had overrun the supply dump and started in pursuit of the ammunition wagons. It was a good bet, said the excited soldier, that the wagons were gone and the column without ammunition reserves. To this Custer quietly replied that it was a poor bet, and that the wagons would show up in due time. Due time proved the very next breath when, careering around the flanks of the watchtower hill from both sides, the mule-drawn ammunition vehicles came, a screaming band of Arapaho in hot pursuit. An ordered volley of Spencer fire from Cook's deadly "boys" took care of the hostiles, and the wagons rumbled up intact to the last mule and white-faced driver.

Custer included both Carmody and the supply dump sergeant in his superior magnanimity. "Now, gentlemen," he said, "if everyone will save his advices and permit me to get on with this matter, we shall be through here in thirty minutes."

Carmody, eying the hills downriver, still believed it would be considerably less than thirty minutes. But Custer kept him and all the scouts, together with the troops, so occupied with his shouted instructions that no time was granted for entering dissents. Throwing Cook's sharp-shooters and Meyers's virtually unused troops into his own main column of the Seventh, backed on the lodges of Black Kettle, he ordered the front-line forces to burn ammunition as if they had seventy, not seven, wagonloads of same. "I want those Indians powder-smoked," he told Meyers and Cook. "I want so much gunpowder burned in their direction that they will think they've dug into a volcano, do you hear?" The officers heard well enough. Charge after charge of the yelling Indian horsemen was broken and turned by the steady roaring of the big-caliber Spencers. Behind this screen of lead and smoke, Custer employed his own troops to complete the planned rape of the Washita.

His treacherous attack on Black Kettle's village had brought him sixty captured squaws with their surviving children. On the icy ground about the lodges lay the bodies of the Cheyenne dead: 103 warriors, sixteen women, eleven small children. Piled high between the gutted lodges was the naked fruit of Indian genocide: 241 saddles, 1,123 tanned buffalo hides, uncounted lodge furs and robes and clothing, 82 rifles and revolvers, 425 axes and lances, 4,035 arrows and bows, 2,185 blankets, scores of lariats, bridles and buckskin parfleches, 535 pounds of gunpowder, 1,375 pounds of bullet lead and finished bullets, and 700 pounds of tobacco plus untold tons of buffalo meat stored for winter use.

This plunder, enormous by Plains Indian standards, was now piled by Carmody and the others in the very middle of Black Kettle's village. Over it was sprinkled the 500 pounds of captured Indian gunpowder. Then the lodges themselves were pulled over by rope and pony and added to the growing mountain of spoils. Custer barked an order and the match was instantly put to the completed work of destruction. As flames burst with a roar into the morning sky, the greasy smoke of the lodges and belongings which had once been those of Moxtaveto, the peace talker, exploded into 10,000 spiraling embers of despair. On the hills in front of Cook's and Meyers's hard-pressed lines, a sudden stillness fell among the hostile warriors. During it Custer spoke raspingly to Micah Carmody.

"Very well, let's have your little coup de grâce, Micah; I believe the time is appropriate. How was it that you put it? '*Kill a Plains Indian and two will spring to take his vacant place—destroy his pony and his heart for war drops dead within him*'? I never realized you were a poet, Carmody." Of a chilling sudden the banter was gone from the thin, high voice. "Get on with it, man. Do it in that clear meadow along the river. I want those red devils to see every shot go home."

Carmody did not answer except to turn the gray mare away.

"All right, Hard Rope!" he called to the old Osage. "Have your braves take the pony herd over there in yonder meadow by the river. The General wants every head in full view of the hostiles. *Hopo! Hopo!* Hurry it up, now!"

The Osages brought forward the beautiful pony herd of Black Kettle's people. At a signal from Custer the execution of the Cheyenne horses commenced. For one hour, unrelieved, the troopers of the Seventh Cavalry kept up the rolling drumfire into the frightened mass of captive animals. Upon the hillsides above, the watching hostiles grew absolutely still. For long minutes no single shot was fired at the soldiers by the red men. Then, with no seeming command from the war chiefs, the Indians began to move away down the Washita. At first they went singly, then in small groups, finally by the hundreds and hundreds. Eastward they went, across the soundless hills and down along the bloodied waters of the Washita toward the lower camps. Their savage throats were silent. The barrels of their forgotten rifles were grown cold and smokeless. Their wild hearts within them were gray and heavy as the broken ice of the river. The war ponies were dead, and dead with them were the wills and minds and spirits of their red masters.

No formal count of the execution among the Cheyenne pony herd was ever rendered by the army, although California Joe later claimed, and emphatically, "Nine hundred head, give or take nary a one." But no count was needed on that day. When the relentless volleys of Custer's riflemen ceased, at last, not a Southern Cheyenne pony stood alive on the sodden floor of the little general's Washita slaughterhouse.

Neither was there remaining upon the brooding hills about the great encampment at Big Bend a solitary mounted warrior of the thousands who had sat in stunned witness to the killing of Black Kettle's herd.

Downstream, whence they had disappeared, the drums of sorrow were already beginning to throb. Beneath the roiling smoke of Black Kettle's burning lodges Custer marshaled his column and left the field. He went westward, back upon his own tracks, abandoning Elliott and two other units not reported. Behind him he left only the smoke and the smell of powder and the stink of death in the lovely valley of the Washita; that and the terrible silence. Yellow Hair had had his way.

The retreat to the base camp on the Canadian was made under forced and fearful march. The troops understood, if their commander did not, the danger of a hostile recovery and following attack. Without their overcoats and with no food or tobacco or coffee, the men were near exhaustion in the bitter cold. The horses, unfed for twenty-four hours, unrested for forty-eight, were in no better condition than their riders. The abandoning of Elliott—the other units had rejoined the march—with the assumption now of the rash major's company being wiped out, sent morale to the breaking point. Custer, sensing this, allowed no halt. Not even so much as a dismounting to tighten cinches was permitted. The retirement was completed with nightfall of the twenty-seventh. No Indians had been sighted.

Next dawn the column pulled out in the early blackness. Crossing the Canadian, the Seventh fled onward throughout the day. No sign of pursuit developed. The silent-eyed captive Cheyenne women continued to stare along the backtrail but their prayers were not answered. Without Black Kettle to talk peace, or Mad Wolf to talk war, no hostile leader came forward to fill the empty opportunity to destroy the pony soldiers. Late in the afternoon of the twenty-ninth the column reached Camp Supply and was safe at last.

Yet for one of the fortunate number there was no safety and no rest at Camp Supply, or at any post of its kind, from that hour forward. With the surviving troopers of the Seventh gratefully billeted in the long rows of stove-heated Sibley tents, the wounded men under treatment in the hospital barracks, and the dead laid in stiff-limbed

state on the frozen dirt floor of the post woodshed, Micah
Carmody sought out Colonel George A. Custer.

The somber scout's progress toward the door of the
Seventh's commander was presently barred by the carbine of a guard corporal. This trooper had the usual military respect for civilian scout personnel. "Sorry, Carmody.
The general ain't seeing nobody. Beat it."

Carmody nodded, eying the youth.

"He'll see me," he answered quietly. "Just tell him who
it is, soldier."

"Can't; General Sherman and General Sheridan are in
there with him. Move on, you hear."

Carmody eased back a step.

"It doesn't impress me any if U. S. Grant is in there,"
he said, voice too quiet now. "You tell Custer Micah
Carmody is out here, and you tell him quick."

"Yeah? What's it about?"

"The Indian girl. Black Kettle's niece."

"Listen, Carmody, I don't care how many Injun squaws
you got on the string. But I ain't busting in on the general. I got my orders."

The corporal's devotion to duty underwent some modi-
fication when Carmody lifted him off his feet by the front
of his winter blouse. He vowed he would see Custer immediately and repeat faithfully each word of Carmody's
message. He was as good as his extracted word but by
the time he returned his courage was restored to its previous disdain of tall mountain scouts.

"General says he'll send for you when things clear up a
little. Says you ain't to worry about your pay; you'll get it
eventually." The corporal paused to savor deliberately
the next tidbit. "Oh, yeah, and he says to tell you the
Injun gal is a prisoner of war the same as the rest of
them squaws, only more so. Now you got any more billy-
doos for the general, chief?"

Carmody, past anger at the trooper and his kind, only
looked at the man and nodded, low-voiced, "Just tell him
Black Kettle and Carmody said good-bye."

The full dark of the Arkansas winter night was down.
Under its sullen black screen, Carmody moved swiftly to
take his leave. For him it was no effort to slip unseen
past the soldier guards watching the loose horse herd.

Nor was it hard work to locate the gray mare and get her neck-roped. The girl's Cheyenne sorrel took a higher degree of skill. But Carmody Indian-talked the animal into standing for the rope and, within minutes, was leading the two mounts away toward the jumble of Seventh Cavalry tack dumped in the service corral. Here he found his own and another good saddle, along with bridles and blankets. Saddling the horses, he booted the short Henry carbines, his own and the beautifully engraved one Bright Hair had been using. Then he borrowed two sets of saddlebags, one filled with oats, the other with dried jerky, and was ready to move out.

Taking the mounts on the lead, he started for the area where the Cheyenne squaws were being held in an open-faced hay shed and feed corral. Tying the horses behind the shed, he circled the corral until he was near the cluster of warming fires the Indian women had kindled. He waited until the guard detail had tramped past, then cupped his hands and made the perfect grunting imitation of an Indian pony's alerting whicker. Bright Hair, crouched to the nearest fire, looked up at the sound and saw the tall scout signal her from beyond the corral fence. After what seemed to Carmody an eternity, she got up from the fire and went into the shed. He did not see her again until a light whisper touched him from behind, saying, "I am here, *veho*; let us go elsewhere swiftly."

Since *veho* meant white man in her strange tongue, Carmody smiled gladly and they went, like twin shadows, back around the shed and to the horses. She had brought with her from the hay shed her Plains Indian dowry of two scorched calfskin sleeping robes retrieved from the blazing shards of her father's lodge. These and the soft look of her dark eyes were all the worldly pledges she ever made to Micah Carmody, and they were enough and to spare.

By 10:00 P.M. the double line of their ponies' hoofprints lay three miles south of Camp Supply. Eight hours later they had recrossed the Canadian and were snugly camped in the shelter of the Antelope Hills. Sixty miles to the north Yellow Hair Custer was being routed from the 6:00 A.M. blackness of his victor's couch to be informed that his pet scout and prize Cheyenne captive had deserted in the unknown hours. To the south and east, forty

tragic miles, Black Kettle was sleeping beside his faithful
woman by the waters of his native Ouachita. With them,
in Elliott's Grass of the Big Bend, slept the eighteen pony
soldiers. Magpie was gone. Mad Wolf was gone. The dog
soldiers were undone. Stone Calf and Big Mouth and Yellow Buffalo were all far away and riding fast. Yet somehow Black Kettle was not gone, and somehow Magpie
and the other dead warriors rode with him still, and not
in vain.

For over all the silence Notamota, the God of the North,
was once more spreading the thick white robe of his will
and way. But the old god was not howling in anger any
longer, nor was he even crying out in bitter laughter at
what fools his children were. Now he was chuckling
behind his white beard. He was happy as he carefully
filled in with his snows the hoofprints of the white man's
gray mare and the red girl's sorrel. And he was smiling
as he drew the soft blanket of his friendly flakes over the
warm, dry resting place of Carmody and the old chief's
niece.

They were well mated those two. Let them dream
there under their sheltered bank in the small, warm cave
they had found. Let them rest now. Let their voices be
tender with the moment. Let their weary bodies relax
to the long-awaited mercies of their young love. Aye,
even withhold one's icy breath, making the outer storm
a little stiller now, that she might miss no word of the
white scout's promise of the fine red cattle he would
bring to graze the fat grasses of this homeland of Black
Kettle's, that she might hear each vow he made of the
countless moons they would prosper here as man and
wife, and of the brightening they would bring unto the
dead chief's valley with the laughter and the joys of their
many children, and the children of those children too.

And now halt the falling flakes altogether. Let no wandering swirl of snow disturb the softness of her answer.
Let the listening white scout understand each full-lipped
whisper that she made him. Let him know that this was
the way in which old Black Kettle had seen it in the
smoke clouds of his final pipe. Let Carmody be certain that
this was the way the aging chief had spoken it to Bright
Hair that last night within the lodge.

Let Yellow Hair come, the old man had said. Let him

have his wanton hour of shameful war. Give him his small moment of willful, wicked pleasure. Then let him go, and let him come no more. Let there be peace, not war, along the Ouachita. And let that peace come with the growing herds and laughing, happy children of the white man and the red girl together. That was how it ought to be in a good land.

Yellow Hair had had his way. Now let Black Kettle have his. *Nohetto.* Let that be the final end to it.

Peace of the Pony Soldiers

In those latter years the tides of fortune rolled steadily against the red man. The Southern Plains Indians, Comanche, Kiowa, Southern Cheyenne, were rounded up and placed upon reservations. There remained then only the indomitable hostiles of the north: the Sioux, under Red Cloud, Sitting Bull and Crazy Horse; some remnants of Northern Cheyenne led by Two Moons and Dull Knife.

Red Cloud went over to the whites, taking thousands of Sioux onto the northern reservations with him. Two Moons and Dull Knife stayed "free," but talked of coming in "when the snow had gone and the new grass had come again." Thus, in the winter of 1875–76 when the ill-famed unconditional surrender order was tendered the northern hostiles—specifically the Sioux—only Crazy Horse and Sitting Bull were admitted "fugitives" and, by the language of the fiat, "deemed hostile."

The order proper, issued by the U.S. Secretary of the Interior and addressed to the Indian Bureau, that bumbling, strange friend-enemy to the harried red brother, was a singular document, if not sinister. In significant part it stated:

Referring to our communications of the 27th ultimo,

relative to the status of certain Sioux Indians resid-
ing without the bounds of their reservation and their
continued hostile attitude toward the whites, I have
to request that you direct the Indian Agents at all
Sioux agencies in Dakota and at Fort Peck, Montana,
to notify said Indians that unless they shall remove
within the bounds of their reservation and remain
there, before the 31st of January next, they shall be
deemed hostile and treated accordingly by the military.

This was under date of December 3, 1875.

It was a fearsome winter, even for that land of bitter snows. The camps of Sitting Bull and Crazy Horse, the
"certain Sioux" and "said Indians" referred to in the Secretary's order, were 240 miles north and west of the nearest agency at which they might be expected to surrender.
The Government runners sent out bearing the news
had not even located the hostile Sioux winter camps by
January 31, the expiration date. Thus, no legitimate opportunity was afforded the wild Sioux to come in. The
army, it seemed, wanted the hostiles to stay away. It
wanted them to fight.

The Indians, supreme realists, understood this well.
Their decision in this light was even more poignantly
tragic. Crazy Horse, that great moody warrior of the Oglala, announced his determination not to force his woman
and children to march over 200 miles through snowdrift
and blizzard wind to reach an agency where no food
awaited, and no real friendship. Even as he spoke, the
lodges of his people, he said, were filled with agency
Sioux who had stolen away and come home simply to get
something in their belllies more nourishing than the windy
promises of the whites. To this, Sitting Bull and his
fierce Hunkpapa band nodded somber agreement. But others had less heart. He Dog, a good friend of Crazy
Horse, led his eight lodges of Sioux out of the Oglala
camp and joined them with the Cheyenne village of
Two Moons; the latter had already told the army that he
and his Cheyenne would come in to the agency and surrender even though the order had specified the Sioux only.
Crazy Horse and Sitting Bull were left alone in their
winter lodges amid the whirling snows of the Big Horns,

listening to the icy winds. They knew that war would
come to the plains with the new grass of spring; the white
man had ordered it so.

The hostile lodges were nestled along Tongue River,
a tributary of the Yellowstone. The weather had turned
blue cold, temperatures plummeting far below zero. Yellow Bull and Tonkalla, dispatched by Crazy Horse some
weeks past to scout the Sioux agency, had just returned
to the winter camp with news big enough for a formal
calling of the Fox Lodge—the Sioux high council—into
emergency session. Crazy Horse headed the meeting, Sitting Bull and the Hunkpapa people having moved to another winter camp of their own during the absence of
the scouts.

Tonkalla made the report, backed by Yellow Bull. He
told Crazy Horse that what they had found out was
exactly what Crazy Horse had suspected: there was going
to be a big war against the Indians in the spring and it
was by the grandfather's orders from Washington that this
would be so. By "the grandfather" Crazy Horse understood his young scout to mean President Grant, and he
nodded quickly for Tonkalla to continue. As quickly, the
latter obliged.

He told the great warrior that many soldiers had started westward from Fort Lincoln far over by the Missouri
River. But snow had fallen very deep, the cold turned
deathly hard, the wind blown night and day. Those soldiers had intended to march all the way through that
snow to the Sioux lodges on Tongue River and those on
Powder River. They had thought to catch the people of
Crazy Horse and Sitting Bull at their winter resting. But
that snow and wind and cold had been true friend to the
Indian, not the soldier. Those troops had turned back to
Fort Lincoln and could be forgotten. So spoke old Spotted
Tail when Tonkalla and Yellow Bull had sneaked into the
main Sioux Agency to visit him on the business of their
war chief, Crazy Horse.

Concluding this part of his report, Tonkalla turned to
his comrade Yellow Bull for confirmation of its accuracy.
The latter, it developed, believed his friend Tonkalla
had been entirely too modest, that snow had been so deep
over there that all the ponies and all the soldiers had

frozen to death in it; not one of them had gotten back
to the big fort by the Missouri. Yellow Bull, of course,
was wishing, not reporting. He was suffering from the
Indian disease of exaggeration.

Tonkalla now tried to cure him of its worst effects by
correcting his wild words to say that not quite all the
ponies and the soldiers had frozen to death—only a very
few really—but that it was true all had suffered a great
deal from the bad weather and had retreated raggedly
back to Fort Lincoln.

The young scout held up his hand warningly, however. There was bad news as well as good. As Tonkalla
and Yellow Bull had come away from Standing Rock
Agency their trail had crossed that of the Cheyenne Little
Wolf. Little Wolf had with him a Crow scout army
deserter. It was the Crow who had the bad news: Three
Stars Crook was coming up from the south into the Sioux
country. He was at Fort Fetterman already. He planned
to march against Crazy Horse, in particular, blaming
him for most of the hostility of the Sioux who still had
not come into the agency. The time for Three Stars'
attack was to be when the moon was new again.

At the mention of General George Crook the council
came alert. Here was a real Indian fighter; a man to be
both respected and feared. It was the immediate opinion
of Crazy Horse that if Three Stars had said he would
come with the new moon, he would do it. With this
statement the famed Sioux was upon his feet. Three
Stars, he vowed, would find the Oglala ready.

Toward that end and upon this very midnight, Tonkalla
and Yellow Bull would go out again. This time they
would go to find Three Stars and learn which way he was
coming. They would determine the strength of the force
he had with him, and its fighting quality. Then one of
them would come back to report to Crazy Horse, while
the other would stay with the soldiers, trailing them
constantly. Meanwhile, One Bull and White Bull, like
Yellow Bull nephews of Sitting Bull, would travel to warn
their uncle and his Hunkpapa of the new danger.

At this point Crazy Horse moved over to face Tonkalla.
As the latter traveled south to find Three Stars he must,
as well, find the village of their Cheyenne brother, Two
Moons, and warn those people that their lodges lay in the

path of the approaching pony soldiers. The Cheyenne
also must not trust Three Stars. They must not think
that their promise to come in peacefully and surrender at
the agency next spring would save them now. Lastly, Two
Moons was to be assured that he and his people would be
welcomed in the warm lodges of Crazy Horse and
his Oglala people, and could stay there until such time as
they might locate a new and safe place for another winter
camp of their own.

Tonkalla and Yellow Bull departed within minutes.
They moved southward through a stinging ice storm. For
four days they traveled and on the morning of the fifth
day, far up the Tongue, they sighted the fires of many
soldiers. These troops proved to be Crook's men. Three
Stars certainly had a strong number with him this time.
Tonkalla guessed it to be 1,000 soldiers, both cavalry
and infantry troops, and with all the foot soldiers mounted
on mules, a very bad sign indeed.

The two Sioux scouts exchanged nervous glances. The
report they would make to Crazy Horse must be a harsh
one. And it must be made very quickly. Three Stars
and all of those mean-looking mule soldiers and pony
soldiers were surely riding down the Tongue in search
of the winter lodges of the Oglala. But first the cursed
Cheyenne must be given a second chance to listen to the
warning.

Tonkalla and Yellow Bull had passed through the
winter village of Two Moons's people only the day before,
and there had faithfully delivered the alerting words of
Crazy Horse. But the Cheyenne people had covered their
ears. They had refused to believe that Crook would mean
them any harm. Their hearts were good for the white
brother and they had already promised to come into
Standing Rock when the snows melted and the new grass
came. They were safe.

Yellow Bull grew very excited, wanting to run the
ponies at once for the Cheyenne camp, and for home. But
Tonkalla, whose name meant "the Mouse," and whose
temperament scarcely matched the title, was cut from a
calmer bolt of red cloth. Not only had he an unusually
calculating mind for an Indian; he had also been to
school at the great Pine Ridge Agency and been taught
how to lie and cheat and steal and figure things out in

the white man's way. So he knew now that he needed some proof of what he and Yellow Bull would again tell Two Moons—some hard proof, which would make a dent even in the old Cheyenne's stubborn skull. He believed that he saw opportunity for that proof in the soldier camp below.

"Look down there," he told Yellow Bull. "The blacksmiths are reshoeing the mules. See? The irons are worn too smooth for traveling on this ice and snow in such a steep country. I think we had better wait until the soldiers have gone on. We need something from this mule camp of theirs. Be patient."

Yellow Bull did a little Oglala barking and growling but he really had a large respect for the brain of Tonkalla. He waited as he was bid and after the foot soldiers had shoed their mules and eaten their food and gone on down the river he and Tonkalla rode down into the abandoned camp.

Once there, Tonkalla sought out the farrier's fire. There he bid Yellow Bull, an enormously strong fellow, to dismount and help him load an old gunnysack with the worn-out mule shoes. Yellow Bull shook his head, calling upon the Great Spirit to witness that Tonkalla had lost his wits and that his head was stuffed with milkweed fuzz. But nonetheless he joined his comrade in cramming the sack full of the discarded iron shoes.

Shortly the bag was full to overflowing, and Yellow Bull slung it over the horn of his saddle. Getting up onto his potbellied pony, he waved his arm and cried out, "*Hopo*, let's go!" and away they went, making very long tracks in the snow.

By circling wide of the soldier column, riding all night through the rough, high hills, they reached Two Moons's camp just at break of day. Sliding their weary ponies to a halt, which showered ice and snow over the entrance flap of the old chief's lodge, they challenged the Cheyenne leader to arise and step forth.

"Let Two Moons come out here and see what a fool he is!" shouted Tonkalla.

"Aye!" yelled his companion to a group of gathering tribesmen. "And let all you great Cheyenne warriors come and see what fools you are also! Ho, He-Dog, where are you hiding, brave Sioux? Are you with the women?

Come here, wherever you are, for you are the biggest fool of them all. You left Crazy Horse when he asked you to stay and help him. Pah! I spit on you. Come out, come out!"

In minutes only, a large crowd of men had gathered. They were talking a lot, a sure sign of apprehension. They sensed trouble and in a moment, when He-Dog came stumbling up and Two Moons emerged sleepily from his lodge, Tonkalla and Yellow Bull gave it to them.

"By the time that the sun is overhead," bellowed Tonkalla, "there will be pony soldiers and walk-a-heaps mounted on mules among you to the number of a thousand men. What do you think of that?"

At once a murmur of grave concern swept the Cheyenne warriors. They knew that the average army expedition, with its awkward baggage and ammunition wagons and its preponderance of green infantry, was intended to impress them, not make actual war on them. They also understood that a column of mule-mounted veterans, supplied exclusively by pack animals and led by a soldier chief such as Three Stars Crook, was something else again entirely.

"Mules? The foot soldiers all ride mules?" He-Dog faltered.

Two Moons was more direct. "You lie!" he charged flatly.

Tonkalla turned to Yellow Bull. "Two Moons says we are liars about the mules. He-Dog hesitates and cannot believe we know soldiers mounted on mules when we see them. What a pity. It seems that we must show them some proof. Go ahead, Yellow Bull. Show them."

Grinning delightedly, the muscular brave heaved the clanking bag from his saddlehorn. Then, even before Tonkalla might guess his intention, he spurred his pony up to Two Moons and emptied the cascade of old mule shoes over the chief's head.

"When dealing with iron heads," he announced into the following pause, "iron proof is required."

The lesson, if insulting, was effective. Within the hour there was not so much as an old moccasin left in the Cheyenne camp.

Bag, baggage, lodgeskin, poles, packs and travois

ponies, the people of Two Moons, together with the Sioux
of He-Dog, were gone from that dangerous place. Even so
they were none too soon. Tonkalla and Yellow Bull,
lingering behind the departure to cover the approach of
Crook, were nearly caught. They barely managed to
get into the pines as the army scouts and the forward
cavalry patrols rode into the deserted village ahead of the
slower mule-mounted infantry.

Beside him, Tonkalla heard Yellow Bull curse angrily.
"By the buffalo's navel!" whispered his fellow Sioux.
"Look who leads the scouts! It is Sitting-With-Upraised-
Hands!"

"What?" muttered Tonkalla. "The Grabber?"

"Yes, the Grabber. May his food turn to ashes in his
mouth!"

"The Grabber" was the Sioux nickname for Frank
Grouard, one of the most able scouts the army had. He
was, by Sioux standards, a traitor. Many years earlier,
young Grouard had been captured by Sitting Bull in a
wagon-train ambush. The Hunkpapa medicine chief had
raised the youth as his own son, a true red man. Grouard
had become one of the premier fighters and hunters
among all the Sioux, an Indian hero. Tonkalla had not
known him well but had heard the nephews of Sitting
Bull, including Yellow Bull, speak of him with vast
respect. Such an Indian-trained man made extremely bad
medicine to have in the camp of the enemy.

When Grouard had reached adult age and gone over
to the army to serve his white blood and white brothers,
Sioux apprehension mounted. But his services had been
in the south against the Cheyenne of Black Kettle, the
Kiowa of Satanta, the Comanche of Quanah Parker.
The Sioux, until the present uneasy moment, had forgotten him with that "out of sight, out of mind" childish
simpleness which had always handicapped them in their
wars with the white man.

But now that Yellow Bull saw this devil back in the
northern homeland leading the hated soldiers against his
own adopted Sioux people, a very different feeling pre-
vailed. It was only the dry clink of Yellow Bull's rifle
being cocked that warned Tonkalla in time to thrust
his hand over the breech of his friend's gun. Calling him

heyoka, fool, and worse, he ordered him to put aside the
weapon, to take his finger from its trigger.

For a moment Yellow Bull glared wildly at him. It was
never safe to run over the feelings of a Sioux warrior.
For an uneasy instant Tonkalla believed his companion
would shoot him instead of the Grabber. Then Yellow
Bull grinned and shrugged and said that it was a natural
mistake he had almost made. He would not shoot The
Grabber now but Tonkalla knew that the traitor must die
soon. He was the finest scout Three Stars had, or the
whole army had, and if left alive would surely guide
those cavalry troops and those mule soldiers squarely
down upon the villages of their people.

Here Tonkalla disagreed. He advised his comrade to
look at the trail that Two Moons had left. That trail was
broad as a buffalo road. The Cheyenne had run like
rabbits, making no effort to cover their going. The
soldiers would need no scout of The Grabber's skill to
follow that track; a child could do it.

Yellow Bull scratched his head, scowled, agreed. This
pesky Tonkalla had a sly mind, just as everyone said.
He was correct about not shooting The Grabber now. It
would be immeasurably more entertaining to kill him
later—and far more slowly.

"All right," he said. "But what will we do instead?"

"Sit very still," urged Tonkalla. "Listen very hard."

They were hidden in the lower branches of a gnarled
cedar at the fringe of the pine grove overhanging the
embers of the Cheyenne cooking fires. Their ponies were
well hidden half a mile distant. They had chosen the site
hoping to overhear something when General Crook should
come up. The risk in it was their lives, of course. But
now they received something for the gamble.

Grouard had no Indian scouts with him. Tonkalla recalled Spotted Tail telling him while at the agency
that the Indian Bureau had succeeded in getting the use
of Indian scouts against their Indian kinsmen ruled out
in the campaign against the remaining hostile Sioux and
"reluctant" Cheyenne.

Thinking back now to the many Crow and Pawnee
outriders of Crook's column which they had seen but the
day previous, the young Oglala shook his head scowlingly.
The white man was very clever. He said he would do a

thing, then did not listen to his own word. The Sioux, the wise ones like old Sitting Bull, said it in this fashion: that the soldiers never did inform their right hand whose throat was being slit by the knife in their left hand. It was a difficult thing to fight. Tonkalla had learned a little something of its subtleties in his brief schooling at the agency. But he was quite relieved, all the same, that The Grabber had come up to the Cheyenne camp without his Crow and Pawnee friends of yesterday's scout. Now the main thing he, Tonkalla, had to worry about was preventing Yellow Bull from shooting The Grabber out of sudden deep-feeling Sioux anger—unbridled Indian pride.

Grouard halted by great luck almost directly beneath their tree.

It seemed the logical place to get in out of the cold wind following a swift look about the abandoned campsite. Very soon old Three Stars Crook came riding up with his cavalry commanders, Colonel J. J. Reynolds and Captain Anson Mills. Mills was a good man like Crook. Reynolds was somebody else, not a good man, not a decent fighter and not very brave. Tonkalla and Yellow Bull knew both officers from former skirmishes. They exchanged glances, held their breath.

"Well, Frank," said Crook, pulling at the frost rime in his long red beard, "what have you found? Where do we go now?"

"They've ducked out for Powder River, I reckon, General."

"Is it the bunch we're after—Crazy Horse's Oglala?"

"I'd say it was, General, yes sir. There's quite a few Cheyenne with them but that ain't nothing unusual. It's Crazy Horse's Oglala, I'm certain."

In the cedar tree, Tonkalla and Yellow Bull looked at one another in amazement. Why was The Grabber lying? He knew as well as they did that this was a Cheyenne village. Why was he telling Three Stars it was Crazy Horse's village, then?

"You're absolutely convinced this is Crazy Horse's band?" The qualifying question, delivered with suspicious sharpness, came from tough Captain Mills. Yet The Grabber only nodded.

"Yes sir, Captain. But I can tell you for double sure when I see the horse herd."

Crook was still fingering his famous red whiskers. Tonkalla noted that he still wore the beard in braids to keep it from flying away in a fight or a hard wind. Now Three Stars held up his hand.

"The weather's very severe," he announced.

"And due to get a site worse," added Frank Grouard.

"Yes, of course. Hmmmm. Well, I fail to see the sense of marching the entire command after this small village, Crazy Horse or not. . . . Colonel Reynolds."

"Yes, General?"

"Take the cavalry troops of Mills, Egan, Moore. Go on ahead and find that village for us. Grouard will move in ahead of you to make certain it is Crazy Horse's village. Do not touch it if it is some other band, particularly Cheyenne. If you make a mistake and attack another band, you will answer to me. Grouard knows those Indians. Bad weather or not, dark night or not, you will have no excuses. Do you have all that?"

"Yes, sir."

"General." It was Captain Egan quickly stepping forward. "Begging your pardon, but there is still some feeling among us that Grouard is sympathetic to the Sioux. You will recall that Sitting Bull raised him. Personally, I think he's loyal to us, but why risk it now?"

"What are you suggesting, sir?" Crook said it quietly, as he did everything, but his high voice was annoyed.

"I think, General," broke in Colonel Reynolds, not overjoyed with his big opportunity to run up on Crazy Horse in the dead of night, "that Captain Egan is suggesting we take along the Crow and Pawnee for this close work. I might say I agree."

"Yes," nodded Crook, eying him. "You might, Colonel. However, I would not. Now, sir, let us to business. You know our orders in regard to using those Indian scouts in combat against other Indians. We have them as hunters and guides, not to be employed in fighting or in punitive scouting before a fight."

"That's fine for the newspapers, General. But we're not in view of the press now."

Reynolds knew such argument was riskful, but he was

afraid of Grouard, and perhaps of Crazy Horse, as well. Anson Mills suffered no such qualms.

"I can vouch for Grouard, Colonel," he said, smiling the assurance, "and he knows he can't fool me. We've worked too much together. Do you hear me, Frank?"

Grouard, absolutely expressionless, merely bobbed his head.

"All right," continued Crook. "Grouard will take you in, Reynolds, and you are to act strictly on his information and his recommendation. Moreover, I suggest you let him give you the best way to go in with the troops. Any reservations now?"

Colonel J. J. Reynolds knew he had gone as far as he was going with George Crook. "No reservations, General," he said.

"Egan?"

"All clear with me, sir."

"Grouard?"

The adopted son of Sitting Bull glanced up at the red-bearded officer. In the entire discussion of his loyalty he had said no word, devoting his time to an enormous cud of dark cutplug tobacco. The thin black streams of the juice were his total contribution to the seminar on his honesty. Now he merely shrugged and spat again.

"I've been ready to go since we got here, General. It ain't me that doubts me."

"Good. Your column will set out as soon as it's dark."

That was the end of it. An hour after sunset, with the soldier camp snug and the supper fires banked for the night, the assault troops moved out. Grouard went ahead of them on foot. The snow was coming harder than ever. It piled more deeply with each hour. The cold was intense. Tonkalla, as he and Yellow Bull stiffly climbed out of their cedar bower and limped for their ponies, guessed that it might be forty degrees below the red line on the white man's glass ice rod. Very, very cold. And very, very dark. He could scarcely make his lips move, as he and Yellow Bull untied their mounts and prepared to part company.

"I think it best that you ride to warn Crazy Horse," he told his companion. "You're stronger."

"And you?" demanded Yellow Bull, at once doubtful.

"I will trail The Grabber, trying to come before him to

the lodges of He-Dog and Two Moons, warning them in time."

"I could do this better than you can. Why don't you go to Crazy Horse?" Yellow Bull was glowering now. He was angry.

But Tonkalla would not be bluffed. "I am looking into the middle of your black heart," he told the other. "I see what you want to do."

"Yes? What is that you see there in my heart then?"

"I see you sticking a knife into The Grabber's kidneys, while all the rest of us, Crazy Horse as well, can go to hell and get shot by the soldiers. Am I right, big bull?"

For a moment Yellow Bull stared at him in a slit-eyed way, frightening even to a fellow Sioux. Then, suddenly, he grinned like a wolf with his mouth full of hot buffalo veal.

"Mouse," he said, "may your sons always feed on hump ribs. You have the brain of a grizzly bear and a fox and a white man. I salute you. *Hookahey!*"

With that, and a curse at his snow-coated pony, he was gone.

There were perhaps three white men in the Sioux country who could run a trail as well as any Indian. Frank Grouard was one of them. When Tonkalla found the camp of Two Moons, the soldiers of Reynolds were already sneaking into position about its sleeping lodges.

The site of the Cheyenne encampment was a low, level bottom in a tight bend of the Powder River. No less than 100 tipis, of which but eight were Sioux, dotted the willow brush and cottonwood timber of the streambanks. Tonkalla's cover was in very close to the nearest lodges, the entire scene being heavily screened by a low-hanging ice fog. This enabled the Oglala scout to "hear" the village better than he could see it. A rusty-voiced old man, the village news crier, was calling out the early morning informations, as Tonkalla wriggled forward between the skulking advance patrols of the soldiers: ". . . Our scouts, sent back by He-Dog, have found no sign of pursuit close to us. They have just now returned with this good word. All is well. Sleep some more . . ."

This announcement, coming to Tonkalla at a moment when he knew the hillsides about him to be swarm-

ing with cavalry troops, caused the young Oglala scout to
curse silently. Apparently He-Dog's scouts had gone but
a short distance along the backtrail of the village. The
wily Grouard, suspecting they would nose back to find
him and his soldiers, had pulled the troopers off the trail
five miles from the village, and held them quietly in the
timber until the scouts of He-Dog had gone home. If
those scouts had followed back another quarter-mile,
they would have stumbled on the hidden soldiers. But
they did not. It was very cold out in the snow, and their
minds were on their lodge fires and the warm, waiting
bodies of their women. They turned around too soon.
Now innocent Indians would die.

Tonkalla stilled his curses. A file of men had loomed
out of the gray fog. They were not Cheyenne. They were
not Sioux. They stopped near enough to Tonkalla so that
he might have spat upon them. He recognized Captain
Anson Mills, Colonel J. J. Reynolds, Frank Grouard. With
them were another captain and a lieutenant whom he
had never seen, or did not remember in that poor light.

"I know it's Crazy Horse," said Grouard forcefully, the
cold smoke from his breath spurting in the dawn chill.
"I've been in his camp enough times. I know his horses,
and I got damned close to those ponies just now. They're
his horses."

"We have got to be absolutely certain, Grouard." This
was the good captain, Anson Mills, demanding rigid ad-
herence to orders. "It's a matter of gravest importance that
we don't hit the wrong Indians in this damnable fog."

"I tell you, Captain, I was close enough to those ponies
to touch their rumps with a willow stick. I recognized
them and I recognized their war markings. I saw Oglala
horses."

"We can't sit here arguing about it, Mills." Colonel
Reynolds, Tonkalla noted uneasily, was just as nervous
as he had been back with Three Stars. A nervous commander was a bad thing. Brave men died when their
leaders were nervous, and died for nothing.

"No, sir," answered the captain. "That we can't. We're
too far in to fall back if we wanted to. We might get
jumped ourselves. How do you think we ought to move
in, Grouard?"

"Yes, Grouard," Reynolds put in petulantly, not liking

to have his troops taken over in effect by Mills. "Speak up, man. You are the man of the hour here. General's orders, you'll recall."

He was waspish with it, and Tonkalla, on his belly in the snow not fifteen feet away, decided that he did not like Colonel J. J. Reynolds very much at all. Were it not for the fact that he owed The Grabber the first shot in the body when the fight should start, he would certainly have thought in terms of putting a bullet into the bowels of this Eagle Chief who whined when he talked and who did not ask any proof of his scouts as to what Indians he was about to start shooting down.

But The Grabber was answering Reynolds now. "Well, Colonel," he was saying, "we will split into four bunches. One bunch to rush the lodges straightaway. Second bunch to follow up behind the first. Third bunch to hit the horse herd and run it off. Last bunch to stay up here on the hillside to keep the Indians from getting out of the river-bend flat and into the roughs behind us here. If we can get the horses and then pin the Indians into that bend flat afoot, we won't lose a lot of them. It'll be a beef shoot."

Tonkalla's dark face contorted. He knew what a beef shoot was. When the Army issued cattle for food to the Indians at Standing Rock or Pine Ridge, the cattle would be put in a pen where they could not get away, and the Indians would sit on the fence and shoot them down with their rifles. *Ai-ee!* What a bad thing The Grabber was saying.

"All right." Tonkalla could understand that Reynolds was going to do it now. "Captain Egan, you will charge the village. Captain Mills, follow in reserve. Lieutenant Moore, place yourself on the hillside. I shall cut off the horse herd."

The Sioux scout's thin face relaxed momentarily. Good. Reynolds had given himself the easy thing to do, but he had given the young lieutenant the hard place to hold, and the one which really counted—up on the hillside. And before Mills or Egan might object to placing the youth in the position of greatest danger, Reynolds had stridden off through the fog to put his attack into operation. Moreover, Mills and Egan had been given the exciting part—riding into the sleeping camp to shoot down the innocent Cheyenne in the confusion and fear of the ice fog and the early hour. So they also went quickly to seek their commands and to get ready. Tonkalla knew he had a very few minutes to spare. But he had learned something by a great stroke of hunter's luck. Lieutenant Moore would be guarding the hills. And Lieutenant Moore was very young and not a little frightened. Tonkalla could see that, fog or no fog.

As soon as Grouard and the officers of Reynolds's staff were well gone, the Sioux broke from his cover and ran the quarter-mile into the village risking a soldier's shot at every leap. Fortunately, the swirling ground fog sheltered him to the last. He reached the Cheyenne camp unharmed and raced down its silent rows of lodges shouting the alarm in both Oglala and Cheyenne.

His hoarse voice brought braves, squaws, old ones and children tumbling and rolling out of the lodges and warm sleeping robes. The warriors sprang quickly to their weapons, and the women to hiding their children and guiding them away from the streets between lodges. In this moment, fatefully, the wind sprang up as well. The ice fog lifted up from the river-bottom bend. Tonkalla, whirling about, could see, not thirty yards from the lodges and standing on a slight rise, the leather-clad figure of Frank Grouard. The Grabber cupped his hand, even as Tonkalla and he recognized one another.

"Mouse! I see you there!" called the white scout. "It's me, The Grabber. Tell Tashunka (he used Crazy Horse's Oglala name) that I am here with the pony soldiers!"

"Wait, wait!" shouted Tonkalla, desperately making the delay sign. "This is the camp of Two Moons! Crazy Horse is not here!"

"You lie! I saw the horses of He-Dog!"

"Yes, he's here; but not Crazy Horse. Don't shoot, Grabber—!"

But the time of talk had run out. Grouard raised his rifle. The crash of it spun Tonkalla around, the bullet raking his left arm. The Sioux was up in the instant. His own weapon, a Colt's heavy revolver, boomed two times. He saw the body of The Grabber buck and jerk to each boom. Usually the Indian could not shoot revolvers very well. But Tonkalla had learned this too from the white brother at Pine Ridge. He saw The Grabber swat at his right armpit as though bitten by a hornet, and then grasp his left shoulder as if bitten through it by a grizzly bear. Tonkalla prayed that the second shot would kill his enemy, and he knew that the two shots together would cripple him. If he lived in the end, he would never be the same. And for this hour of the terrible attack on the peaceful village of old Two Moons, the soldiers would have to fight on without the help of Frank Grouard.

It was a crucial thing to knock The Grabber down and get him out of the way. Tonkalla shouted the news to the Cheyenne as they came running up to help him with his own wound. Their war hopes were heartened by this knowledge, and the hearts of the fighters were made instantly larger. And just in time. The troops of Egan were galloping into the south end of the village. Tonkalla knew that the soldiers of the dreaded Anson Mills were waiting immediately behind him. He yelled at Two Moons and old He-Dog to ask if they were agreeable to him, Tonkalla, being the war leader there. The two chiefs shouted back, "Yes, yes, you tell us how to fight, Mouse; you have been right all the time!"

Thus it was that an Oglala subchief, little more than a boy himself, and unknown to the Army at the time, commanded the great fight that the Cheyenne put up against the treacherous murder attempt of Reynolds and his pony soldiers in the Powder River winter camp of old Two Moons, the "peace-talker" chief who had already surrendered weeks before and who had promised to bring his people into Standing Rock when the snows melted.

Tonkalla ordered He-Dog and Two Moons to rally their warriors and hold back Egan until he, Tonkalla, might round up the women, children and older men and get them moving out of the beleaguered camp. "Fight the soldiers," he told the chiefs, "with the thought that they are trying to kill all of you!"

So instructed, the Cheyenne dug in and, with but a handful of warriors fighting birth-naked in the bitter snows, held up the entire command of Captain Egan for thirty crucial minutes. They even had begun to drive back the demoralized white troops when the reserves of Anson Mills were thrown into the fight and, of course, that broke the thin Cheyenne line.

But the thirty minutes of the heroes had been enough.

Tonkalla had herded the terrified women and children and all of the old people of the village into one place near the side of the river bend where the hills commenced to rise toward the position of young Lieutenant Moore. He had inspired the people to be calm and to obey him, telling them that they had a youthful chief before them, with soldiers who did not want to fight. They had but to follow him, to continue doing what he told them.

"I was sent to you by Crazy Horse, remember that," he said; and they grew quiet and answered that they were ready, for such was the great reputation of the mighty Oglala warrior. Even an emissary of his, even merely a boy such as this skinny Tonkalla, this wise and courageous "Little Mouse," was very big medicine.

"*H'gun!*" growled the old men. "We are with you, Oglala. Go ahead. We will see that our people come after you."

"*Hookahey!*" yelled Tonkalla, signaling to He-Dog, his fellow Sioux. "We are all ready over here. Bring back your fighters to go with us. We are breaking for the hills through the soldiers of the young lieutenant on this side."

"Coming, coming!" called the battle-scarred chief. "*Hopo!*"

"Wait!" demanded Two Moons, moving toward them now with his Cheyenne heroes. "What of the ponies? We can't leave our dear horses! *Ai!*" His nomad's heart lay first with his priceless horse herd. But Tonkalla was not thinking of horses; he was thinking of women and babies and the lives of his red friends.

"Forget the horses!" he shouted angrily. "Run with us for the hills on foot. Horses can't go into those deep and high places. Come on; I'm trying to save your people, not your ponies, you old fool!"

"*Hopo! Hookahey!*" screamed He-Dog, brandishing his Winchester. "Everybody follow the Mouse. Lead the way, Mouse."

The rush for the high ground followed. The Cheyenne, led by the two Sioux, He-Dog and Tonkalla, and finally now, by the aging Two Moons, and defended in the rear by the incredibly brave warriors who had held back Egan, charged up into the rocks and brush of the lower rises in an angry, deep-shouting wave of desperation. Young Lieutenant Moore, waiting in the rocks above, saw that his forces were directly between the Indians and the freedom of the rough country behind his position. It was then that he did the strange thing which the Cheyenne never forgot. As they came upward, their women struggling and falling with the papooses on their backs and in their arms, with the old persons falling and crying out for aid, with the children whimpering for lost parents but coming on bravely, despite their terror, the officer shouted to his sergeants to pull the troops back on either side and to provide the fleeing Cheyenne with an avenue of safety through which they might escape without further terror or panic. Lieutenant Moore not only failed to fire at the Cheyenne, he helped them to get away. And if Tonkalla the Mouse should live to be 110 winters old, he would never think that this young white soldier was a coward, or that he showed fear that day. He showed love.

"*H'gun! H'gun!*" he called to the white-faced officer, as he led the escaping Indian horde past him. Lieutenant Moore did not speak Sioux. But he understood gratitude and the nature of a fellow soldier's salute. He put his fringed cavalry gauntlet quickly upward, saluting the Oglala's fierce shout, and that was the last that Tonkalla saw or heard of him.

From their rock-girt emplacements high upon the hillside, the Indians poured their rifle fire into Reynolds's soldiers in the deserted village below. Tonkalla ordered the Indian fire slowed and then halted altogether as it became obvious that the white commander had no intention of following the red foe into those powder-smoked rocks. Colonel J. J. Reynolds, despite the urgings of Anson Mills to keep up the pursuit, had seen all he wished to see of the "peaceful" Cheyenne. By now he understood that Grouard had lied to him and that he, in turn, had blundered grossly in attacking the officially surrendered band of Two Moons. It was his purpose to retire as speedily and with what honor he might yet manage. And in the semihysteria of the man who knows he has committed murder, he now compounded the crime with an action of utter irrationality, which was designed, as so many a similar atrocity, to cloak the fact of the original wrong.

Tonkalla watched this enormous stupidity now with unbelieving eyes. His fellow Indians, crouching with him, shook their heads in total disbelief. Was this Eagle Chief obsessed? Was he mad as the loon? Having driven the enemy in rout from his home, having won the field and all the rich spoils upon it, what was he doing? Was he putting his frightened and weary soldiers to warm, snug rest in the captured lodges? Was he preparing a big feast of the tons of buffalo meat hanging in the lodges, so that his hungry men might feel strong once more? Was he ordering his best riflemen to surround and shoot down the pony herd, so that the Indians might not return and recapture it? Was he sending back scouts and messengers to tell Three Stars Crook what had happened, as Three Stars had been heard by Tonkalla and Yellow Bull to order him to do? Was he wisely loading many of the captured packhorses with good meat and warm furs to feed and shelter his soldiers on the march back to Three Stars' camp? No. Not Eagle Chief Reynolds. He was doing none of these reasonable things. He was piling every ounce of Indian possession, including all of the 108 lodges, into a vast pile and burning it in a flare of fire which could be seen forty miles away from its greasy and black smoke climbing into the blue winter skies.

Oh, there was one small lodge left standing. It was left by order of Captain Anson Mills to shelter one blind old squaw who could not see to follow her comrades up the hillside. This one small lodge was the sign of his fine honor which the white man left behind him at Bloody Snow Bend of the Powder River.

When darkness fell that day of the Bloody Snow fight, Tonkalla with a picked band of warriors swept down upon the soldiers from the howling belly of a new blizzard. Not only did the daring Sioux and his Cheyenne companions recapture and run off the entire pony herd lost earlier, but also they stole the column's band of beef cattle. The troops were left with no mouthful of food save for the very horses they rode. Reynolds's men were starving, yet he had destroyed wantonly enough prime meat to feed Crook's entire command for sixty days in the field. His troops were riddled through with gunshot wounds and with frostbitten limbs, yet Colonel Reynolds had ordered burned a small mountain of warm furs and sheltering tipis. Little wonder that Crook arrested the man upon sight, placing him on file under severest charges. But Three Stars' action was too late. The damage was done and would now never be undone.

Many of the Cheyenne in the sleeping village were agency Indians. Some of them were there with proper leaves from Standing Rock to visit their wild relatives. Others were present as peace envoys sent out by Standing Rock. The presence of clearly marked agency trade goods in the lodges, and the protests of these agency Indians during the fight, must have demonstrated the innocence of Two Moons's people to the troops. The officers of these men had to know within minutes of their ordered assault, and well before any real damage had been wrought by either side, what Indians these were whom they were attempting to kill. And they had to know, beyond reasonable or tenable question, that Crazy Horse and his Oglala bad faces were not among those about to die that morning.

General Sherman tried to smooth fresh, clean earth over the blood and ashes of the ugly thing with his subsequent strange proclamation that *"the result of Reynolds's fight was only the destruction of the tipis of the Indians, with their contents."* But General Sherman was very wrong; in all of the long, unpleasant history of the Army upon the Indian frontier, no commander had ever been more wrong.

With the recapture of the Cheyenne pony herd, Tonkalla ordered the survivors to mount up and start the journey through the night. With daylight the retreat was moving well. The heavy snowfall and bitter temperatures held, preventing any possible pursuit by tracking. But several old persons had made their last rides during the freezing blackness of that night, and four very young children with them. When he knew that enough miles had been put behind by the laboring ponies, Tonkalla sent for the old warrior, He-Dog.

"My chief," he said quickly, when He-Dog had come up, "I must ride ahead with all speed to bring this news to Sitting Bull. Will you see that Two Moons does not slow down in the march nor stop to rest again? You must

bring him along with his people to the village of Sitting
Bull as quickly as you are able. Do you understand?"

"I will see to it," promised He-Dog. "I have been a
fool, boy. You have made me brave again. Ride with
great care."

Changing to a fresh horse, Tonkalla set off alone through
the blizzard. It was long after dark that night when the
snarling and yelping of Indian dogs told him a village
lay ahead. Sitting Bull saw him at once, for while the
two had not met previously, the famed chief knew Tonkalla to be one of the trusted lieutenants of the war chief
Crazy Horse.

Here let it be said, and to Tonkalla's certain knowledge, that all talk of jealousy or rivalry between Crazy
Horse and Sitting Bull was thin rot. To Crazy Horse, Sitting Bull was his respected "uncle," and the accepted
civil head of all the Sioux Nation. By the same token,
Sitting Bull regarded Crazy Horse as his "nephew" and
the uncontested war leader of all the tribes. Tatanka Yotanka (Sitting Bull) was the lawmaker. Tashunka Witko (Crazy Horse) was the warmaker. It was an arrangement known to all the Sioux and obeyed by them. Accordingly, Tonkalla was a little nervous facing the great
man at last.

Sitting Bull was a short, powerfully broad man with an
enormous head and an impassive face, wide between the
eyes, wide of forehead. His eye-color was an odd gray,
not brown or black. Also the eyes were set very level for
an Indian, not slanted at all. His hair was feeling the
iron of many winters. It showed silver-gray as the badger's tip hairs. Tonkalla believed, seeing him thus, that
he must have sixty winters. He was seated by a small
fire in the center of his lodge when the young Oglala
entered. In his hand was a long pipe festooned with eagle
feathers. Merely glancing up across the fire, he grunted
to his visitor, "*Hohahe*, welcome to my tipi. Close the flap.
It's cold on my legs."

"*Woyuonihan*," said Tonkalla, paying him the respected gesture of touching the brow with the fingers. "I am
Tonkalla the Mouse, adopted son of Crazy Horse. I come
with news."

"Even so," answered the old man, "don't be hasty. Are
you hungry? Cold? You want a smoke?"

"My news is bad, Uncle." The young Sioux grimaced unhappily. "I cannot eat or smoke with such a heavy heart within me."

"Of course. When a man's heart is heavy, his tongue is not to be trusted, however. You had better have some hump ribs."

Tonkalla was forced to interrupt, saying that on the morning of yesterday's sun he had crept in and heard Three Stars talking to The Grabber about killing the Cheyenne of Two Moons. Three Stars was looking for Crazy Horse, but The Grabber had lied to him and told him the village of Two Moons was that of Crazy Horse. The next morning early, the pony soldiers had followed up and fallen on the village of Two Moons, burning all the lodges and driving the people into the blizzard. Tonkalla was sorry to tell Sitting Bull about his son, The Grabber, but he had seen The Grabber there with Three Stars and heard him speak his lies.

The young Oglala filled in the remaining shameful details of Reynolds's cowardly attack. When he had finished, Sitting Bull put aside his pipe. Softly and with great force, yet with almost a trembling in his deep voice, he commenced to speak. He said that ever since the Indian Commissioner had made the Laramie Treaty with him many summers gone—eight snows had fallen since that day they touched the pen for all time—the white man had lied to Sitting Bull and cheated him and stolen from his people. But he had maintained the peace which he had promised to do. He was a man of great suffering. He knew much patience. In his nature he was a gentle man. Yet he had been a great and desperate fighter too, in his younger times.

Now he had taken many insults from those greedy white people, and that perhaps was as it should be. A chief must be able to suffer, holding back his anger. For himself presently Sitting Bull wanted nothing. But the soldiers had attacked the Cheyenne brothers of the Sioux people. They had done it in the dead of night and when the Cheyenne wore no paint and when there was not even talk of war. Those Indians of Two Moons had promised many weeks before that they would go into Standing Rock in the spring, when they could get through the snow. The soldiers had known that. Now the same soldiers would try to kill the Sioux, and keep trying to kill the Cheyenne, their brothers. Those soldiers did not want peace; they sought only after war.

Now the young Tonkalla came to Sitting Bull telling him of these bad soldiers, and Sitting Bull was losing the last of his gentleness. No more of patience remained to him. He was become very angry now. And when Sitting Bull was angry many things became different for all. It saddened him to say it, but he saw a dark time coming . . . a dark time and a very dark thing with it. He fell silent and he and Tonkalla sat for many minutes passing the pipe and saying nothing. At last the young brave spoke.

"Uncle," he requested, "may I now go to see that buffalo meat and warm bed spots are prepared for our poor Cheyenne brothers who come with He-Dog through the snows behind me?"

"Yes, my son. Go, and go in peace; yet say a prayer to Wakan Tanka as you do. Soon there will be war."

As the survivors of Reynolds's raid drifted in during the dark hours of that morning, they were fed, clothed, made warm and whole again. All the following day preparations were made for emergency removal of Sitting Bull's Hunkpapa camp. Minutes only after the arrival of Tonkalla, runners had gone out to summon the chiefs of the Nation to a war council on Tongue River, where the lodges of Crazy Horse were pitched. The young Sioux was sent ahead to apprise his Oglala chieftain of the situation. Thus it was that he came presently to the gathering site of that great war camp on the Tongue, where so much of Indian history was to be plotted.

Present at the council which met within three days were the Sioux White Crow, Gall, Two-Bull-Bear, White Bull, Gray Eagle, Old Bull, Elk Nation, American Horse, Yellow Bull, Black Moccasin, Paints Brown and the Cheyenne Hump, Bob-Tail-Horse, Comes-In-Sight, Wolf, Two Moons and Half-A-Horse. Tonkalla sat with his adopted uncle, Tashunka Witko. His friend Yellow Bull sat with his real uncle Tatanka Yotanka. The latter began the speeches. By contrast with his usual way, he was brief.

"The whites are a great lake around us," said Sitting Bull, "and the Indians are an island in the lake's middle.

We must stand together or they will wash us all away. These soldiers have come shooting. They want war. All right. We will give it to them."

Crazy Horse now arose, greeted by an acknowledgement not afforded even Sitting Bull: the guttural *"hun-hun-he!"* admiration growl reserved for the greatest heroes only. The tribute seemed the more eloquent by the known gravity of the hour. For never out of the Sioux minds was the fact that the slender Oglala chief was the mightiest warrior in their fierce history—and none of Sitting Bull's great powers of civil government and law-settling could overshadow that martial power. Crazy Horse was, by common consent of the army commanders who met him in the field, the greatest natural cavalry leader of modern times. Beside him, Little Phil Sheridan and Yellow Hair Custer were only school soldiers, only civilized, ordinary men on horseback. The Oglala was a legend. And as a legend he stood there tall and dark-skinned in the leaping light of the council fire.

He made a figure to be etched upon the mind forever, whether that mind was simple and savage, like Yellow Bull's, or complex and partly educated to the wiles of the white man, such as that of Tonkalla the Mouse. Lean, pantherish, unspeakably fearless, ominous alike to the eye of his red brother and his white, the war chief of all the hostile Sioux now spoke with a brevity even greater than Sitting Bull's.

"Our Uncle Tatanka has put the tongue of his words to the angry sadness crying in the hearts of us all. A war will come now. I will lead you."

The council broke up on a final instruction from the dour Sitting Bull; an instruction which cost many a white man his scalp, many a soldier his life shot away, many an innocent white traveler his wagons and horses, milk cows and treasures, wives, mothers and children, in the terrible months to come; an instruction which smashed Three Stars Crook and his vaunted "mule-mounted infantry" completely back upon their supply base at Goose Creek; an instruction which was to run red with the blood of untold brave troopers the whispering buffalo grass of an as yet nameless stream beyond the Rosebud and the Tongue.

"Runners will go at once," ordered the Hunkpapa chief,

"to every hunting band of Indians yet free upon the prairies. Also runners will go to every agency of the Sioux, Arapahoe and Cheyenne standing to the sunward of the Missouri. Tell all of these Indians, 'It is war; come to my camp which will be at the Big Bend of the Rosebud River; there let us all get together and have one more big fight with the soldiers!' "

"*Hopo! Hookahey!*" In response the deep voices of the assembled chiefs bounded off the wind-buffeted skins of the council lodge.

"*Wagh!*" cried Crazy Horse, throwing his Winchester high overhead. "Let us die as free men, unafraid!"

Then suddenly the chiefs were gone, the great lodge stood empty and the Indian die had been cast. Tonkalla went quietly into the night. He knew he had listened to the valedictory of a brave people. What he could not know that he had also heard in the dark lodge upon Tongue River, was the true answer to Reynolds's raid upon the Cheyenne, and to the mean lie covering that raid by General Sherman. It was not the wanton destruction of the peaceful lodges of Two Moons's people which Reynolds wrought within the ice-fogged bend of Powder River five days before; it was the deaths of 226 gallant officers and men three months later.

For the name of that waiting unknown river beyond the Rosebud and the Powder and the Tongue was the Greasy Grass. That was its Indian name, of course. The white man knew it better by another name. He called it the Little Big Horn.

Way of the War Chief

On the fourth day of their flight northward from Fort Reno, Oklahoma, toward their lost homeland in high Wyoming, the Cheyenne of Little Wolf reached the Cimarron River. At the place of the crossing Little Wolf, who was the war chief of the escaping band, ordered a halt. Here, he said, they would pause to water and graze their horses and to rest the women, children and old people.

Yet even while the poles were being raised for the buffalo-skin coverings of the distinctive Cheyenne lodges, a gray horse troop of the Seventh Cavalry, quartering down from Fort Dodge, Kansas, in search of the homesick Indians, caught sight of the encampment. Without reconnoitering the Cheyenne position, or considering their own situation, the troop charged the hapless fugitives. It was hilly, cut up, rough brush country, the kind which had always been difficult for white cavalry, and there were, as well, no more than twenty minutes of shooting daylight remaining. The clash proved brief and bloodless.

This was not the old Seventh Cavalry of Yellow Hair's day but a new outfit of beardless boys and West Point-fresh officers without significant plains experience. The only sign to mark them professional brothers of the boot-tough bravos who had found oblivion in the shallow hills of the Little Big Horn two years ago was the proud regimental guidon with its big red 7 and white U.S. fluttering palely in the twilight. A battalion of such horse soldiers should have thought twice about attacking sixty Cheyenne of war age; a solitary troop under a lieutenant who had never before seen a wild horseback Indian should have given the idea no thought whatever.

Only the determination of the Cheyenne to avoid shedding white blood at all costs on the homeward march saved the green troopers. As it was, they were permitted their first dash through and disordered scatter of lodgepoles, furled skins, cursing squaws and yipping children. In the wild course of this ragged charge the valiant cavalrymen injured four camp kettles, three pack saddles, an ancient village mongrel and a blind baggage mule. After that, Little Wolf felt it was his turn and took it.

As always when on a war march his braves had picked their night horses and tethered them alongside each lodgesite. Before the gray horse troop could re-form for its rush back through the Indian camp or even slow its mounts to make the initial turn, the Cheyenne were mounted and running swiftly up behind them. The young lieutenant, demonstrating promise of some future as an Indian fighter, learned the game with equal quickness. On the instant he waved his brave followers onward along their present course, a course which would take the gray horse troop as far and as fast and straightaway from the shouting Cheyenne as clumsy Government horseflesh might manage. The "battle" was over before it was fairly joined.

Little Wolf, all the same, did not linger on the Cimarron to savor his tactical superiority. That lone troop could have been the advance patrol for Maheo knew how many other pony soldiers. Also, green recruits or not, the Cheyenne remembered that red-and-white guidon with the 7 in its lower half. They remembered, and they thought of Sitting Bull and Gall and Hump and the others who were fled or gone before the anger of the cavalry. Silently the lodgepoles and skins were repacked. Quickly the women and the children and the old people remounted. With full darkness the band was once more on the endless march northward. Forty-eight hours and ninety miles later, another sunset and another darkness came swiftly down.

Peering into the western cloudbank of that sixth twilight the wizened Little Chief, medicine man of the weary tribe, grew vastly uneasy. He told Dull Knife, the head chief, to forbid the squaws to unpack the lodgepoles just yet and warned Little Wolf to keep his warriors mounted and the line of march unbroken. He, Little Chief, would first need to make smoke and consult the sacred medicine arrows about this place. His feeling was that this was a very bad place to camp. The Cheyenne medicine man predicted better than he could know. Dismounted behind the flanking rises of ground to the west, tensely watching the halted Indian band, were four troops of regular cavalry—160 men, eight sergeants, four lieutenants, two captains and a full eagle colonel from nearby Fort Dodge.

But Maheo had not forgotten his Cheyenne people. The troops did not correctly interpret the slow ceremony being conducted by the old shaman. They presumed, from Little Chief's waving of the pipe and his chanting intonations, that he was merely blessing the campsite. Accordingly, they waited. It was far less dangerous to let the Indians get off their ponies and begin erecting their lodges before rushing them. It also made later reports of women and children killed less liable to investigation. In a fight at a campsite all such "accidents" were professionally acceptable. So the colonel waited for the Cheyenne to get down from their shaggy mustangs. But Little Chief's pipe smoke smelled bad to him and suddenly the colonel saw that the Indian column was not dismounting but was moving again. And moving on a high lope straightaway toward the long valley of the Arkansas.

The colonel stood in his stirrups. He waved and shouted for the bugler to blow the advance. The latter blew hastily and with sour key. Away swept the troops up and over the crests of their ambushing rises of ground. Down upon the rear of the fleeing Indian column they raced, the colonel and his bugler still trying to make their respective noises of command ring with proper authority. It was too late in the twilight for such second efforts. No white troops, superior force of numbers to the contrary, ever whipped a band of High Plains horseback Indians in a running fight.

The Cheyenne cut away from the main trail, raced for

the cover of the opposite eastern series of ridges, got their
women and children and old people safely behind these
ridges, turned and struck back wickedly at the leading
troops. The soldiers were driven back, disorganized, on
the open ground of the riverbank. With sharpshooting
detachments of Cheyenne warriors pushing both flanks
of their retreat, and with the accurate rifle fire of the
old men on the ridge striking them from above and beginning to take toll, the order was passed to leave the
field. This the troops did with shameful alacrity, but were
spared further casualties by lack of Cheyenne pursuit.
Within ten minutes of the first squalling bugle note, the
shooting was over. But for the Cheyenne, only the shooting.

No fires could now be lighted for cooking. No lodges
could be set up for shelter. They had a twelve-hour
grace of night's darkness in which to rest themselves and
dry-graze their horses. There was little water left in the
buffalo-paunch waterbags, the supply having been used
up in the long ride from the Cimarron. Only a few
pounds of fly-blown agency beef remained to them. This
ration amounted to less than two ounces for each of the
old ones, the weaker women and very small children.
The warriors and the boys past ten years of age ate
nothing, drank only the cold night wind.

For Little Wolf it was a lonely time. The war chief
went by himself up on the ridge so that he might think
where only Maheo and the stars and the sad cry of the
prairie wolf were his companions. It was here an hour
later that his sister-in-law found him.

"Come down now," she said to him. "Lie quietly and
rest."

"I cannot," he answered. "My heart will not let me
sleep."

The woman nodded. "Your nephew cannot sleep
either. He stirs within me."

"He is a Cheyenne," said Little Wolf. "He knows, even
in the womb, that his people are on the last trail."

The woman fell silent. She was younger than the war
chief, not even half his age. Yet thinking of the long
years between them, Little Wolf did not feel very old;
the words and worries of this swollen mother made him
forget the years, made him remember only the moment

which was now—the moment of his choice for the Cheyenne People.

"Hold your silence a little longer, woman," he told her softly. "I must think for all our people, not just for my nephew who stirs within you."

"Yes, Brother," said the young squaw. "*Naamáta*, I obey."

Little Wolf nodded. He did not otherwise answer her declaration, and his glance was far away, scanning the backtrail, seeing the way it had been on the fateful night of decision . . .

At Fort Reno near Darlington, Oklahoma Territory, three gaunt Cheyenne chiefs crouched in a smoke-stained cowhide lodge and watched soundlessly as the tired smile on the face of a fourth Cheyenne chief faltered, faded, finally went vacant. Iron Mountain, the forty-first of Dull Knife's tribesmen to set forth upon the last long ride into the Cheyenne Land of the Shadows since the band's arrival at Fort Reno the previous year, was dead.

Little Wolf, the fighting chief, stood up. The other two chiefs remained beside the dead comrade, making the holy signs for a peaceful passage above him. Little Wolf raised his pipe. He blew a puff of smoke in the four cardinal directions of the Mother Earth, and one toward the smoke-hole opening in the lodge's peak.

"It is done," he said. "Bring the shield, Little Chief."

The latter obeyed quickly and without question. Little Wolf was the man of greatest power among that fiercely savage and independent people. If the older Dull Knife ruled the tribe, Little Wolf ruled the entire nation. He was a gentle man among his own kind but terrible to cross or to delay when he might believe the welfare of the people to be in danger.

So Little Chief went quickly to the rear of the lodge and took down from its tripod of willow poles the bullhide war shield of Iron Mountain. Returning, he placed the shield carefully upon the dead chief's breast. He then scooped a small handful of *hesec*, the blessed mother soil, from the tipi's floor. Mounding this earth in the center of the war shield, he commenced the minor-keyed intonations of the Cheyenne Death Song.

Outside the lodge Iron Mountain's women caught the

first notes of the dirge. They began to sway upon their haunches and to croon aloud the eerie cadences of the chant. There was no other outcry, no weeping. Within the lodge Little Chief's incantations ceased.

Dull Knife looked at his companions. "Who will be the next to die?" he asked them. "How long must we wait?"

It was then September, The Month of the Cool Moon. They had waited too long already. Little Wolf knew this. His dark hand reached for his Winchester.

"We will go tonight," he said.

"It is truly a bad thing," murmured Little Chief. "None of us are young men. I myself am quite old. Yet I have seen no evil like this sickness since the Vomiting Death." He referred to the cholera epidemic in 1849 in which more than half of the Cheyenne Nation had perished. But Dull Knife waved his words aside.

"This is no brother to that sickness," he said. "We would not be dying now if we were well in our hearts. It is not the people's bodies which fail here, but their spirits. We are all homesick, that is the trouble. It is killing us one by one."

"We will wait no longer then," repeated Little Wolf grimly. "Now we will go home and be sick no more. I say tonight."

"Yes," nodded Little Chief. "Let us go this night to Agent Miles and tell him of our decision."

He spoke of John D. Miles, Indian Bureau Agent for the Darlington Reservation, a respected friend of the Cheyenne and a man in whose essential fairness each of the northern nomads showed a savage's trusting faith. Still, any decision of the band to inform their agent they were leaving the reservation was a most serious and final one. The very simplicity of the old medicine man's agreement that they now do this thing struck the chill of that decision's true meaning into both his companions.

It had been little more than a year since the band had come in voluntarily and surrendered to General Crook at Fort Robinson in the sand hills of Nebraska's northwestern corner, mere miles from the beloved homeland of Wyoming. Subsequent treachery of the white man—his denial of Crook's word to let the Cheyenne stay in the northland, indeed return to Wyoming with all their baggage and horses—had sent the band to the hot and humid lowlands of Oklahoma's central plain. In the year of their banishment the twin plagues of dysentery and malaria, against which the mountain-bred northern Indians had no natural immunity, had decimated their ranks. On a starvation diet of rotten beef, weeviled flour and maggoty bacon the people had weakened and died like quarantined cattle in the inescapable welter of their own filth. Now, ravaged by hunger and disease, with only a few muzzle-loading rifles, less than two days' hoarded supply of food and a small remuda of grass-thin ponies, the question had been called on a march of 800 miles across an alien barrier of three states and four army departments; a friendless land which twenty-four hours after their departure from Darlington would be swarming with aroused white settlers and pursuing U.S. cavalry troops bent upon a common holy war—killing Cheyennes.

The ultimate decision was given by Little Wolf to his old friend, and far gentler man of his people, Dull Knife. "Aye," he said, low-voiced. "Let us go to Miles and tell him we are going home. And *this* time, my brothers, we will do it. Do you understand me?"

The others paused, watching him. Little Wolf was tall for a Cheyenne. His skin was nearly black, the color of smoked buffalo-hock leather. He was a man for other men to remember, once seen. Some would write of him as "ugly of face and head." Others would say he had "the muscular repugnance of a snake." But these were white men, not Indians. Looking at him now, Dull Knife and Little Chief saw the silver cross which the great warrior wore as his battle charm upon his breast. They saw the round otterskin hat and the curling otterskin hair tubelets which encased his waist-long braids. They saw the fringed black buckskin hunting shirt and the famed yellow-and-black trade blanket which encased him from the waist downward. But above all, they saw the burning look in the eye of Little Wolf, and they both nodded very cautiously.

Dull Knife said that they understood him but that they would like to know what it was that he intended to say to Agent Miles when he actually stood face to face with such a good man. In response, Little Wolf's voice grew softly bitter. He said that he would tell Miles that the

Cheyenne people had been reared far up in the north country among the pines and mountains and the cold snow waters; that in that country they were always healthy, all of them; that there was no sickness and that very few of the Cheyenne died. Now, however, since they had been in the hot south country, they were dying every day. This was not a good country for mountain people. The Cheyenne were afraid and they wished to go home again to their high country.

"That is what I will tell him," nodded Little Wolf.

Dull Knife returned his nod and shifted his glance to their comrade, Little Chief. "And you, Brother?" he asked.

The aging medicine man answered that he would tell Miles that a great many of the people had been sick; that many had died; that he himself had been sick a great deal of the time since he had been brought down here into this smothering southland, homesick and heartsick and sick in every way; that he, Little Chief, had been thinking lately of his native Wyoming and the fine home he had up there where he was never hot and never hungry. And also where, when a man wished something to eat, he did not ask for it by begging, but took his bow and went out and shot it—an elk, a deer, a buffalo, anything he wanted. That, he vowed, was what he would tell the agent.

Dull Knife thanked him and turned back to Little Wolf. "And what will you say," he asked, "when Miles has heard your wish to go home and has said no to you?"

When Little Wolf answered, it was as though he knew that he spoke for a long time from then, and not for himself. "When Miles has said no to me," he said, "I will take his hand in mine, using my left hand because that is the side of my body upon which my heart lies. Then I will say to him, 'My old friend, I am going now to my camp. I do not wish the ground about this agency to be made bloody, but now listen to what I have to say to you. I am going to leave here. I am going back north to my own country. If you are going to send your soldiers after me, I wish that you would first let me get a little distance away. Then if you want a fight, I will fight you and we can make the ground bloody at that other place."

The war chief hesitated, putting his lean hands upon

Dull Knife's bowed shoulders. "Do you understand me now, my brother? Do you see finally what is in my heart and mind? What it is that I will do when Miles has said no to me, and I have said yes to him?"

It was the tribal leader's turn to hold the silence, and to let it grow while he thought of the meaning of Little Wolf's words. It was *death* of which the war chief spoke; death rather than further dishonor; death in preference to continued imprisonment; death in freedom as against life in slavery. The pronouncement had already been made. It remained for Dull Knife only to anoint it; only to bless it with the people's word; only to speak for the women and the children and the old ones, who would die as surely as Iron Mountain had died if he now said yes to Little Wolf.

The old chief drew seven times upon his smoldering pipe before his stooped shoulders straightened and were thrown back and the dark light of pride-in-race and of his chieftainship of such as Little Wolf showed flashingly and for a last fierce moment in his aging eyes.

"I understand you, my brother," he said. "May Maheo watch over us." Then, quickly, "Let us go home . . ."

On the ridge above the resting camp, Little Wolf's young sister-in-law reached forth in the darkness to touch the warrior's arm. She spoke to him urgently, asking if he would not now come below with her, would not lie down those few hours until dawn to restore his own weary body. But the war chief shook his head. He had not done with his looking back, he told her. His mind and heart were still seeing the trail they had followed to this place . . .

The fall night was as still as the whisper of summer wind in dry grass. The unshod ponies of the five Cheyenne made no sound as the animals topped a starlit rise of ground and came to a halt. While the lathered ponies flared their nostrils and lifted eager heads to the smell of the water below, their masters held their silence. Behind them, to the south and east, lay Fort Reno and Darlington, a fireless, foodless march of forty-eight hours on horseback. Before them lay a nameless prairie river. Beyond the stream waited 700 miles of open plains between them and the borders of their northern homeland.

"What water is this?" asked Dull Knife of the dark-skinned chief beside him, while pointing to the stream below him.

"I am not certain," replied Little Wolf scowling. "But I think it is the Medicine Lodge."

"It will do, whatever its name," ordered Dull Knife. "Red Bird—" He called the name into the darkness. A small rider moved his mount forward from between those of the other two Cheyenne scouts. He was seen to be a boy, of perhaps as many as twelve or thirteen winters.

"Yes, Grandfather," he said to Dull Knife. "I am here."

"Go back quickly to the people," the chief told him. "I inform them we have found good water with some cottonwoods for the cookfires. Bring them here at once."

The boy wheeled his pony. He kicked the animal into a gallop, racing back toward the 250 women and children and fifty rear-guard warriors who composed the straggling column of the Cheyenne retreat. Watching him go, the old man muttered to Little Wolf with weary pride.

"He is a worthy grandson, eh? He will make a warrior one day. I charge his care to you, Hokom-xaaxceta."

Little Wolf nodded, then corrected him sharply. "The boy may one day make a worthy grandson; he is already made a warrior."

"Aye," said Dull Knife sighing. "When the days grow short the years grow long. He should be hunting rabbits and birds with blunted arrows and happy laughter."

"Late or soon," grunted Little Wolf, "a man will become a man when it is his time." Then, in a deep voice, "Come, let us go down there and scout that water."

At his words the two other scouts moved forward, ready.

"Yes," agreed Bull Hump. "Let us go scout the water and set the signal fire for the people to come into."

"We must make it a very small fire," added Wild Hog cautiously. "Just large enough to fill a Cheyenne's eye, not one twig larger. It must not be big enough for a pony soldier to see."

"Do not worry about the pony soldiers," rumbled Little Wolf. "I will watch them for you. Meanwhile, we must hurry. The night is our friend but she will not cover us forever."

There was no trouble getting the people up and the camp made by the nameless stream. Nevertheless, the fugitives found it difficult to close their eyes. The frosty black hours crawled by. Four o'clock and the first streak of the false dawn found Little Wolf still atop the lookout ridge, still scanning the murk of the prairie to the south, to their rear. Taking a final look, he turned to the thin warrior who had come up from the camp to relieve him of the guard.

"All right," he agreed uneasily. "I will go and get some sleep now. But watch most carefully when the real daylight comes. I will be in the lodge of Tangle Hair, remember."

Beyond an expressionless bobbing of his dark head, the young replacement gave no answer. Nor did he need to. His name was Aeno-anos, Yellow Hawk, and of all the Cheyenne his eyesight was the most keen. The camp was safe with such a one watching over it. And for the next two hours there was indeed nothing but peace and stillness over the silent camp. Then, with the new sun rimming the gray wasteland to the east, Yellow Hawk's famed eyes grew suddenly fierce with far straining. The next moment he was bounding down the slope toward his sleeping comrades. He did not wait to seek out Little Wolf but ran crying with each leap downward, "Cavalry! Cavalry!"

At this dread warning Little Wolf sprang from his buffalo robes within the lodge of Tangle Hair. As he raced out of the lodge he was already pumping the first shell into the chamber of his Winchester.

"Where, where?" he called to Yellow Hawk. "How many are they? How far off yet?"

"They are to the south," shouted back the young brave. "I would say about one mile. Behind the lookout ridge there. A big number this time. I would guess 200 at least."

"How are their horses? Can you say? Do they look strong?"

"Yes, they do. They move well, at a brisk trot. They are picking up their feet clean. They leave little dust."

"Bad, bad," frowned Little Wolf. "It will mean a fight."

"No, Brother!" Dull Knife had come up in time to hear the remark. "There must be no fight here. I will go out and talk with them. You stay here with the people."

Little Wolf put his hand on the chief's arm. His tone was not angry but it was very strong.

"*You* stay with the people," he said. "*I* will go out and talk to the soldiers—with my gun."

Dull Knife did not argue. Neither did the other men now hastening up. They all understood the change in things. This was war. Little Wolf was the war chief. He was taking command. "Be careful," he warned the Cheyenne. "Do not any of you shoot until the soldiers have fired first. Make them shoot first. Have your guns and your horses ready to be behind me when I go out to talk to them. If they kill me, *then* you can fight."

Minutes later he was on the open prairie beyond the lookout ridge listening to Ghost Man, an Arapaho Government scout known to him as an Indian whose word could be trusted. The Arapaho told him the troops were from Fort Elliott in Texas. They were young troops and nervous. The officer with them was new as spring grass. He had never been out after Indians before. It would be the best idea of all if Little Wolf would please come over with Ghost Man and have a nice friendly talk with that young officer and calm him down a little.

"For Maheo's sake," added the Arapaho fervently, "keep your old people still and your warriors well back on top of that ridge while we go to talk!"

Queried by Little Wolf as to the troops' orders, the Arapaho said that he believed the Cheyenne would have to surrender and be returned to Fort Reno and Darlington at once. The only promise offered them in return was the old one of better rations and more decent treatment of their other wants. Little Wolf replied that he would never surrender but that he would come over and talk with the officers and then maybe something more useful might be mentioned.

"You tell them," he instructed the nervous scout, "that we do not want to fight them but that we will not go back. We are leaving this country. We have no quarrel with anyone in it and I will hold up my gun to show that I do not wish to fight with the whites." With these grave words he raised his rifle overhead with both hands in the peace sign. But even as he did so, he concluded abruptly by warning the Arapaho that the Cheyenne intended to go on to their old homeland to stay, and that the troops must not try to stop them.

Ghost Man, noting the growing number of Cheyenne warriors along the ridge behind the war chief, departed at once across the prairie toward the impatient white commanders. As he did, the subchiefs Wild Hog and Tangle Hair began to have difficulty holding their young men in check upon the ridge. Unconscious of this fact, Little Wolf remained alone on the buffalo grass below, intent on watching the army troops across from him. Presently his gaze was rewarded. He saw the guidon of the troop wave in a wigwag; then a white pennant was run up beside it and the troop commander edged his horse out of ranks and a few steps along the plain toward Little Wolf. Ghost Man came with him, signaling by hand for the Cheyenne war chiefs to be assured that the truce flag would be respected by the soldiers.

Little Wolf cautiously set his pony in motion forward. Behind him his young men edged farther down the ridge. It did not appear now as if they were nervous, but more as if they were only moving up to occupy the ground their war chief had just left. Wild Hog and Tangle Hair, Little Wolf's primary lieutenants, later insisted that this was the only purpose of the move—to get a better view of the parley to follow.

But Ghost Man had spoken with a straight tongue about those young troops from Texas; they were as green as the spoiled gall juice from a sick she-bear. Whether the shots were fired from their lines on command as a warning for the forward-edging Cheyenne warriors to stand where they were, or if they were let off through what was well named "horse Indian nerves" among cavalry veterans, will never be ascertained. Whatever the cause, a ragged volley broke from the troop position almost the moment that Little Wolf started his pony forward, and one of the bullets smashed stunningly in a ricochet off the ribs of the war chief's mount. The scraping blow knocked the little mustang off its feet, seeming to have also injured, if not killed, its famed rider.

In fact, Little Wolf was not struck at all. He was scarcely even shaken up by the fall, having managed to get free of the horse. But as quick as he was in leaping to his feet to signal his men that he was unharmed—that the thing had been an accident and of no fighting account—he was forever too late.

There was an instant yammer of war shouts from the Cheyenne young men. Ghost Man, that Arapaho son of a she-coyote! He had betrayed their leader! He had killed the great Little Wolf! Even as the latter ran waving his gun and crying out for the warriors not to fight, they swept past him across the buffalo grass toward the white troops, howling the Cheyenne wolf howl. The firing became general in seconds. And within half a minute a full-scale "Indian brush" was under way.

When nightfall of that September 11th brought an end to the day-long exchange of wild riding and reckless shooting on the part of the angered Cheyenne, with the ragged and mainly ineffectual volleys of the recruits, three pony soldiers had paid the eternal price. Consigned to the same timeless future, as well, was the hapless Arapaho emissary, Ghost Man, shot at hand-close range through the heart by Little Wolf himself in the most reckless coup of the day. For such a close and a long fight, casualties were surprisingly light. Yet to Little Wolf the three dead troopers seemed as grim a toll as thirty might have been. For the war chief knew the price of white lives in that land.

Sometime before dawn of the twelfth the Cheyenne struck their lodges and disappeared northward into the rough hill country of the Cimarron badlands. Behind them the time for peace lay hopelessly glazed in the staring eyes of three fair young pony soldiers who would never see Fort Elliott or Texas again. Ahead now lay only that other time, that ugly, wicked time which Dull Knife had so long prayed would not come once more to his people. It was the time of the bullhide shield and the black charcoal greasepaint. It was the time of war . . .

"Now will you come with me, my brother?"

The woman had seen Little Wolf turn at last from his southward peering, and had seen him shake his head as though to clear from it some vision or remembrance which came with a bad feeling to him there upon the ridge above the sleeping camp.

"Yes," said the great warrior, voice low and seeming very weary. "I will go with you, but not to sleep. It has come to me how it must be for us now. Take my arm, woman. It is steep here. How is the young life within you, Sister?"

"Strong!" the woman replied, smiling, as they started downward. "As the seed, so the seedling."

"No, Sister," said Little Wolf with his gentle humility. "As the soil, so the sprouting. Remember always that it is the mother who is the earth."

The scouts under Yellow Hawk were sent out by Little Wolf shortly after midnight. The Cheyenne, unlike others of the horseback Indians, traveled by night when the need was dire enough. Their courage was thus of a unique kind defying even age-old fears of the supernatural. When loved ones were in peril, when the people were dying today and would be dying tomorrow and the next day and the next, the scouts rode out by dark. If it were black as a dead bull's gut, as it was that moment, and if every departed Indian shade had come above the earth to prowl in pursuit of living red men, they would still ride out. It mattered only so much as to require that the braves redouble the medicine signs they took with them.

Little Wolf waited with Dull Knife, Wild Hog, Tangle Hair, Tired Horse and the boy Red Bird. A pipe was soon lit and passed among the men. When it came to the war chief, he glanced at his nephew seated beside him in worshipful silence. Taking a draft of the acrid smoke, Little Wolf exhaled and gave the pipe to Red Bird. The boy stared back at his uncle, unable to believe his act. But against the starlight he could see the quick bobbing of the famed warrior's round otterskin hat.

"Go ahead," grunted Little Wolf. "Smoke."

Red Bird put cautious lips to spittle-laden stem. Closing his eyes, he gritted his teeth and drew manfully in. He coughed in a strangling manner but, fighting the smoke as any nephew of Little Wolf's should—nay *must*—he recovered, eyes streaming. As he gasped for breath Tangle Hair kindly observed that it was cold sitting there in the night air and that perhaps such a small warrior should wrap his blanket more warmly about himself. Old Tired Horse charitably agreed, adding that it sounded to him like quite a bad cough and that he trusted the boy would mind it carefully. Still choking, Red Bird passed the pipe

to Tangle Hair, who sucked noisily upon its cold stem to
contribute his share toward covering the lad's embarrass-
ment. When the latter could do so, he asked his fierce
uncle if the passing of the pipe to one of his few winters
was not a considerable honor, present circumstances remembered. But Dull Knife interrupted to tell him not to
disturb the war chief, who had far greater concerns. He
then asked Little Wolf about the condition of his sister-
in-law.

"She smiles," answered Little Wolf, "but she is afraid."

"We're all afraid," said Wild Hog. "And why not?"

No one wanted to reply, or sought to. Tired Horse in-
quired uneasily about the overdue scouts, suggesting that
one of the present group ought to have accompanied them.
To this Tangle Hair replied that Little Wolf had sent
Yellow Hawk in charge, the best man for the job, with his
great eyesight. Wild Hog concurred, adding that the war
chief always sent the right man.

Little Wolf laughed softly for an instant in the gloom.
"Old friend," he said, "do not seek to make me forget
with flattery that fine shag of tobacco you stole from me
at the agency. No one always sends the right man."

The boy Red Bird, seeking to challenge this, suggested
that Maheo had sent the Cheyenne the right man to lead
them in the person of his legendary uncle. If not so, he
demanded, then how had the people come this far in such
a terrible journey? This loyal tribute only served to upset
Little Wolf, who sharply rebuked the youngster for such
prattle and ordered him to be still and to stay still. Warriors spoke, boys listened. Red Bird fought his tears,
shamed and humbled but silent.

Compassionately Wild Hog began commenting on what
a lovely night it was. He said he could not recall seeing
the dawnstar so big and bright. It made him think of the
old days, he mused, and he wondered if Dull Knife remembered those times when his, Dull Knife's name had
been Morning Star, and when they all were young men
and the prairies and mountains were young with them,
and all the girls pretty! "Ah, those were the times, cousins,
those were the times . . ." He sighed, trailing off the
words. Little Wolf suddenly said that he had just felt the
beat of pony hoofs through the earth beneath them. The
scouts were returning.

Their news was bad, all bad. Up there, between the Cheyenne camp and the Arkansas River, they had found a big encampment of white men waiting. These were not soldiers, but men from the settlement at Fort Dodge. Their horses were not grazing either, but were on picket lines near the parked supply wagons, and all of the men were heavily armed. When this news was given, old Tired Horse wanted to believe the Dodge people could be buffalo hunters. After all, it was the Cool Moon, the time to begin getting in the winter's meat. But the war chief knew better, and so did Old Tired Horse. Buffalo hunters did not arm their sentries, nor flank their sleeping spots with all-night fires.

Those white people was not hunting meat; they were hunting Cheyenne. What those white men wanted was a chance to kill Indians in safety and comfort. So ran the thoughts in Little Wolf's mind as he listened to the scouts.

"Well, my brother," asked Dull Knife heavily, "what is to be done now?"

What was to be done then was very little, and exceedingly long of odds. Little Wolf knew that. Their ponies would not stand another long night march to swing wide of the white camp. The faithful little animals had traveled a hundred miles the past two nights and days under heavy loads and without rest or even good grass and water. The way of the war chief in this hour at the Arkansas Crossing was desperate, but it was clear to him. It was a choice all had prayed to escape. Now they stood where prayer would not answer for them; where they must answer for themselves; where, indeed, Little Wolf must answer for all of them, even to the last hungry, half-naked child.

"There is but one thing we can do now," he said at last to Dull Knife. "You know what it is. I will let you tell the others so that they will know their chiefs speak with one tongue."

Dull Knife nodded.

"Aye, Brother," he said, words heavy with the meaning of the choice he knew Little Wolf had made. "It is an evil thing that this time should come to us. Maheo must be sleeping tonight. Yet I cannot deny what my heart knows, and what Little Wolf's heart knows. If we kill a pony soldier who is trying at the same time to kill us, it is bad enough. In this case the white men call it war and think far less of it than other dyings. But if we kill a settler who is at the same time trying to kill us, if we slay any white man who is not a soldier yet is shooting at us, the white men will call it murder and will seek out the Indian and hang him high upon the gallows with the rope."

The old chief paused sighingly. But then his voice grew deep with emotion. "Still," he said quietly, "the war chief is right. We do as he has decided, or we surrender and go back to the agency. Now I do not ask you which you want to do. I know your answers and I honor them. Yet if anyone will speak, let him speak."

"*I will never go back.*" The low words were Little Wolf's. With them he was not expressing an opinion, but issuing an order. The others understood this.

"I am with you," said Wild Hog.

"And I," grunted his friend Tangle Hair.

"And I, and I, and I," added the scouts who had gone out with Yellow Hawk.

One of the scouts, Bull Hump, struck his wide chest and snarled. "I will count the first coup; we will kill them like their spotted cattle caught in a pen at the agency!"

The ancient shaman, Little Chief, who had drifted up through the early darkness of the new day in time to hear the words of the warriors, raised his hands to the heavens. In his hands they all now saw the white doeskin case of the sacred medicine pipe of the Cheyenne People. Muttering, they made the holy signs and bowed before its revered symbol.

"Maheo is not sleeping," said the old man gently. "He is praying for us. Let this thing be done in the war chief's way. That is the prayer our Great Father is making. Believe it, and go forth strong. Follow Maheo and the war chief!"

Dull Knife's people believed. And they followed Little Wolf as the sacred pipe had said. With the first streak of dawn the Cheyenne charged the white wagon camp. They killed one man, severely wounded eight more. The settlers fled in disorder back to the north bank of the river. The Indians did not pursue them into the shallow stream, or across it. They wanted only time and a little water there. They were granted both these pre-

cious things before the Dodge Citians could regroup on
the far side, and before the unfortunate colonel and his
sleepy bugler could awaken to the task of the new day
and come up on the belated gallop to take them in the
rear. The Cheyenne raised grateful eyes to the pinken-
ing sky above them. Maheo had not been sleeping, after
all.

That seventh day of the homeward flight the objective
of the fugitives was to get as far as possible to the west
of Fort Dodge—and out of the reach of its relief troops—
before attempting their own crossing of the river. Because
the pursuing colonel understood this situation, he kept
close. He was always within rifle shot and always pushing the fleeing Cheyenne. No deaths were counted on
either side, but the toll in nerve-wear upon the harried
Indians was severe. However, nightfall found them safely
west of Fort Dodge, and of the large settlement of Dodge
City.

As for the colonel in the field, he retired for the night
expecting the Indians to try an early-dawn crossing of the
river. He thus stationed his troops on the *far* side of
the stream. But Little Wolf was a light sleeper. During
the quiet of the night he and his tireless scouts rode ten
miles farther west of the Indian camp and discovered an
isolated camp of white buffalo hunters. These hunters
were to all appearances unaware that there might be a
hostile horseback Indian within a week's march of the
Arkansas. But with first light of the new day they discovered that there were several such in the vicinity; nearly
300 of them, to be precise. With that same daylight, the
cautious colonel cursed in his sleep-matted beard, while he
stared across the shallow Arkansas at a Cheyenne campsite as lonely of Indian life as a crater on the dark side
of the autumn moon.

Meanwhile the Cheyenne found that the buffalo hunters' camp contained eighteen freshly killed cows, thirty
fine Sharps heavy buffalo rifles and three packmule loads
of modern brass-cased ammunition for those fine, long
shooting rifles. The camp also contained seven of the
luckiest white buffalo hunters in history. When Little Wolf
told them that none of them would be harmed who cared
to set forth on foot at once across the river, not a man
among the white veterans chose to debate the camp creed

of their profession: "Never bicker with a balky mule, a
tailed-up buffalo bull, nor a hot-eyed horseback Indian on
the run." They pulled out as instructed, leaving even
their precious tobacco pouches, than which only their
dirty long-haired scalplocks were more dear to them.

An hour later, full fed for the first time since leaving
the Darlington Agency and driving ahead of them the
ammunition and fresh meat-laden packmules of the buffalo hunters, the Cheyenne crossed the Arkansas. It was
the morning of the eighth day of the flight, the seventeenth
of September, 1878. As the last travois pony splashed
out upon the far bank, the homeland still lay 500 miles
to the north and west.

For four days the position of the band went unmarked
on the military maps beyond the Arkansas. While the
various C.O.'s fumed and fretted and called innumerable
staff meetings, upward of 4,000 troops from three Army
departments converged on west central Kansas to box
the fugitives below the Nebraska line. The military telegraph keys clattered around the clock. Orders and coun-
terorders flashed from post to post throughout the commands of the Platte, the Canadian and the Arkansas.
Field columns from Forts Laramie, Wallace, Lincoln,
Dodge, Leavenworth, Kearney, McPherson, Hays and Ri-
ley curried the Kansas plains with a cavalry comb 350
miles wide and 200 miles deep. The pony soldiers rode
their staggering horses down to the last set of shoes in the
farriers' wagon boxes. Beardless troopers cursed, salty sergeants wept, field-grade officers contemplated resigna-
tion. All in vain. The Cheyenne had disappeared.

It was the evening of the fifth day from the Arkansas
that the military maps were updated. The entry was
marked with a grim black X on the Smoky Hill River a
hundred miles below the Nebraska border. In that place,
six hours earlier, Colonel William H. Lewis had made the
strategic blunder of getting between Little Wolf and
water which had to be crossed. Colonel Lewis had with
him three companies of mule-mounted infantry, a troop
of veteran cavalry, a supply train of field and ammunition wagons. He saw suddenly in front of him a misery-
cloaked ragtag of 250 Cheyenne, old men, women and
children, headed by no more than fifty starving reserva-

tion bucks in cast-off Army coats and filthy issue blankets, and all of them caught out in the open flat of a streambed bottomland.

It seemed a military opportunity complete with the elements of surprise, favorable terrain and the clear chance of a brevet in the field for the lucky army commander. Colonel Lewis ordered the charge forthwith and straightaway from the front. His bugler blew a sweeter note than that of his brother-colonel below the Arkansas. Away thundered the cavalry, the mule-mounted infantry lumbering in their wake. This time they had the Indians. There was no ridge for them to run to; no river for them to get across and fort up in the timber of the far side. Nor was darkness near enough this time to save them. Colonel Lewis had his brevet.

Indeed, less than five minutes later the rash officer did have his promotion. But the Cheyenne rifle shot which made him a brigadier was the same one which made his wife a widow. It came from Wild Hog's stolen buffalo hunter's new Sharps bullgun. The colonel was laid beneath a wagon tarp and on his way back to Fort Wallace within the hour. In a second and third field wagon behind the one which bore their dead leader, jolted a dozen of his troopers, severely wounded. The heavy Sharps rifles, at such powder-burning range, were fearsome weapons. Flaming forth as they had, when the troops expected the Cheyenne to be armed only with a few old low-powdered muskets, their effect had produced panic in the Fort Wallace column.

The blue-clad troopers were still shaking from the effects, still peering back and pushing their horses hard, when sundown cut off their view of a possible Cheyenne pursuit. But they had pushed and peered in vain. And Colonel Lewis had died for nothing. All the Indians had wanted was water. All they had ever asked was to be let alone. They had not changed this thinking in the moment of white disorder. There was no idea, ever, of pursuit. Only of flight. And, Maheo willing, of freedom.

Little Wolf paused neither to mourn his dead nor to hold the traditional scalp dance of victory. He forced his weakening followers across the Smoky Hill that same evening and drove them on through the night. Dawn and 400 fresh troops rushing up from Fort Larned to the south found nothing at the battle scene save disappearing travois tracks and the scattered remains of raw buffalo bones gnawed and discarded on the march. The Cheyenne had once again evaporated into the clear prairie air. This time it was many days before the military maps made another correcting location within their rapidly shrinking perimeters. When they did, a singular change had taken place.

From their October 2nd appearance above Frenchman's Fork of the Republican River in southern Nebraska and through the ensuing days of their crossings of the Kansas Pacific trackline below Ogallala, the South and North Platte Rivers west of that settlement, and the Union Pacific roadbed beyond Sidney Barracks, the Cheyenne had begun to kill the white man wherever he found him—or his woman, or his child, or his old ones.

Tonoesehe, the Month of the Cool Moon, was gone. It was nineteen days into Hissikevinhis, the Dust and Dirt Blowing Moon, when Little Wolf halted the Cheyenne column for what he knew would be the last time in his command. The place of the halting was the south bank of a small tributary to the Niobrara River, far north and west up into Nebraska, within but one more pony ride of high Wyoming, and of home. The time was another sunset as gray and cold as any they had known on the long march from Oklahoma. The ragged survivors drew up behind their war chief, huddling silently together. They seemed as lonely and as lost as the whistle of the October wind.

As they waited, Little Wolf called Dull Knife aside. "Well, my brother," he asked, "what do you think?"

"This is a good place," answered Dull Knife. "The people are tired, the ponies are tired, I am tired. We will camp here." He paused, lifting his head, inhaling deeply. "This is the last camp before our homeland. I smell the pines in this cold wind."

"It's a sad smell in some strange way," murmured Little Wolf. "Is it not odd, my brother, that we fear to be joyful? That coming home hurts the heart instead of healing it?"

Dull Knife did not reply for a moment. He peered across the little stream westward, toward Wyoming.

"I feel what you feel," he said at last. "What is it?"

The war chief took a silent moment in his turn.

"I believe I know, old friend," he said finally, nodding.

"Yes?" Dull Knife watched him, sharing his sadness.

"It is that we have no home any more."

The stillness fell between them then, and Dull Knife did not answer him except to turn his pony slowly away. "I will tell the women to unpack the poles," he said.

An hour later the last lodge was pitched, the last cooking fire kindled. The last shreds of fly-blown bone and bloody hide from the single settler cow slain the previous day were simmering in the boiling kettles. When the final ladle of this putrid broth had been apportioned among the women and children, the warriors and old men, having eaten nothing, tightened their loincloth strings in lieu of a better supper. Then they lit up their pipes and sat back to await the outcome of the council presently going forward in the lodge of Dull Knife.

For a very long time Dull Knife and Little Wolf stayed in the lodge. The waiting for the men outside grew unbearable. Finally the fires died away and the haranguing of the squaws and the fitful hungry cries of their children were withdrawn beneath the muffling covers of the tattered tipis. In the ensuing greater stillness of the camp, the voices of the two chiefs could be heard contending in guttural Cheyenne argument. The voice of Little Wolf sounded deep and forceful, increasingly heated. That of Dull Knife seemed slow, hesitant, continuingly restrained and cautious.

Now the two voices ceased altogether. The entrance flaps of the lodge stirred. Little Wolf strode out and toward the fire where the warriors and subchiefs waited. Behind him came Dull Knife, walking like an old man, his chin upon his bearclaw necklace, leathered face showing the full weather of his fifty-eight winters. At the fire's edge the war chief halted. For all the angry set of his features, his words fell with a peculiar gentleness.

He told them that Dull Knife and he had come to a parting of the trail. The old chief had his eyes in one direction while Little Wolf saw only the other way. Dull Knife believed that the people were already safely home, that the long march was over, that all could rest now and be happy. Little Wolf said that Dull Knife could

smell the pines of Wyoming from this camp. Because of
this, he was ready to stay here where they were, beside
this small stream, and wait in peace for the coming of
the pony soldiers. Dull Knife believed the people must
trust the white man again, that if they did they would all
be allowed to go home from Fort Robinson over into Wyoming when the new grass came. Their ponies would be
fat then and he was certain that this time Three Stars
Crook would speak with a stronger tongue to the Father in
Washington. In the end then, the Cheyenne would be
happy, for they could go and hunt the buffalo and smell
the pines of Wyoming for all of time that remained.

Little Wolf stopped speaking and stood watching his
fellow tribesmen. The stillness became a tangible thing.
It shut down over the fire and the scowling men as closely
and bad-aired as a sweated horse blanket. It was Tangle
Hair who finally spoke, demanding to know what Little
Wolf had to say for himself, what his own words were.
The war chief quoted an old Cheyenne proverb saying
that a white dog would not change color because the snow
hid his true coat. Three Stars had lied to them once. He
would do so again.

Little Wolf did not trust any white man. He would not
wait where they were for any white soldiers. Neither
would he go in and surrender at Fort Robinson again.
He warned that the people were not truly home yet. He
felt they must go on, and swiftly, until they saw once
more the Tongue River and tasted in their mouths its
clean, cold waters as before. Then they would be home.
Then they could rest and be happy.

Lone Crow waited a moment, then querulously asked if
that were all the war chief had to say. To this the face
of Little Wolf grew dark again. No, it was not all, he
informed them. Let the people listen well to the rest of
it. They had an opportunity in this camp; they faced a
final decision that same night. Little Wolf's fierce eyes
stabbed at them. He raised his arms toward Maheo. If
the Cheyenne now went on toward their old homelands,
brave and always prepared to fight, the white man would
honor them. They could make a real peace with him,
with honor for both sides. He would keep it too, for the
Cheyenne would have made it in strength. Yet if the
people now went into Fort Robinson crying, "Pity us, we

are weak from little food and long journeying; help us, we surrender to you like tired women," the pony soldiers would laugh at them and send them all back to the hot country.

"No matter what Three Stars Crook tells us," he shouted suddenly, "that is what he will do to us!" Dramatically, he broke off again, lean hand raising his beautifully engraved Winchester rifle above his head. *"Hear me, my brothers. Remember what I say. Remember it a long time. Peace is never put into the laps of beggars!"*

Once more the uneasy silence fell among the subchiefs. None of them would speak in favor of Little Wolf. Finally the old medicine man, Little Chief, waved the sacred pipe and pronounced in behalf of Dull Knife and surrender. One by one, the other members of the council shamefacedly sided with the cause of peace without honor or any safeguard other than the white man's word.

The war chief waited until the last man of them had grown still, then spoke. "All right, it is time for the sticks," he said.

Little Chief brought out the buckskin medicine quiver which held the voting sticks. Each man took one of the shafts of polished cedar. If he meant to go with Little Wolf upon the uncertain trail which led away west to freedom, or to death, he would thrust his stick into the ground in front of the war chief. If he meant to stay with Dull Knife, following the safe trail of surrender and good faith, he would place the stick upon the ground in front of Dull Knife. The vote began.

Nothing further of bitterness or anger now showed in Little Wolf's face. But when the last stick had been voted, not one shaft stood upright in the ground before the war chief. In the pause that followed, and before the war chief might rise and depart, a last voter who had not been invited and who held no rank in the council stepped out of the darkness beyond the fire.

He was a very small warrior and a very angry one. He took from his own ragged hunting quiver a single sorry-feathered shaft and stalked over to stand in front of Little Wolf. *"Enitoeme!"* cried Red Bird. "I honor the war chief!" And, with the cry, he plunged his arrow into the ground before Little Wolf and stood back glaring at the astounded subchiefs.

"Cowards," he said to them.

Red Bird lay awake in the gloom of his mother's lodge. He stared across the darkened space, not seeing the blanketed forms of his mother and two smaller sisters. He was still seeing the look which had come over Dull Knife's face when he, Red Bird, had broken into the council to plunge his arrow in front of the war chief. Dull Knife had said nothing to him, nor had Little Wolf. The other chiefs had risen and walked away, all of them in silence. Then Dull Knife and Little Wolf had followed them, leaving Red Bird alone by the council fire with his great fears of the punishment which must come to a small boy for such a transgression of tribal custom. The worst of it was that Little Wolf had left his arrow in the ground. He had not pulled it up and taken it with him. Red Bird had dared the love of his grandfather and the anger of the other chiefs to plant that arrow saying he would follow his fierce uncle. And Little Wolf had refused his voting stick.

The Cheyenne boy was still awake when the frost-pink autumn sun rolled up from beyond the sand hills of Nebraska. He started nervously when he thought he heard outside the lodge the fall of a moccasin. Then he felt his belly pull in tightly and draw up like green rawhide when the entrance flaps parted and Dull Knife peered into the lodge's darkness.

"I am here, Grandfather," the youth managed bravely. "I have been waiting for you."

"Shhh!" cautioned the old chief. "Come on out to the fire, boy. Quickly now, before the squaws commence to stir."

Red Bird tiptoed past his mother and sleeping sisters. He shivered when he reached the outside. Dull Knife had melted some creek ice in a small pot and steeped some shags of willow bark in it. He offered the boy a buffalo-horn cupful of the acrid tea. Red Bird took it, drinking gratefully. It warmed and filled his pinched belly, bitter as it was.

"Haho, thank you," he said, bowing. "I am ready now, Grandfather."

"Listen, boy," said the old man. "Behind my lodge you will find two good ponies tethered, the black mare and the roan gelding. Take your pick of them and ride for Fort Robinson. I want you to tell Three Stars we are here and ready to surrender. Last night after the sticks were voted in the council many of the young men, not liking that the vote went against Little Wolf, vowed they would follow the war chief. I want the soldiers to meet the rest of us as quickly as they can, before more of our people waver. Your uncle will lead his followers into the mountains west of here. They will try to get all the way home. I think they are wrong, and I don't want any more of my people going with them. Hurry now. Do as I say."

Red Bird gulped hard but shook his head. "Grandfather," he replied, "I cannot do it. When I put my arrow into the ground before my uncle, I knew what I did."

Dull Knife watched him a moment, then nodded. He reached forth a gnarled hand and patted the boy's thin arm. He was smiling, even if in a saddened way.

"What else would I expect from my own grandson," he said with great pride. "Of course you will go with your uncle."

For a moment Red Bird could not reply. His throat hurt and it would not work so that the words of gratitude came out of it as they should. But at last he had them framed.

"Grandfather," he said, "there is just one question on the parting. If my uncle did not doubt my heart, why did he leave my arrow in the ground? Why did he not take it up and bear it away with him to show he had accepted me?"

Before the old chief might answer, the war chief spoke for himself. He had come up through the shadows while they talked, hearing all they said. Now he confronted Red Bird.

"When we have gone away from here," he said, "and when these fires have grown grass over them and this camp is forgotten, your small arrow will still be in that ground. I have ordered it. It will remind our people that one boy among them had more courage than many warriors."

Red Bird's pulses pounded so heavily it seemed they must break through his veins. The pride of it was more than an Indian boy might bear with composure. He could not speak. He could not act. He could only stand and wonder and stare with unbelieving eyes at the war chief of all the Cheyenne.

Little Wolf had donned his full regalia. He had on his best hunting shirt, beaded and quilled in a blaze of color and strung with dyed horsehair and ermine tails from shoulder to wrist. His long hair was meticulously braided, its single glossy coil hanging across his right shoulder after the fashion of the fabled Masihkota Band. He wore his trademark head circlet of black otter fur. The burnished silver cross which was his dreaded battle charm glowed resplendently upon his wide chest. With his skully face, narrow eyes, broken nose, knife-scarred mouth and skin dark as smoked leather, he towered in the breathless eye of Red Bird's imagination like some great giant against the angered red of the morning sky. Motionlessly the boy awaited the war chief's will. What happened then is still repeated with tribal pride upon the Montana and Wyoming reservations.

Little Wolf, facing Red Bird, brought forth from its elk-hide scabbard his noted, and notorious, engraved Winchester. "We may not meet again, Nephew," he told the boy. "Your way lies with your grandfather, not with your uncle. Dull Knife is old and needs you at his side. One day young blood will be wanted for a new leader. You will be ready when that time comes. You will go with your grandfather and listen to his council. He is wise and full of love. I live only to fight and to be free. War is my way. My life has taught me that peace and freedom cannot thrive as brothers. But Dull Knife believes otherwise. The people, most of them, want to believe with him. But they are old. Their time has gone by and they have learned nothing. The children, though, will know another day; they may learn the secret. Go with your grandfather and see if he can teach it to you. I cannot."

He turned to Dull Knife. "Peace, old brother," he said. "Maheo ride with you."

Red Bird thought that was the end of it, but it was not. Little Wolf returned to him again for the final time. The look on the great warrior's face was saying good-bye. "And you, little Red Bird," he nodded. "You put your arrow at my feet when you thought I sat alone. See now!" he concluded with sudden, savage pride, and holding forth the legendary Winchester. "Your uncle does as much for you; he returns your arrow!" With these words he placed the priceless rifle upon the ground at Red Bird's feet. Drawing himself erect, he touched his brow in the Cheyenne sign of deepest respect toward the small grandson of Dull Knife. *"Enitoeme,"* was all he said, then turned and was gone into the gray mists of the morning.

He did not look back. When he had passed from sight into the swirling ground fogs of the new day, Red Bird saw him no more. For the boy, as for history and the 148 of his tribesmen who would follow Dull Knife along the white man's road to peace and brotherhood, it was the same. The fierce and fearless Little Wolf had said his requiem farewell. His time, too, was gone by. He was the last war chief of his people.

In the ending, as in the beginning, he took his way as only his wild heart could lead him—*to freedom or to death.*

Maheo's Children

Barracks at Fort Robinson, Nebraska, measured 18 × 36 feet. It had been designed to house twenty-four troopers. There was a double tier of plank bunks along either wall. In the aisle between tiers was scant room for a Sibley heating stove—which had been torn out—and two dozen foot lockers. Into this foul-aired prison, at the end of their heroic flight from Fort Reno, Oklahoma, were now herded the 151 surviving men, women and children of Dull Knife's northern Cheyenne.

The stoic captives made the best of their failure to reach the green pines and cold, clear air of Wyoming. Fort Robinson was better than Fort Reno. It was better even if the temporary post commander, Major "White Hair" Weston, had locked them up when he had promised they might remain free. It was better even if Major Weston now said they might have to return to Oklahoma, when before he had told them they could stay in Nebraska. White Hair was still their friend. They had to trust him. All the other soldiers and officers hated them and were afraid of them. Especially Captain "Black Hair" Jackson, who was commanding the soldiers now hammering the boards across the small windows of B Barracks, shutting out the fresh air and the sunshine. That was a bad thing. He went to one of the windows and peered out between the rapidly closing "bars" of rough boarding.

"Why are you doing this to my people?" he called out. "We had the word of Major Weston that we could stay here as free men. Now we are put in a prison like dogs and wild animals."

Captain Jackson, accompanied by the post interpreter, Alec Raynald, went up to the window. "You gave Major Weston your word that the Cheyenne would not try to escape, and you lied," the officer said. "Bull Hump ran away and you kept quiet about it."

"That was only one man. He was afraid, wild, headstrong. I could not control him. Where is Major Weston? Let me talk to him."

Alec Raynald, who had married a Cheyenne woman and who was trusted by Dull Knife's people, made the sign of apology. "Let me tell you how it is," he said. "Major Weston has ordered that you will have no food and no water until you are able to control your men, until you can promise no more trouble. You have yourselves to blame for this, old chief."

"What does he want us to do?"

"You must give him a paper signed by your council of elders. The paper will say that you promised no more escapes, and that the tribe will begin to get ready to go back to Oklahoma in peace. Do this and food and freedom will be yours again."

"That is all?"

"No, it is not. You and your nine headmen will be held as hostages until the march is under way. If any warrior, or even any woman, attempts to escape, one of the hostages will be shot. And one of the hostages will continue to be shot for each Cheyenne who tries to flee on the way back to Oklahoma."

The Cheyenne leader received the news in echoing silence.

"I am sorry, my father," Raynald called nervously to him. "You and I may know it is not your fault, but the soldier chiefs don't see things as we do. Please accept the order, I beg of you. Think of your women and children."

"I am thinking of them," answered Dull Knife after a long, long wait. "But if this ground is made red again, we cannot help it. We gave up our guns and shook hands with Major Weston. He told us we could stay here. Now he says we must go back to the hot place. We won't ever do that. White Hair lied to us."

"No," said Raynald vigorously, "he did not! Your memory fails you in your anger and sorrow. He told you from the first that he would *try* to let you stay here. He warned you he might not succeed with the higher soldier chiefs. You know that."

The silver-haired Cheyenne shook his head. "He said he hoped we could stay at Fort Robinson. He said he would try his best to see that we stayed here. Then he said he was pretty sure we could stay, and all the time I kept warning him that if we could not stay, we would die."

"That is a true thing," admitted Raynald. "But it is also true what I say when I remind you of his warnings."

"I do not say you lie, friend Raynald." The old chief's wrinkled hand swept around the circle of his people who had gathered behind him at the window. "For ourselves, we warriors, we men, do not care. Cold and hunger are no strange food to us. But here are also women and little ones. Here are five babies yet on their mother's milk. Here are four squaws heavy with young. Red Bird's mother is one of them; she will bear her child before another sun. What will the babies drink when the dugs of their mothers run dry? How will we wash Red Bird's little brother or sister when it comes? Where are Major Weston's answers to these questions?"

Raynald could not reply, and shook his head. Dull Knife watched him through the cracks between the window boards. His fine old eyes were unblinking. It seemed to the interpreter that the Cheyenne chief stared at him five minutes.

"All right, Raynald," he said finally, nodding. "I know Major Weston's heart is good for my people. I know that he can truly do no more for us. But Maheo, my God, will not let me believe it, and I cannot lie to my people any longer."

"You mean you will tell your people to go back peacefully?"

"Ah, no," said the old chief softly, "I did not say that. You tell Major Weston that we are here on our own lands now. We will never go back to the south. Tell him he may kill me, and starve our women, and freeze our little children, but he cannot make us go back to that terrible place."

"Think now," said Raynald. "That is all? The end of it?"

Dull Knife nodded. He raised his right hand, chopping it downward in the Cheyenne sign indicating that talk was cut off.

"Yes, Raynald," he said. "That is all."

The next moment only the boarded-up ugliness of the barracks window looked back at Alec Raynald. The Cheyenne had turned their backs on him, and on Major Weston's words.

The very old squaws, the smaller children and pregnant women were given the soldier bunks. The others stood or crouched or lay curled in shivering misery on the remaining bare wood of the floor. Such primitive sanitation as was possible they practiced. Where the stove had stood, the floor had been cut away to provide bottom draft. This place was used as a rude toilet. By severe Indian discipline the smallest walking child was made to relieve itself here. Yet even before the first day was gone, the accumulated odor made even warriors grow faint. Some of the older persons, or the ill, vomited from the stench.

The cold, for the babies and old ones crowded in the bunks, or for the women and walking children packed in the center aisle, was barely endurable. The men and half-grown boys, hunched to the outer walls beneath the paneless windows, were helpless. They awoke with hoar frost furring their nostrils and with the thick spittle frozen upon their lips where they had licked them to moisten the cracking dryness of thirst in fitful sleep.

At first the pangs of advancing starvation were fed with Dull Knife's assurances that, with the squaws and young ones involved, White Hair Weston would surely relent. The suffering for water, less easily assuaged, became acute as early as noontime of that first day. Still, the bewildered Cheyenne band could not bring itself to understand that its good friend, White Hair, meant to deprive the people of water. Food, yes. But not water. Not to little children and to women big with child.

Dull Knife and his nine headmen peered from the boarded windows as the first sun waned. They saw the chains and the padlock still on the door where Black Hair

Jackson had put them. They saw the armed troopers, stationed at forty-feet intervals around the entire building. They met the watchful, unfriendly stares of the soldiers. Those soldiers were angry with the Cheyenne. It was very cold to be standing guard. But for Dull Knife and his headstrong people, those soldiers could have been inside a warm barracks toasting by a Sibley stove. Now they saw the Indians peering forth at them, and they cursed the redmen and told them to get back from the windows, and to stay back from them. With nightfall the band began to wonder about Dull Knife's faith in Major Weston. A little powder snow fell and was scraped from the window sills by the women for rationing among the children and babies. The men began to mutter.

With the second dawn all the snow was used, the last of it going to mothers with nursing babies. Still there was no word from Major Weston. The muttering of the men became an ugly, dry-throated growling. Death could be accepted in better ways than dying in a trap. They had weapons. Had Dull Knife forgotten that five complete Winchester rifles and eleven good Colts revolvers had been smuggled into B Barracks under the clothing of the squaws and hidden in the cradleboards of the papooses, each part of each weapon separated from its brother part and carried on another person? Did Dull Knife also fail to remember that much ammunition for those sixteen guns had been brought into the prison room in the same secret way, right past the soldier guards of Captain Black Hair Jackson? The old chief had better begin to think harder about his good friend, Major White Hair Weston—harder, and much faster!

That eighth of January, 1879, crept by, hour after suffering hour. At last the smallest child ceased its weeping, its tiny body dehydrated of tears even, its infant mind dulled beyond the power to answer the stimuli of its spasming belly. And still Major Weston did not come. But then, just at sunset, Captain Jackson appeared outside the front windows. The officer was alone, a bad sign. He called aloud for Dull Knife to come to the window. He spoke in English, another bad sign, for Black Hair Jackson had some fair command of the difficult Cheyenne tongue. So when the old chief came forward in response

to the order, his tribesmen clustered behind him, uneasy
in their hearts.

"Well," said Jackson unfeelingly, "have you and your
mule-headed people had enough? Are the women good
and hungry? The babies drying out? Wouldn't you all like
a good drink of water? Some hot food?"

"What do you really mean?" asked Dull Knife.

"You know, you damned old rascal. Are you ready to
sign Major Weston's infernal pledge, and come on out of
there?"

Dull Knife shook his head.

"Where is White Hair? I won't talk to you. I won't
make any pledge to you. Where is Major Weston? Is he
afraid to come and see what he has done to his Indian
friends?"

Jackson knew very well where Weston was. He was over
in the officers' mess drinking black coffee and fighting his
desire to plead with the Cheyenne. He *couldn't* say what
needed saying, do what needed doing, to these sneaking
red devils, so he'd had to let Jackson do it for him. But
the junior officer was not inclined to explain this very
human fact to the Cheyenne. The sooner they believed
Weston had tricked and deserted them, the better.

"You will talk to me, or to no one," he told Dull Knife.
"Major Weston has ordered me to deal with you. When
you're ready to talk, send the sergeant of the guard to
me, not Major Weston."

He did not wait for Dull Knife's reply but strode away.
The aging Cheyenne watched him go, his tired heart settling within him like a broken millstone into deep, dark
water. He turned slowly from the window. His leathered
features were composed, but as he raised his gnarled hands
toward his waiting followers they were trembling visibly
in the winter twilight.

"My children," he told them quietly, "we have but one
friend remaining—our lord Maheo. Let us talk with
him ..."

Throughout the endless cold of the third night the
Cheyenne chief crouched with Little Chief, his second-in-
command, in a far corner of the barracks. With them they
had the sacred bundle of the Cheyenne medicine arrows.
Until dawn they sat alone imploring Maheo to listen to his

red children and to answer them. But Maheo did not answer. The only reply was the whistle of the January wind keening along the ridgepole of the barracks; that and the crunching of the feet of the patrolling soldier guards, as they stomped back and forth in the hard-packed snow.

By late afternoon Dull Knife realized the end of resistance was very near. His people had been four days and nights without food and water. The old ones were now too weak to move from the bunks. The nursing mothers were forcing what little spittle of their own they might draw into the mouths of the babies so that their tiny tongues would not swell and protrude in dryness to strangle them. The older children lay motionless upon the floor, eyes dulled with thirst fever. The grown men and teen-age boys held loose bullets in their mouths, sucking them to induce a flow of saliva. When the old chief saw Tangled Hair, a proud warrior, drinking his own urine, he raised his face to Maheo and knew his God had forgotten him. He knew, as well, that the soldier chiefs had beaten him.

It was 5:00 P.M. and nearly dark when he went to the window and called out to the sergeant of the guard. This happened to be a six-foot, five-inch, part Cherokee Oklahoman named Jack Henry Lundy. He was a behemoth of a man with, as he himself put it, the "moral fortitude of a wet mouse." Neither was Sergeant Lundy a facile thinker. But he had an Indian's grace of spirit and could speak Cheyenne.

"Yes, Father," he answered Dull Knife's hail, "here I am."

"Big son," said the Cheyenne, "we are finished. Go and tell Black Hair Jackson that I will talk to him."

"I hear you, Father. I'll go right away."

"An old man thanks you," nodded Dull Knife wearily. "Tell Black Hair we are ready to send a man out to talk."

This time when he hurried up through the settling dusk, Jackson did not come alone. Behind him came a file of carbine-swinging troopers. These soldiers he ordered to flank the doorway, right and left, carbines on the cock.

"Lundy!" he snapped.

"Yes, sir?"

"Get on the door. I want just *one* Indian to come out

of it, you understand. The minute that one Indian is out, you get between him and the door—the closed door. The squad will fire point-blank if there is a break of any kind, even one other man or a woman or child sticking his nose out of that barracks."

"Yes, sir. All right, on the double, men. Move in here."

The squad drew in, tight. Their faces looked unnaturally white in the ghost light of the early winter darkness. They pushed their trapdoor Springfields forward at the ready.

"I'm opening the lock now, sir," said Lundy. "Shall I tell them to send out their man?"

"One man," repeated Jackson harshly.

"Father," called Lundy, "who will be coming out?"

"You will see him," answered Dull Knife. "Open the door."

The remark, in the context of the stillness which suddenly surrounded B Barracks, made the big sergeant uneasy. He glanced at Captain Jackson.

"Go on, go on; what's the matter with you?" the officer demanded. "Open the door."

Lundy unhasped the padlock and moved aside.

There was a stir of sound within the building. The door scraped open. A single Cheyenne stalked out. He tried to walk tall, to overcome by sheer will his physical weakness, but he was unsteady on his feet. Lundy sucked in his breath. Dull Knife had chosen his "peace talker" with dangerous abandon. Or had it been deliberate design? The man was Wild Hog, a notorious "white hater."

The brave tottered up to Captain Jackson. "I am ready," he said, snarlingly. "Take me to White Hair Weston."

Jackson recoiled as though the Indian had spat in his face. "All right, my friend," he seethed, "I *will* take you. Sergeant! Grab this insulting devil."

Lundy was a career N. C. O., with twenty years in service. His spirit might be with the Cheyenne, but his body and soul belonged to the United States Army. He grabbed, and quickly. Yet, swift as he was Wild Hog was swifter. The brave twisted away like some wild beast. He uttered a piercing cry and dashed back toward the barracks. A nervous member of the guard detail at the door hipped his carbine and fired at a range of five feet. Wild Hog stopped as though he had crashed into an invisible cliff. He seized his ruptured belly with both hands

and went loop-kneed down into the snow, making no
sound.

For the instant the barracks door stood unguarded. It
burst open without warning. Lone Crow, the life friend of
Wild Hog, ran out and toward his fallen comrade. Two
soldiers, one from each side of the doorway, leaped to cut
him off. Their driving bayonets speared Lone Crow in mid-
flight, pinning him like some gaunt red mouth, transfixed.
The force of the meeting blades lifted the Cheyenne warrior free of the ground, then dropped him bleeding and
crying aloud in the agony of his hurts, alongside his
stricken companion. The sight was too much for Left Hand,
Lone Crow's great friend. Indeed the valiant brave did not
seem to see the flashing bayonets of the soldiers. He
seemed to see only his friends hurt and helpless on the
bloody snow. He saw, too, the swinging, open, beckoning
doorway of B Barracks. With a coughing war cry, half
blind rage, half starving weakness, he charged the soldier
guard.

Sergeant Lundy, seeking to save his life, leaped forward
between the desperate brave and the guard detail. Barring his own Springfield, he tried to knock down Left
Hand and subdue him. But suddenly he knew that the
Cheyenne meant to kill him, was crazed beyond capture.
Acting in a purely defensive reflex to save his own life
now, he put all his great strength into the swinging arc of
his carbine's steel-shod butt. The weapon crushed into the
face bones of Left Hand, caving them into the yielding
skull behind them, the head splintering with the certain
sodden "give" which almost inevitably foretold death. Left
Hand slumped in his tracks, dropping as empty-eyed and
uncomplaining as a slaughterhouse beef.

Only a heartbeat had ensued since the harsh words of
Captain Jackson's order to seize Wild Hog. Yet history in
the hands of willful, angry men is never more than a heartbeat from blood on the snow. Captain J. T. Jackson was a
willful, angry man. For one sinister moment he held history in his hands, and the ground was made red at Fort
Robinson, Nebraska.

Weston was in the officers' mess with Surgeon Cummings and three company lieutenants, Benton, Thomas
and Stienberg, when the muffled reports of rifle shots put

a period to Cummings's description of gangrene surgery at Shiloh and Second Manassas.

"That was Springfield fire," said Benton.

"From over by B Barracks," guessed young Thomas.

"The Indians!" concluded Stienberg.

"Come on," ordered Weston, moving for the door. "Something has gone wrong over there."

He was met at the door by Captain Jackson, just arrived from the barracks. "Major Cummings," said the latter, seeming scarcely disturbed. "There are three pretty sick Indians on the snow over there. I suggest you may be useful."

Cummings left at once with the lieutenants, leaving Weston to face Jackson. "All right, Captain," he said, face drawn, "what have you done?"

"Not a great deal," answered the other. "Dull Knife sent word to me that he was ready to have a man come out and talk. The Indian they chose for this assignment got nervous looking at all that freedom and made a break for it. I had the men on order to fire instantly upon any such move. Trooper Taylor shot the emissary Indian. Two more then ran out of the barracks behind him. One was bayoneted, the other rifle-butted."

"Dear God," said Weston. "How badly are they hurt?"

Jackson actually laughed in answering the distraught query. "Well, the one with the cracked head is unconscious. Hard to tell about him. I'd say he was a goner. The bayoneted one will likely be all right. He got it through the fleshy chunks of the buttocks from both sides. I don't know about the one Taylor shot. He got it in a bad place, of course. However, he was still kicking and squalling when I left."

Something in the nearly cheerful way he finished up unleashed the rare bite of Weston's temper.

"You don't seem particularly affected, Jackson," he grated. "Do you enjoy shooting down unarmed hostages?"

With the odd quirk of honesty which was one of the purer metals in his flawed character, Jackson straightened. "You know better than that, sir," he said quietly. "There are 151 Cheyenne in that barracks building. They have been without food and water for four days and they have constantly warned us they will die before they will be taken back south."

"But, good lord, Jackson—"

"I'm sorry, Major. There are simply no buts about it. If you have to kill one or two of them to keep from killing all of them, it's a cheap price to pay for keeping your command neat and clean. Indeed, for *keeping* it in any condition." There was a veering return to the youth's callous disregard for the gentle Howell Weston. "I might remind you, Major," he concluded, "that you authorized me to take over these Indians, and that you might have quite some problem convincing a review board of your reasons for authorizing me. There is going to be trouble over this break, if any of those three Indians die. The sob sisters in the Bureau will see to that. Now I suggest, sir, that we work together in this thing."

Major Weston raised his head. His silver-gray hair was rumpled, his calm, sensitive face ashen with fatigue. "You mean, don't you, that I should sanction your brutality?"

"Call it whatever you choose," said the other, hard-eyed, "but sanction it. If you do not, I shall not sign the report on this matter nor take responsibility for it. It's still your command, Major, even though you've lent it to me in deference to your love for Dull Knife's people."

Weston dropped his gaze again. If not defeated, he at least had no real idea of victory. He *could* have no such idea. His moral inability to effect personally the starvation order with Dull Knife and the Cheyenne permitted no military defense.

"Well, Jackson," he said wearily, "perhaps we're getting ahead of ourselves. The three Indians may be all right."

"*Perhaps*," said Captain Jackson with deliberate cruelty.

The stillness was still holding between the two men when the door scraped open once more and Surgeon Ralph Cummings put his head in scowlingly. "Just dropped by to give you the bad news," he said. "They'll live."

"Thank God," breathed Weston. "How seriously are they injured, Ralph?"

The post surgeon waved a hand disgustedly. "The one that got it in the stomach should be dead of shock right now and would be if he were a white man. But the bullet was too high to smash the pelvic girdle, too low to strike the kidneys. I don't think it did a damned thing save pass through him. He's already stopped bleeding. The one Lundy hit in the head with the rifle butt is coming around. The one that got bayoneted is already on his feet —walked over to the infirmary unaided. They're brute animals. Some of our boys who saw the holes in them are a site sicker than the Indians!"

He slammed the door and they could hear his footsteps crunching off in the snow. Weston looked at Jackson and quietly put the remaining problem. "That's that then, Jackson. Where do we go from here?"

"Nowhere," rapped the other. "If you want my opinion, sir, we're out of the woods. I will guarantee you not another damned Cheyenne will put his nose out that B Barracks door—not ever!"

Major Weston thought uneasily of some of his junior's previous rash opinions and "guarantees" concerning these same Cheyenne—the no food or water had been Jackson's idea—the taking of Dull Knife and the nine headmen as march hostages was another of his "realistic disciplines" —and with the thought the senior officer knew a moment's surge of conscience and courage. He *knew* Jackson was wrong. He *knew* that even now, he, Howell Weston, ought to take back his abdicated command and put the fiery captain on report for his mishandling of the Cheyenne spokesman just now. But he also knew that report would have to include his own complicity—and somehow he could not face that.

To acting Major Howell K. Weston, what happened to him in the Fort Robinson command had to be the last mile on his military road. Knowing all of this, the grayhaired C.O. tried one more hopeful grasp upon his slipping control of the situation. He made himself believe that Captain John Tenney Jackson had learned a great deal about Indians through his own patience with them. He forced himself to think that as of that present January 9, 1879, Jackson *had* to understand the Cheyenne and *must know* what he was talking about when he claimed to have them rigidly in hand. He, Weston, could even be grateful, he told himself, that Jackson was there with that iron hand. And, moreover, in view of that iron hand, any reasonable officer must accept as simple military reality Captain Jackson's harsh assurance that not another Cheyenne would dare try B Barracks' padlocked door.

Not another Cheyenne ever did come out of B Barracks by way of its padlocked door, and Captain Jackson's guarantee was never violated. But that guarantee covered only the door. It said nothing about the windows.

The wind died with the sun that night. The moon came very early. By its wan light the Cheyenne made ready. While the blood of Lone Crow, Wild Hog and Left Hand was still warm upon the snow, the council of elders gathered for the last time about Dull Knife. In the time that it took Little Chief to make the four sacred signs, the vote had gone around the circle. It went for war.

"We must all die now," Dull Knife told his people. "But we shall not die shut up in this soldier prison like dogs. We shall die in the open, fighting."

It was Wild Hog's gaunt woman who answered for all the others. *"We shall die like Cheyenne,"* she said.

A muscular brave named Shield was appointed war leader. He had been a scout for Three Stars Crook in the wars of '76 and '77 against the Sioux. He knew the confines of Fort Robinson. Beyond the fort—once safely beyond it—he could remember the distances and directions of every march toward their Wyoming homeland. All listened with brooding intentness to his words.

"Beyond this prison of ours is the river. When we have crossed it, we will make for the bluffs which lie beyond it. But on this side of the river, there is that bridge by the sawmill. Am I right?"

The braves nodded quickly and he went on. "We will make for that bridge. The water is running too strong and our old ones and women and young ones cannot risk the thin ice. They must go by the bridge, and we must guard them as they do. I want the five best men to shoot our five rifles there."

This time the nods of his listeners were not so swift. The price those "five best men" would pay at the bridge would be their lives. But the hesitation had a hard Indian reason far divorced from any fear of dying. To lose one's life that a comrade might escape was highest Cheyenne honor. But the five rifles were worth fifty fine warriors, and who was chosen to fire them became a matter of life and death for 151 fellows, not just of death for five men.

Little Chief stepped forward in the silence. He laid

upon the bare floor the five reassembled rifles. Pausing a moment, he reached down and picked up one of them. "Naturally I shall take the first gun," he said.

Hunts Alone, a morose, unpopular man, picked up the second rifle. He scowled defiantly at his watchful comrades. "Wild Hog was kind to me once," he said. "I never repaid him."

"I am a lonely bachelor and have no one who cares what I do," announced Noisy Walking and took up the third weapon.

"Well, I have a woman," admitted Big Beaver reluctantly, "but she talks too much and I would rather have a good gun."

When he had made his selection of the two remaining rifles, Yellow Hawk, the great shot, grinned disdainfully. "You have left the best one, emptyhead," he gibed. "I claim it."

There was no more talk after that. The eleven revolvers and ammunition for all guns were rationed out swiftly to the acknowledged best marksmen of the band. The warriors opened their medicine bags and began to paint their faces, using the black charcoal death color heavily. The women piled all of the march equipment—what little there was of broken knife, dented pan, ragged cover—under the escape windows. The men tied spare army blankets about their bodies, but left their hands free to fight. Shield put two of his riflemen on the right-hand window, two on the left. The time was then.

"Are you ready?" he whispered to the left-hand pair.

"The moon is good now," grunted Hunts Alone. "I can see the guards clearly through these cracks."

"He speaks for me," agreed Noisy Walking. "A blind squaw could hit a weanling chipmunk from this distance."

"Are you also ready here?" asked Shield, gliding to the right-hand window.

"My guard is already dead," answered Yellow Hawk, his famed eyes narrowed along his rifle barrel, where it followed the tramping of the nearest sentry. "Say the word, Shield."

"Big Beaver? How about you?"

"Well now, Brother, I don't know that my guard is *already* dead, but I think he won't feel too well in a minute. I can hit a crippled bull stuck in the mud from close range. I recall one time we were up on the Mussel-shell River stealing horses from the Absarokas. I shot five of the enemy that night. Of course one proved to be a squaw, but the light wasn't as good as it is here tonight. Besides, she was big enough to—"

"Shut up, you fool!" ordered Shield. "I didn't ask you for the history of your great shooting eye!"

"He lies anyway," put in Yellow Hawk. "I was on that trip. He only shot three, and *two* of them were squaws."

"I am ready, Shield," said Big Beaver. "You had better say the signal word before I shoot somebody *inside* this building."

At this dissension the old chief, Dull Knife, stepped forward with raised arms.

"My people," he said, "pray with me now. We are going in a moment. It is time to say good-bye. Listen to us, Maheo . . ."

Outside B Barracks two of the patrolling sentries came to a startled halt as their paths met and as the eerie chant of the Cheyenne death song stole across the winter still-ness.

"Mother of Mary!" said the first soldier, the short hairs on his nape rising instinctively. "What in the name of heaven are they doing in there? Holding a red Injun wake, or what?"

The second trooper shivered. He had been with Mac-kenzie when the latter had trapped and burned Dull Knife's village on the Red Fork of Powder River in '76. He had heard this sound before, and he was not shivering now because the mercury stood at 14° below zero on the post thermometer.

"No, my God," he whispered to his companion, "they're saying good-bye to one another. They're getting ready to die." Private Paddy O'Shea was correct. But the Chey-enne death song was meant for white men as well as for red.

An Indian rifle shot ruptured the stillness, ending Dull Knife's prayer. The bullet struck Paddy O'Shea in the head, killing him instantly. His fellow sentry died with more sound because he was hit through the body and had time to cry out. As he did so, four more troopers

were shot down and the front of the barracks was free
of soldier guards. At once the Cheyenne was pouring
through the splintered boards of the windows and racing
for the river.

Shield died first among them. He went down in a burst
of soldier fire from the astonished guards at the rear of
the barracks. Red Bird, the twelve-year-old running in
the Indian pack behind Shield, seized up the fallen warrior's Winchester. A lunging soldier attempted to wrest it
away from the boy and Red Bird shot him in the face.
Another soldier leaped at the youth, trying to bayonet
him. Instead, his blade went home in a fellow trooper
closing in at the precise moment, and the Cheyenne boy
ran free with the priceless Winchester toward the sawmill
bridge.

Covering the youth's escape, Big Beaver and Yellow
Hawk killed two of the remaining three guards and
wounded the third. In that same incredibly fast-moving
blink of time Sergeant Jack Henry Lundy, who had
been screened by the barracks, came racing up. Turning
to follow the women and children toward the bridge,
Yellow Hawk yet had the quickness to snap a shot from
the hip at the towering soldier. It took Lundy in the fleshy
part of the shoulder, spun him twice around and knocked
him flat. He came to his knees spitting snow, frozen dirt
and parts of front teeth, his Cherokee blood mixed in
freely and on the boil.

"All right, you Cheyenne sons of she-dogs!" he bellowed
into the night. "You just shot the wrong sergeant!"

As officer of the guard, he was wearing an army Colt
sidearm. He had never fired the revolver, being a rifle-
man by service and hill-country tradition. But seeing the
Cheyenne who had shot him making his escape toward
the sawmill bridge, Lundy decided he would learn the
Colt in a hurry. Leaping up, he heard the calling of
the confused troopers now stumbling out of the other
barracks. "This way, boys!" he roared. "Follow me! They're
hitting for the sawmill bridge!"

Next moment the fire from the Indian rearguard at
bridgehead forced him to dive for cover into a clump of
cottonwood. Here he was promptly joined by his barracks
mate, Sergeant Sam Meeker, and six veteran G Troop

privates, first reinforcements to reach the immediate area.

"Sam," said Lundy, "there's four, five of those red devils got Winchesters. One of them winged me. He'd be in the bunch holding us pinned down while his people get over the bridge."

"This ain't hardly news," replied Meeker, a good-natured Tennessee sharpshooter. "Try again."

"I'm going after the one that hit me," said Lundy calmly. "It ain't an order, but if you or any of the boys would care to accompany me, it would warm my old heart considerable."

"You're accompanied," drawled Meeker. "Get going."

Lundy darted out of the cottonwood cover, Meeker and two of the troopers following him. Where they broke into the open moonlight, they were less than fifteen yards from bridgehead. Yellow Hawk shot both of the soldiers with the two sergeants before Lundy fired the Colt into his face from arm's length. Meeker, one jump behind, shot Hunts Alone through the lungs and bayoneted Big Beaver as the slow-witted brave was levering his gun. Hunts Alone fell into the water and was momentarily lost. But his bumbling companion tumbled off the bridge ramp onto the jagged shore ice. Meeker shot him in the back of the head as he tried to regain his feet.

Noisy Walking, the last of the suicide warriors, threw his empty Winchester aside. Drawing his knife, he charged Sergeant Lundy. The big soldier did not have time to sidestep. He turned his rear toward the Indian, putting his hip into the arc of the striking blade. The weapon ground into the heavy muscles of his buttock. Reversing his body with a curse of pain, Lundy barred his arm across Noisy Walking's throat, brought the helpless brave close into his own body, and shot him twice in the spine with the Colt revolver. Throwing the lifeless Cheyenne from him, he heard Meeker calling from beneath the bridge ramp.

"Hey, down here, Jack Henry! I got me a crawler. Toss me your popgun."

Glancing over ramp's edge, Lundy saw Hunts Alone crawling from the water onto the shore ice. The mortally wounded Indian was whimpering like a hurt dog. He commenced dragging himself in a blind circle on the ice, coughing and strangling on the blood welling from his ruptured lungs. Lundy tossed the Colt down to Meeker, who killed Hunts Alone as unemotionally as he would have destroyed a cavalry horse injured past service.

He started to rejoin Lundy on the bridge, but the latter suddenly muttered, "Stay down, stay down!" and leaped over the ramp to join him. "Hole up, Sam," he whispered, shoving his comrade in under the bridge. "The red sons are coming back for those rifles!"

Overhead a party of a dozen Cheyenne thudded up and began frantically searching for the fallen Winchesters of the suicide guard. Miraculously all four weapons had landed on the bridge and were swiftly recovered. The Indians departed as desperately in haste as they had returned. Beneath the ramp of the sawmill bridge the two sergeants exhaled gratefully.

"No use being a pig about it, Jack Henry," said Meeker. "There'll be plenty of Indians to go around even after General John Tenney 'Custer' gets here with the 'regulars.' You and me might as well relax meanwhile."

"That shines, Sam," nodded Lundy soberly. "Besides, I ain't got no real belly for what's coming to them poor devils when Jackson gets up here." He pointed up the river where the voices of those Cheyenne cut off from the bridge could be heard calling one another in the moonlight and shadow of the winter night. "I reckon you and me can believe we was caught in a corner and had no actual choice. It ain't going to be like that up yonder."

"It ain't," agreed Meeker. "Not with Jackson in the saddle."

Lundy nodded and pulled out his tobacco pouch. The two old soldiers loaded their pipes. They smoked in short drags, exhaling thinly so that the blue fragrance of the Burley would not rise to expose their position. And in the time required for their pipes to burn down to the heelcakes and commence rattling spittle, they saw and heard the full gamut of that action for which Sergeant Lundy had no real belly.

Up and downstream from the bridge the cries and struggles of the Cheyenne continued. Perhaps half of them had escaped across the bridge. But the remainder, in particular the old men and squaws and some small children lost in the darkness from their parents, had missed the bridge trail and tried to cross on the rotten ice. Many of these broke through and drowned. A few got on over the stream. The less resolute of these stragglers, yielding to the terrible thirst of four days, threw themselves down at water's edge to fill their shrunken bellies with the icy black water. These it was who paid the real price of freedom for the others. Jackson's soldiers, coming up to the river in force now, defiled above and below the bridge. On order, and with murderous timed-fire cadence, their rifles barked and snarled. For ten minutes while Meeker and Lundy stayed huddled beneath the bridge ramp, Jackson raged up and down the soldier line directing the slaughter of the Cheyenne trapped on the fort's side of the river by their eagerness to drink. Only when the last target ceased to move, the last Indian voice to cry out in agony, did the black-haired officer order the rifles stilled.

The stillness was terrible. In all of it was no Indian sound. Lundy and Meeker knocked the dottle from their pipes and climbed back up onto the bridge ramp. Neither said anything or needed to. Both had been in this silence before. They knew what it meant. The only Cheyenne remaining in range of Jackson's Springfields on the banks of the White River at Fort Robinson, Nebraska, were those Cheyenne never again to know thirst or hunger or hopeless crying in the night for Maheo to protect them.

Jackson's re-formed troops double-timed over the sawmill bridge. Weston was up with them now. Out in front moved Alec Raynald and three Sioux trackers. But the trackers were not needed. Four inches of fresh powder snow lay on the ground. The wind was dead. The temperature was fifteen or twenty below. In the day-bright glare of the moon, the Cheyenne trackline could be read with merciless clarity by all.

Beyond the bridge, heading for the bluff to the west, the warriors had whipped the tribe into a cohesive unit, making the track still easier to follow. The soldiers picked up speed, virtually trotting now where they had been shuffling before.

"If I know them," panted Jackson to Weston, "they will hole up in the bluffs. That's why I decided to push them on foot. Had we waited to mount up, they would have been half way to Wyoming by now. As it is, we'll have them back in that barracks by midnight, by God!"

"Yes, yes." Weston nodded. "You were right."

He said no more. Howell Weston was not an Indian fighter. Before inheriting the temporary command at Fort Robinson, he had been a staff officer with no field experience whatever. All he knew of the savage Cheyenne was that they preferred their dogs boiled, took a little coffee with their sugar, were unduly kind to all children and made beautiful bearskin coats, one of which they had given him in token of gratitude for his receiving them with honor and dignity at Fort Robinson.

He sighed deeply for breath, struggling now to keep pace with the much younger Jackson. Well, there was nothing for it but to struggle now, he thought. He had covertly turned over his command to the younger man when he saw he himself did not possess the combat officer's "iron" with which to deal on Indian terms with Dull Knife and his displaced people. There was no point, and no possibility, in reconsidering the decision then. Rather, and far rather, it was a time to listen to his rough-minded junior and perhaps thus to learn a little yet about handling hostile red men.

Howell Weston did in fact learn a little something along these lines within the following thirty minutes. When the fight at the bluff was all over, he had to admit that Captain Jackson had been at least partly right. The troops, if not the Indians, were back in their barracks by midnight. But they were back without any live Cheyenne prisoners, and with the freezing bodies of their own dead and wounded jolting in the beds of the hastily brought up field ambulances.

At the bluffs the Cheyenne turned and fought like tigers. They gave the troopers nothing to fire at save the muzzle flashes of their guns, and these were never in the same spot twice. It was a ghost fight for the Robinson command, made up largely of new recruits from Fort Lincoln. And when, within the first twenty minutes, they had taken their eighth casualty without hearing a single Indian scream in signal of a return hit, they lost their existing small stomach for trading shots with phantom foes who gave no sign of being flesh and blood.

At the same time Captain Jackson understood he had

blundered badly. Being generally a good soldier, however, and always a smart one, he also understood how to correct such blunders. In giving the order for the retreat to post, he took gracious care to pass the honor to his superior, letting Major Weston issue the shameful words and inherit the entire onus for them.

Captain Jackson was not only fighting Indians; he was campaigning for the command at Fort Robinson. He had a concrete belief that the two matters were inextricably involved. He must beat the Cheyenne and Weston with them. It was no way to commence such a maneuver by having his own name associated with a battle report which must contain a killed-in-action listing of at least ten men, with an as yet uncounted number of wounded.

As for Weston, he only sighed again and gave the order to fall back, still wanting to believe in J. T. Jackson.

In the bone-cold dawn, the long column of cavalry, infantry and artillery snaked across the sawmill bridge, around the northerly base of the White River bluffs, and angled out into the open plains toward distant, legendary Powder River.

The trail, if anything, was more clearly marked than it had been the night before. The black spoor of death lay along it now. By four o'clock that afternoon of January 10, the troop column was sixteen miles west of Fort Robinson, and Major Weston had counted the huddled bodies of fifteen Cheyenne since crossing the White at daybreak. These dead, upon examination, had proved unwounded. They had simply dropped out of the Indian line of march and frozen where they fell. For Sergeant Jack Henry Lundy, riding with his C.O. at column's head, these snowdrifted bodies marked far more than miles of trail. The fact that the fleeing Cheyenne had made no effort to carry away, or even to cover their pitiful dead, provided the Indian-wise Oklahoman with a chill not born of the January air.

"Best hold up here a minute, Major," he said quietly.

Weston waved the halt, not even questioning Lundy's comment. These two were not new to one another, having served the Union in the same regiment. There was between them an unspoken well of memories, if not affection or respect. And Weston knew of Lundy's "nose" for Indians.

"What is it, Jack?" was all he said.

Lundy pointed ahead. "See that limestone rise yonder? The one with the scrub timber crowning it? You'll find moccasin tracks going up this side of it but none coming down the other."

"You think they're laying for us on top of the rise?"

"They got to be, Major. Best set up your howitzers and dust them out of there. You got an hour of good firing light yet."

Again Weston nodded acceptance, seemingly without thought.

"All right; relay it to Jackson as an order."

"Should be a short relay," said Lundy grinning. "Yonder comes General Custer on the high lope," he added sarcastically.

Jackson slid his horse to a stop beside them a moment later.

"What's the matter, here, Lundy?" Incredibly his demand went to the sergeant, rather than the C.O. "Can't you follow the trail? A blind squaw could see it!"

"Yeah," said Lundy, shifting his quid of Burley and spitting a stream of amber into the snow in front of Jackson's mount. "But I ain't been mistook for a squaw lately, and I sure ain't lost my eyesight either—*sir*."

"You insolent devil!" shouted the enraged officer. "You're talking to *me!*" He said it to Lundy, meant it for Weston. "I won't have your damned insubordination, do you hear?"

"Lundy thinks the Cheyenne are dug in on top of that rise," interrupted Weston patiently. "Will you please go on up there, Captain, and give it a pounding with your howitzers while the light is still good?"

"*Lundy* thinks?" Jackson turned from white to red. "Sir, I've been studying that rise, too, and I—"

"Captain Jackson," said Weston, "you will please relay the order to the artillery, sir. Quickly."

Jackson fought for control, barely managing to achieve it.

"Yes, sir," he said. Then, wheeling his mount to face Lundy, handsome features contorted, "I beg your pardon, *Colonel* Lundy, sir; it won't happen again—*I promise you!*"

Watching him gallop off, Weston shook his head slowly. "What a pity. He's far and away a better officer than I am. I only wish he weren't so impetuous—so cocksure."

They rode forward in silence, seeking the best position for the howitzer battery. Lundy did not reply to his C.O.'s statement for perhaps a full minute. When he did speak, his words, for all their softness, carried a world of power for Weston.

"Major, sir," he said, "Captain Jackson ain't half the officer you are. He ain't a tenth. He ain't nothing . . ."

The howitzers were brought up. For forty-five minutes and until darkness blotted out the target, they pounded the top of the elevation. Upward of a hundred rounds of six-pound grapeshot were dumped onto the hilltop before the light went and Weston ordered the battery silenced. It did not seem possible that a living thing could have survived the efficient way in which Captain Martin Hayes walked his barrage up and over the hill and back across it, yard by rock-shattering yard. Yet, when the throats of his howitzers were swabbed out and Lundy led a volunteer patrol up the shell-pocked face of the rise, the five Cheyenne rifles stabbed instantly downward.

One trooper and his horse were killed, two other troopers seriously wounded.

"That's enough," said Weston quietly to the reporting Lundy. "We won't take any more casualties like that."

"What do you mean, 'like that,' Major?"

"From here on, Lundy, we'll trail them until they surrender. We will keep them under pressure by artillery fire when we must, and that is all. They cannot escape us and I will not accept further casualties merely to hasten their understanding of this."

The huge sergeant reached impulsively through the darkness to take his arm.

"Major, hold on a minute. It ain't *time* you got to save here. It's yourself."

"How's that, Lundy?"

"Sir, when them Cheyenne leave their dead behind like they been doing, they're not meaning to give up. You're going to have to wade on in and take them. And that means every man, woman and kid among them. Hang it all, sir, there simply ain't no other way you can hang onto what's left of your chances to keep this command!"

He stepped back, embarrassed by his own vehemence and familiarity. But Weston only let his shoulders droop sadly.

"Thanks, Jack," he said, "but it's already too late to save my command. I don't have it any more. I gave it over to Jackson—I let him take it from me—when we put the Cheyenne in B Barracks. The only thing I can do now that makes any sense whatever is to try and save those remaining poor devils out there in that black cold, and I mean to do *that*."

"It's a beautiful thought, Major," answered Lundy, looking away. "But it won't win you *this* fight."

Sometime during the brief utter darkness between sunset and moonrise the Cheyenne stole down off the hill and cut up the dead cavalry horse. And sometime between moonrise and dawn of January 11, refreshed by the frozen blood and flesh, they got off the far side of "Howitzer Hill," escaping once more to the west.

All that was found among the shell craters were the torn parts of five Cheyenne bodies. No, there was a sixth body, but this a matter of medical, not military interest.

"Hmmm," mused Surgeon Cummings, turning the form of an hour's-old infant with the toe of his boot. "Born yesterday on the march. Froze here last night. Mother's gone on with the tribe. God, what vitality!"

"Maybe it was borned dead, sir," suggested his orderly hopefully.

"No chance of that. Navel's clotted and closed. Well, let's go, Hankins. Jesus, but it's cold up here on this damned ridge!"

The orderly hung back, staring down at the tiny form. Making sure Cummings was not looking back, he hastily lifted the dead infant into a shell crater, covered it gently with a blanket of scraped snow. It was all the grave ever given Red Bird's small brother.

One other inconsequential event took place before the command left the hill. Weston and Jackson stood on the western rim of the rise, scanning the trail of the vanished Cheyenne. Jackson was the first to lower his field glasses. "Well," he challenged, "what are you going to do?"

"I'm going after them, of course," said Weston, still

studying the long line of moccasin tracks stretching away
toward Powder River.

"Good. I'll go down and get the column moving."

Now Weston lowered his glasses. "I said *I* was going
after them, Captain."

"You are *what?*" demanded the other incredulously.

"*I* am going on after the Indians. *You* are going back
to Fort Robinson."

Jackson grew profane and insubordinate. Weston waited
him out, repeated the order firmly, dispassionately. "You
are going back to the post. I am going west after the
Cheyenne. I shall take G and H Troops of cavalry, Lundy's
and Meeker's, plus Hayes's mounted artillery. Stienberg
and Davis with their C and D Rifle Companies will follow me in dismounted reserve. You will take the remaining cavalry, F and G Troops of the Third, return, secure post, begin rounding up any stragglers in that
vicinity. When I get back we shall add up our respective
scores and see where we stand, both personally and in
relationship to the command. Then we can turn the matter over to General Crook in Laramie, and you and the
devil can take it from there. Dismissed."

Jackson cursed some more. He wheedled when that
failed. He even resorted to hard, honest combat logic. In
the end he turned away without a word, sending his
mount down the slope full gallop. Lundy, coming up for
orders just in time to get a look at the color of the captain's face and the shank-deep manner in which he
jammed his spurs into his horse, grinned happily.

"Nothing he won't choke on, I hope," he said to Weston.

"If he does, Sergeant," answered the latter pleasant-
ly, "you may take credit for the casualty, thank you."

"How's that, sir?" Lundy's eyes narrowed. Something
had happened to his friend the C.O. since they had talked
the evening before. Weston hadn't used that easy, old-
time way, much less the crooked, half-shy smile, since
arriving at Robinson.

"What do you mean, Major?" he prompted cautiously.

"You recall our conversation last night, Lundy? It put
me to thinking of myself for a change. Of myself, Jack,
not some other man who I am not. Just me, Howell Weston." His face calmed, the voice smoothing with it. "A
man can't live his life over; he can't be something God

never intended him to be. But he can *try*." The shy, crooked smile twisted his mouth corners again. "I just *tried* something, Lundy, and I *did it*—something I ought to have done four months ago when I was ordered to."

"Sir?" frowned the big sergeant, not yet understanding.

"Taken command, Lundy; I've just taken command," said Major Howell Weston and reached for his horse's trailing reins.

While it was a virtual certainty that Dull Knife and the main force composed the band on Howitzer Hill, it was suspected that many of the older Cheyenne, together with some smaller children, had become separated from the Indian column during the first night's march west of the White and were yet at large somewhere to the rear. In the relentless drive to maintain pressure on the old chief's group, there had been no time to detach a force to collect these stragglers. It now became Jackson's responsibility to do so, using Raynald and the Sioux trackers, while Weston ran the main pack with Jack Lundy's help.

The quarter-blood Cherokee sergeant was well up to the work. For the following five days he kept Weston's troops exactly where the grayhaired C.O. wanted them—close up but just out of rifle range of the fugitives. The Indians made three more stands but Weston would not come to them. There were a few desultory exchanges of ineffectual small-arms fire, and twice more it became necessary to wheel up the howitzers and dislodge the Indians from some particularly well-chosen cover. Examining the last such place, Weston was convinced that most of the survinging Cheyenne were suffering shell-burst wounds. The area was a charnel house of blood and blood-soaked blanket-bandages. Lundy winced and said, "It looks like a pigsty on slaughter day," yet not one Indian body was found and the weary sergeant knew that dawn would bring only another day of the seemingly endless pursuit. He was right. But it proved a very short day.

Repeating their previous pattern of holing up at night and slipping through the white lines in the darkness preceding the coming daylight, the Cheyenne on that sixth dawn fled once again westward. Then, with full sunrise and the first clear sighting of the inexorable cavalry

column once more closing upon his staggering followers,
Dull Knife called the final halt. Atop the rocky, treeless
crown of the Hat Creek bluffs, only forty-four miles from
their beloved Powder River, the Cheyenne dug the last
rifle pits and prepared to meet Major Weston and Maheo.

The former did not keep them waiting. By 7:00 A.M.
his howitzers were pounding the Wyoming blufftops. Four
hour later, Captain Martin Hayes wheeled his battery out
of position and reported back to Weston: from here it
was up to the riflemen—Company F, 4th Field Artillery,
had just lobbed its last shell onto the Hat Creek highlands.

At once, and typically, Weston ordered Lundy forward
with the white flag. Wiser to the ways of his red relatives
than was his compassionate commander, the big Oklahoman obeyed reluctantly but with total care. His eyes
never left the Cheyenne rifle pits. It was thus he saw
the warning flash of the sun on their aiming barrels in
time to swing his pony and send him thudding for the
troop entrenchments. Forced by the show of relentless
hostility, Weston did not hesitate. It was by now clear
to him as to Dull Knife that Hat Creek marked the last
mile in the homeward flight of the Powder River Cheyenne. As Lundy had warned, these Indians were not going
to surrender. As Dull Knife had said, they were never
going back to Oklahoma. And as Wild Hog's fierce woman
had foretold, they were going to die like Cheyenne.

"All right, Lundy," said the Robinson C.O. "Move in."

Under Lundy and Meeker, G and H Troops of the Third
Cavalry invested the bluffs north and south of the Cheyenne position. Lieutenants Benton and Thomas, official
leaders of G and H, went along obediently. As in most
such tactical squeezes, the sergeants took the combat, the
officers took the credit. Neither rank complained of the
arrangement. It was army.

The flanking heights commanded the Indian rifle pits by
fifteen feet of elevation. For six hours and until the early
dusk closed over the field, the eighty Springfield carbines
poured in their murderous salvos of ordered fire. The
Cheyenne replied sporadically but their Winchesters were
outranged and their ammunition was down to the final,
priceless rounds. As darkness halted the execution that
night of January 16, Dull Knife had been supplied with

Major White Hair Weston's answer to his last-stand prayer and now awaited only Maheo's.

When midnight passed with no sign from his god, and the black hours crawled toward daylight with nothing but the cry of the winter wind to reward his lonely vigil, the old chief told his people that it was time for them all to say good-bye to one another—time for the warriors to shoot the women and the children and make the final suicide charge upon the soldier trenches. Maheo had abandoned his people. They could not live another day. So they would die together and by their own choice. It was the Cheyenne way. All would now prepare.

Yet even as he spoke the words and those among his listeners who could still move began dragging themselves toward him to receive his blessings and to touch the sacred arrows, Maheo relented of his long persecution.

The wind died unexpectedly, totally. The stillness smelled of hope. High Bear, last of the grown warriors who was whole and sound, raised his head. He sniffed the cold, quiet air, his voice stirring eloquently.

"Do you smell that?" he cried. "Snow, Father! Big snow! Don't you smell it? A storm is coming, fast and hard."

"Aye, it may be coming as you say," agreed the old chief. "But it comes too late, my son."

"No, never, don't say that! Maheo has sent us a sign!"

"He has sent us a blanket," corrected the old man dispiritedly, "to cover us when we are dead."

"A blanket will cover many things, Father," said High Bear excitedly. "This blanket will cover your tracks away from this place!"

"What is that you say? *My* tracks?"

"Yes. Yours and those of the women and the little ones who can still walk. When the snow starts and the wind is crying loudly, you are all going out of here. The storm will not fail you. It will cover all your tracks by morning. The sun will show the soldiers nothing."

Dull Knife shook his head sadly. "The sun will show the soldiers that we are still here, my son. I am not going."

High Bear, too, shook his head. But firmly not sadly. "You are going, Father," he said. "You and all who can walk."

The aged chief looked at him frowningly. "But you don't talk of yourself. That shows you are thinking something you haven't told me. See, you can walk, you are not wounded. Yet you don't say you are going. Why is that?"

High Bear straightened and stood tall before his chief. He placed the muzzle of his Winchester upon the top of his own right foot and pulled the trigger. The heavy bullet shattered the bones, toe to ankle.

"All those who can walk," repeated High Bear quietly, "will go with you when the snow comes."

The first flakes fell an hour before daylight. Within minutes the wind followed them. Shortly the snowfall thickened, the hammer of the wind increasing to gale force. With half an hour of darkness remaining, there were four inches of fresh powder over the old, hard crust and the howling wind was piling Maheo's god-sent blanket deeper with each gusting blast.

The good-byes atop Hat Creek bluff were quickly said, the last embraces silently given and returned. Only minutes before daybreak, Dull Knife and his small band of unwounded slipped over the crest of the rifle pits and were gone.

There were nine of them—the old chief, Red Bird's mother, two other squaws, four younger children and the twelve-year-old Red Bird himself. As the "warrior" of the party and at the insistence of High Bear and the other heroes remaining on the bluff, the proud boy accepted one of the treasured Winchesters, together with the last three cartridges which would fit it, as an honor sign from his people. Dull Knife's escapees had no other weapons, no food, no blankets. Their desperate objective —the Pine Ridge Sioux Agency—lay 179 miles away. They did not look back as they crept down the narrow defile of a blind gully which gave hidden egress from the bluff downward. Through it they passed north of Meeker's troops, alerting none of the cold-numbed white sentries. Behind them, where they lay sharp and black upon the new snow's glaring whiteness, their moccasin tracks were already filling to the brim with blowing new flakes. High Bear's prophecy now seemed assured; the coming sun would show the soldiers nothing.

But High Bear was wrong. The wind fell and the snow-fall commenced to thin within minutes after the Cheyenne passed Meeker's position. The flakes ceased coming altogether by 5:30 A.M. The wind was dead by six, having lasted just long enough to blow a nice blue hole in the heavy cloud above the Hat Creek bluffs.

Lundy's and Meeker's troops reopened with their carbines at 6:15. There was no reply from the Cheyenne.

Shortly the cavalrymen were joined by the infantry of C and D Companies, which had come up during the night. Even the artillerymen liberated Springfields from the infantry supply and headed up the slopes to be in on the kill. Encircling the redoubt of the hostiles were presently no less than 300 white riflemen. Not an officer or man among the number understood how many of Dull Knife's original 151 fugitives were still alive to fire back. Lundy's guess, given Major Weston when the C.O. came up to the lines about 8:00 A.M., was terse.

"Maybe thirty of them left, Major. With likely no more than five or six of them able to get off an aimed shot."

In response, Weston's sensitive features tightened to lines of genuine despair. "This is the end then, Jack?"

"Afraid it is, Major. You want another white flag waved?"

"Is there any use in it?"

"It'll look good in your report, sir."

"Very well, go ahead then."

Lundy ripped away a yard of canvas gun-cover from the nearest howitzer. He snagged it upon the bayonet of his short Springfield, stepped free of G Troop's covering boulders and into the open sweep of the blufftop. He walked out ten paces and stopped, waving the flag. Of the four Cheyenne shots which answered the gesture, one shattered the Springfield's bayonet stud and fluttered Lundy's surrender cloth to the ground. The sergeant beat the second volley of Indian fire back to his own breastworks by a shameless, face-first slide. Regaining his feet, he saluted Weston.

"Well, Major, you convinced now?"

"Yes, Jack. Advance in skirmish order. Keep firing until you are into them. Be as quick as you can about it."

"It won't take ten minutes, sir." Lundy wheeled on the waiting members of G Troop. "All right, boys; let's go."

As G Troop started forward, the other outfits followed in. The ring of white rifle steel shrank in upon the Cheyenne position with stealthy, nervous speed, its near-300 rifled throats snarling in the deadly rhythm of timed, deliberate fire. The four Indian guns spat thinly—once—and fell still. No trooper was hit. There was no other fire from either side.

At forty paces from the Cheyenne, Weston, walking with Lundy, ordered the halt. "Take a knee rest and be ready to fire," he told the nearest men. "Sergeant Lundy, go forward and offer them one more chance in their own tongue. Go quickly, please."

Lundy saluted and started in. He had no fear in his heart, only pity now. Ten yards from the silent rifle pits, he stopped. "My brothers, it is all over; come out in peace," he called. At the words, three Indian figures tottered up out of the pits. One had a camp ax, one an empty Winchester clubbed by the barrel, the third a Camp Robinson butcher knife.

With these weapons the three charged stumblingly toward the astonished white riflemen behind Sergeant Jack Henry Lundy.

Without command, a hundred Springfields blasted the stillness. Two of the Indians were torn bodily apart and were dead before the echoes of their hoarse war cries faded. The third lived long enough to stagger within a few feet of the motionless Lundy. There the stricken Indian halted, staring at the white soldier. Then, as his eyes went wide in disbelief, the swaying figure took the rusted knife in both hands and plunged it rippingly into her own vitals.

Yes, the third and last of the Powder River Cheyenne was a squaw. It was Wild Hog's woman. With her savage act she had lived out her dark prophecy, dying like a Cheyenne. There was only silence after that on the Hat Creek bluffs, and the Dull Knife raid was over.

Major Weston stood at the south rim of the tiny crater which had housed the Cheyenne final stand. It was a natural amphitheater in the bluff's top, a dozen paces in diameter, four or five feet deep. In it were twenty-eight emaciated Indian bodies, all that remained of a once feared and powerful people. *But were they all?*

The only unbroken snow on the blufftop lay now before Weston. It had been protected from the advance and trampling of the troops by a small gully so choked with boulders and slide rock it had not been considered passable. The possibility that the Cheyenne—some portion of them—might have escaped by this route still was not apparent to the white commander. And for a very evident reason. The Indian moccasin tracks which *did* show in the snow were coming from the gully, not going to it. The Cheyenne, despite the gully's impassable appearance, had used it in gaining the bluff, and that was all. They had certainly not, *any of them*, used it in departing.

Major Weston, on the point of shrugging off the matter of the gully, as had his staff before him, turned to find Sergeant Lundy at his side. Lundy kept his voice down, merely hunching a shoulder in the direction of the narrow declivity. "Major, let's you and me mosey down that draw a piece. I got something I want to show you."

As they started off, some of the junior officers showed a disposition to follow. Lundy was scowling instantly. "Sir, we ain't going to need no help on this," he said. "You'd best give your boys something to do."

Weston, taking note of the scowl, waved to Captain Hayes. "Martin, we're pulling out directly. See that everything is ready. You others, too. I won't be a minute."

Lundy led the way to the gully, deliberately scuffing at the Cheyenne tracks on the route. A few yards into the defile and safely out of sight of the troops above, he halted and pointed ahead. Weston gave a startled look. Once into the gully, the Indian tracks reversed themselves. Now they lay pointing away and down the narrow opening.

"Good lord, Jack. Some of them did make it out."

"Yes, sir. They walked backward into the gully, then lined out and beat it. Raynald and his Sioux scouts would have been onto this in a minute, but the way it is, Major, it's only me and you and the old man knows about it."

"The old man?"

"Dull Knife, sir. He ain't among them bodies back yonder."

"You're certain, man?"

"Yes, sir. As far as our troops are concerned, Dull Knife could be any one of them old Cheyenne back in the rifle pits. But not for me, Major. I knew him. He ain't back there."

Weston stared at him a long moment and spoke very quietly. "Very well, Sergeant. Where does that leave us?"

Lundy returned his look. "I make it out this way, Major. There's nine of them in this bunch that got away. One growed man, three squaws, four little kids, one bigger kid. They ain't been gone over two hours. They may have made seven or eight miles, no more. They're weak and sick and starved. It's getting colder with the wind dropped. The prairie, past these roughs, is all wide open. They haven't a chance."

"Eh? How's that?" Weston seemed bemused, uncertain.

"They're ours if we want them, Major. All we got to do is go after them."

Weston did not answer for such a stretching time that Lundy commenced to grow edgy. Someone was bound to follow them down from up on the bluff before too long. They had to get out of there, if they were going to. "Major, sir, what do you say?" He moved closer to the staring C.O. "You ain't but one question to answer now: What do you want did about following them Indian tracks?"

Major Weston turned slowly, putting his back to the Cheyenne trackline. His frown lines were gone. His lean face was at rest, his gray eyes gentle and untroubled. *"What Indian tracks, Lundy?"* he asked and went past the sergeant, up and out of the gully to the troops above.

The shallow earth atop the Hat Creek bluffs was frozen as brittle hard as the Wyoming limestone which underlay it. No attempt was therefore made to bury the Cheyenne dead. Nameless, they were left uncovered where they lay. The troops were formed up and marched out within the hour. Camp was made early that afternoon. The column was under way again with daybreak of the eighteenth.

Leaving the troops under Martin Hayes, Weston pushed ahead accompanied by Lundy and Meeker. They halted at noon to boil coffee and grain the horses. Lundy, never at rest in Indian country, climbed an elevation to scan the local terrain. He was back presently to report a strange troop of cavalry headed their way. "Angling up from the south," he told Weston. "Most likely some of General Crook's pets from Laramie."

At the mention of Crook, Weston's face shadowed. Lundy understood the reason. He straightened and stood almost protectively at the C.O.'s side as the officer of the approaching troop appeared over the rise and rode down to meet them.

"Major Weston?" greeted the youngster. "Lieutenant Foreman, sir. Headquarters Company, Laramie. I've been looking for you." He smiled, straining it a bit. "Looks like we're a little late for the fun, eh?"

"If you mean the Cheyenne, Lieutenant, yes. They're all dead." He watched the other man a moment. "Did you say you were looking for me?"

"Yes, sir."

Weston nodded. "Tell me, Lieutenant, when did Captain Jackson's report reach General Crook at Laramie?"

Lundy's eyes narrowed. This was a shot in the deep dark by Weston. The young officer, however, not understanding this, replied without hesitation.

"It was the tenth or the eleventh, sir. I'm not certain."

"I am," said Lundy. "Make it the eleventh. He was with us on the tenth. He sure didn't waste any time getting to that telegraph shack, did he, Major? And after you asking him to wait till you got back and the two of you could compare notes before contacting Crook. The lousy little brass-kissing son of a she-dog."

"That will do, Sergeant." Weston rebuked him without sharpness. "Well, Lieutenant, I suppose you can't tell us anything about the general's reaction to all this trouble up here at Robinson? I mean, he didn't say anything to you?"

The young officer shook his head. "No, sir, just told me to get started and find you in the field if I could. That, and to hurry you along back to post, if I did find you." He paused, whether out of relish or sympathy Lundy could not decide. And Weston did not try to. "But I can tell you one thing, Major. You won't have to wait very long to find out for yourself what that reaction was."

"Oh? How is that, Foreman?"

"General Crook, sir, he's waiting for you at Fort Robinson."

Crook, in his patient, kindly way, made it as easy for Major Howell Weston as any general officer in his position might do. He ordered the office cleared, instructed the guard to admit no one, even sent his own adjutant out of the room. When the door had closed behind the latter, he spoke concisely and gently, employing the straightforward, merciful manner one honorable gentleman will take with another, in his brief review of Weston's palpable failures in command at Robinson. He concluded with the earnest hope that Weston would remember that he, Crook, greatly regretted what he had now to tell him.

In the ensuing silence, Howell Weston took a last, lingering look through his favorite parade-ground window. When he had finished, he squared his thin shoulders and faced Crook. "Yes, sir. I understand, General."

Crook stood up, came around the desk, stopped.

"You are hereby relieved of command, Major. You will report to General Sheridan at Fort Lincoln not later than 1 February. I'm truly sorry, sir."

Weston saluted, saying nothing.

Watching him narrowly, Crook's famed hard blue eyes softened. "Weston," he said, "we both know that you did your best. No man is expected to do more."

Howell Weston nodded. "I wonder," he said softly, and turned and went out, never looking back.

He left at six the next morning, when the sergeants were barking out roll call on the parade ground and the remainder of the post was in its most deserted hour. He had said his few personal good-byes the previous evening; to Meeker, Lundy, a handful of embarrassed troopers, come to take his hand and stammer some fashion of awkward, heartfelt farewell. Now all that lay ahead of him was the frozen slush of the company street and its ending at the main gates. On a borrowed brown and undistinguished troop horse, looking neither right nor left, Major Howell K. Weston rode his lonely way out of Fort Robinson, Nebraska.

The remaining encounters were wordless things, accidents only of the route and of the day's beginning routine. Newly promoted Major John Tenney Jackson, gold oak leaves agleam in the pale sun, stepped from the C.O.'s

office on his way to his first staff breakfast. He stopped
when he saw Weston and drew himself up properly and
held it. Coming up to join him, Post Surgeon Cummings
heard the crunching of the horse's feet in the cold snow.
He looked down the street, saw Weston approaching,
added his stiff respects to Jackson's. The deposed C.O.
rode past them. There was no bitterness in the way he
accepted their presence without acknowledging it. They
understood.

"Poor devil," grimaced Jackson when the rider had
turned the corner of the headquarters building and was
gone. "You can't help feeling sorry for him. Too bad.
Just no real guts."

Surgeon Cummings first nodded, then shook his head,
finally flushed guiltily and said nothing.

Past the farrier's shed and the quartermaster's supply
depot, turning past the post guardhouse for the gates,
Weston sat his homely mount in continued silence, eyes
straight ahead. From the iron-barred grating of hospital
cell 17, a wasted dark face watched the white officer
drew near. "*Eneamen,*" said Left Hand quietly to his
companions. "Come to the window, my brothers, and see
who passes by. It is White Hair Weston. They have done
something to him. They have hurt him. Turned him
away."

Wild Hog and Lone Crow dragged themselves to the
window, perspiring to the pain of their unhealed wounds,
and to the jangling weight of their leg irons. The sound
of the harsh bonds clanking and bumping carried to Weston. He checked his horse, peering toward the guardhouse. In a moment he saw the three Indians at the
window of cell 17, and in another moment recognized
them. Gravely he swung his mount to face them. Raising his left hand, he put the fingertips to his brow
in the Plains Indian gesture of deepest parting respect.
As soberly, the injured warriors returned the sign, their
hearts stirred.

"I must say this," announced Lone Crow to his comrades, "he never lied to us; we lied to ourselves."

"They have tried to take his pride but they didn't get
it," said Left Hand. "See how straight he sits on that
ugly horse they gave him."

"*Enitoemel*" Wild Hog called the Cheyenne courage

word with impulsive suddenness to Weston. "We salute
you, White Hair!"

Weston sat taller yet on the brown horse. Watching
him ride on, the Indians understood that. Pride was their
whole life. Pride and freedom. They knew this soldier
chief had found both things in his failure at Fort Robinson.

At the main gate Lundy had the guard detail. He was
dozing in the warmth of the morning sun behind the
sentry box when the guard corporal put his head around
the corner of the small building and called, "Brass ho,
Sarge. Look alive!"

Lundy peered around the corner and pulled his head
back. "It's *him*," he said to the corporal. "Hit a brace
and hold it."

The two soldiers stepped to the edge of the military
wagon road and came to attention. As Weston passed
they snapped their salutes and broke them off sharply.
He returned the salute, not checking his horse nor looking their way, but both troopers swore later that they
saw it. When he left Fort Robinson, broken in career
and stripped of command, Major Howell Weston was
smiling.

They watched him then as he put his horse up the long
rise of the wagon road eastward from the post. And they
watched him still as he pulled the bony animal in at the
top of the grade and sat him for a moment uncertainly,
as though looking back for the last time on the scene of
his failure as an officer and a commander. Another moment and he had turned the horse and was gone from
their sight.

The guard corporal shook his head, puzzled. "Now what
the hell do you suppose that damn grin was all about?
I'd give a week's pay to know what he had to be smiling
about!"

"Save your money," said Lundy. "I can tell you for
free."

The big sergeant fell silent, looking far away and across
the snowswept crest of the wagon road rise. At last,
and satisfied, he turned back to the corporal. "He was a
better man than Jackson," he said softly. "*And he knew it.*"

The Last Warpath

He was a very old man. The woman with him was old, too, although she was not yet fifty. The woman was the old man's daughter, and she helped him now to climb the last of the slight rise. When they had reached the top, they stood panting for breath. It was cold, for the autumn was well gone.

"This is the place," said the old man, when he could speak. "I remember it as yesterday."

The woman said nothing. Broad of face, seamed, wrinkled, dried and smoked of hide and feature and frame, sturdy legs bowed, hands taloned and calloused with hard work, spine permanently curved forward and arms hanging long almost to the knees, she was only another poor scarecrow of the proud race which had died in this silent, empty place those six autumns ago. Hunger, fear, flight, hiding, the awkward humility of the imprisoned soul all showed in the lines of her dark face and gaunt form. There showed, too, in the limp with which she followed the old man, and the crooked scar which disfigured her face from brow to lower jaw, the torments of the living wounds of war which made her forty-seven years seem as the old man's seventy-eight. This woman had once been—well, she had once been not as she seemed now, not old and not broken and not ugly.

"It seems uneasy here," she said finally. "As though those ghosts of our people remembered this place, even as you do, Father. As though they might be standing here with us, looking down at Wounded Knee."

"It's a gray day and very dark," suggested the ancient warrior. "There are no ghosts. Not any more. But there were ghosts on that day. How long has it been now, Moheya?"

"Six years, Father. It was 1890. In Maxhekonene, the hard frost moon."

"December," said the old man, using the white man's word deliberately. "In the last week."

"Yes."

"Big Foot was the Sioux chief. He was a ghost dancer; he had those poor Sioux people all stirred up. They thought the buffalo were coming back from heaven to bring food once more to the Indian. Poor people."

"Yes, very poor."

The wind whined over the crest of the rise. It whipped a powder of snow to mound against the patched and torn moccasins of the woman, the broken-countered workboots of the old man. The frost from their breaths whirled away like pipe-smoke and was gone.

The woman put her shawl about the old man's shoulders and stood close to him protecting him with the warmth of her body and its strength.

"Come, Father. Now you've seen it again, let's go away. It's not good for you to stand here making your heart cry."

"Doesn't your heart cry, Moheya?"

"You know that it does."

Behind them the bony packmule which stood back-hunched to the gaining wind, waiting for them, brayed in complaint.

"You see," she said, "even the mule knows enough to go where it is warmer and kinder to the heart."

The old man shivered but did not want to go.

"See the creek and the dark timber of its banks," he said. "The channel is the same as on that day. I can still see the lodges pitched along it and through the woodland. Out beyond, in all that flat valley, were the pony herds. I can hear again the barking of the dogs, the thin tinkling of the bell mare's brass song, hear the beautiful

distant laughter of the children, the callings of the old
grandmothers who looked after them. Do you see where
that dry gully runs this way from the creek, Moheya?
Where the old wagonbed is showing the ribs of its topstays
there in the snow? That's where the soldiers dug the
trench when they came back after the blizzard. That's
where they buried the Sioux."

"One hundred and thirty-eight Indians," said the woman, "and thirty-one soldiers."

"But the soldiers were not put in the trench."

"No, only the Indians."

The old man nodded. His eyes were rheumy with the
cataracts of many winters, yet now for a moment they
saw clearly again. He pointed below.

"There is where Lieutenant Casey was shot in the back
by Plenty Horses. It happened when Casey came with
his Cheyenne scouts trailing the Sioux of Big Foot to
this place. Plenty Horses met Casey. He smiled and
shook hands with him. When Casey rode on, Plenty
Horses shot him from behind."

Now the woman nodded. The toil, the pain, the living
and the dying of her years seemed to darken her wide
face. She had been at Sand Creek long ago; she had
survived Custer and the Washita, Carson and the Palo
Duro; she knew what it was to be struck, to feel the flesh
tear, the bone shatter, the body bear tortures to kill the
soul and the spirit.

Still she was a Cheyenne, still she saw things as they
were, nor would she lie even to herself. "It was wrong
of our people to track their brothers for the soldiers,"
she said. "A terrible thing."

"Brother against brother," said the old man. "I remember it. I came back here with the burial party, identifying
the dead for the soldiers, helping roll the bodies in."

"But you weren't with the scouts."

"I was too old."

"Is that all, just too old, Father?"

"No, there was more."

The woman knew that he would say it now, and that
then they could be gone from this lonesome, cold knoll
above the ghostlands of Wounded Knee.

As she waited, she glanced at the old man's face,
close to hers. She saw a thing there which she was not

supposed to see, which she would never admit to seeing. The old man was weeping silently.

She brought the frail body nearer to her own, gathering it in the shelter of the ragged shawl. "Go ahead, Father," she said. "Tell it."

The old man straightened. His hair, as white as the snow which whirled about them, still roached thickly above his forehead, fell in gleaming double braids below his waist. The dark eyes, dimmed with time and the memories of terror, and now with tears, burned for a moment as fiercely as the half-century gone. In the time of a long slow breath, he was once more the war chief, the fighting Cheyenne, the son of Whistling Elk and Lighting Swan, the final blood of the ancient Shahi-yena squaw Goodfeather.

"It was not I who said it," he told the woman, "but old Little Wolf, who was there when the Cheyenne scouts were there. He saw how it was. He stood with me on this very knoll where we stand now. Here is what he said:

Our officer was dead, killed by Plenty Horses with that shot in the back, that handshake and that smile. Some of our scouts, four or five of them, were dead also. At first I was angry with that Sioux, and all of his people. Then I saw all of those people lying broken apart and covered with blood, the warrior, woman, old one and child alike, and my heart broke and I cried. My sorrow, I thought, was for the wantonness of it, but then it came to me what I was really seeing on that snowy ground. It was not those broken bodies of my people, my brothers the Sioux, not only that, not just the blood and the bones and the broken bodies—had not I seen all of that a hundred times before? Aye, and worse. What it was that I saw this time, I had never seen before, and it was a terrible thing. There on the ground before me lay a man that I knew. It was Big Foot. He was so near to me that I could see his eyes open behind the clear ice which covered him. He was on the ground, reaching upward. He was holding out his arms, pleading for someone to help him to get up. He was looking at me so I spoke to him.

Lieutenant Casey's scouts laughed at me. They said I was getting old. Hearing things. They said they heard only the whistle of the wind answering me back, but I heard Big Foot's voice. He was telling me what it was that I really saw there on that icy ground where he lay frozen, body skin to marrow bone, reaching out for help. He was telling me what we Cheyenne—the scouts of Casey—had done there that grim day. *We had not killed the Sioux; we had killed our own people, we had killed the Cheyenne.*

The old man was not quite at the end of his tale. He wiped his eyes, only to remove the little ice lines on the lashes, to brush the moisture brought by the cold wind.

"Little Wolf," he said, "looked out once more across the blowing snows of Wounded Knee, then turned to me with a look of sadness which went into my heart like a knife.

" 'My old friend,' he told me, 'we will never fight again. Now truly Maheo's children are all dead. We are the last Cheyenne.' "

The woman, who had heard the story each autumn in the hard frost moon since the battle's fighting, even from this same ghost-ridden rise, patted the old man comfortingly.

"It's time to go now, Father," she said. "The fight is over. The soldiers are all gone. Come on."

She led him down to where the packmule waited on the slope below. Strong as she was, she had some difficulty getting the old man up into the worn safety of the mildewed cavalry saddle. When he was settled, workboots firmly in the rusted iron stirrups, she smiled up at him and spoke a Cheyenne word of reward, as though to a small child.

But the old man was a chief. He was looking far away, seeing again the buffalo, the red buttes, the war bonnets, the wide blue skies of high Wyoming and of home. He sat very straight on the bony mule.

The woman led the animal downward and away from Wounded Knee. When she reached the bottom of the slope she halted to make sure the old man was still comfortable in the saddle. When she touched his hand she felt more than the cold of the hard frost moon. But she was a Cheyenne. She only crossed the waxen fingers upon the saddle's pommel, lacing them there swiftly with a thong of rawhide so that the silent rider would not slip sideways and fall off. Then she went on, out across the monotonous flat of the valley, toward the distant hills and the dark timber, leading the mule.

When the gusting ground snows closed behind the plodding figures, Spotted Wolf was dead and the last warpath was covered over.

WILL HENRY

CHIRICAHUA

"Some of the best writing the American West can claim!"
—Brian Garfield, Bestselling Author of <u>*Death Wish*</u>

Led by the dreaded Geronimo and Chatto, a band of Chiricahua Apache warriors sweep up out of Mexico in a red deathwind. Their vow–to destroy every white life in their bloody path across the Arizona Territory. But between the swirling forces of white and red hatred, history sends a lone Indian rider named Pa-nayo-tishn, The Coyote Saw Him, crying peace–and the fate of the Chiricahuas and all free Apaches is altered forever.

The Spur Award–winning Novel of the West
___4266-5 $4.50 US/$5.50